UNDER THE
SLAUGHTERHOUSE

UNDER THE
SLAUGHTERHOUSE

R. D. AMUNDSON

iUniverse, Inc.
Bloomington

Under the Slaughterhouse

iUniverse books may be ordered through booksellers or by contacting:

iUniverse
1663 Liberty Drive
Bloomington, IN 47403
www.iuniverse.com
1-800-Authors (1-800-288-4677)

ISBN: 978-1-4759-7086-9 (sc)
ISBN: 978-1-4759-7088-3 (hc)
ISBN: 978-1-4759-7087-6 (ebk)

Library of Congress Control Number: 2013900531

Printed in the United States of America

iUniverse rev. date: 02/08/2013

Prologue

Every now and then, on a scale large or small, life seems to remember that fairness and justice were once words of meaning, and are still sometimes needed to strike a balance in the affairs of men.

Story has it old Tucker was responsible for the naming. Others said he simply went there to die. Maybe he did, no one could say for certain.

The old fellow had lived in the village for as long as anyone could remember. A widower, he had no one, except the occasional company of Aran, the village orphan. Tucker helped the boy out whenever he could, which wasn't often, but what he did pass on to the youngster was the Gift of See, enabling him to foretell the future, and the future he foretold was now.

Silhouetted against the iron gray of the early morning mist, the aged man was no more than a shadow with his back bent under the weight of his worldly possessions, each unsure step raising a small puff of dust.

"Hey, Tuck, where you going?" hollered young Aran from atop his perch, a hut sized boulder in the middle of Green Meadow.

Raising a bony finger, Tucker pointed straight ahead, to the east. "Whither, by the sea," he answered the lad, his voice cracking under the weight of many years. "Whyn't you join me?" he invited, his voice taking on a shriller note.

Devoid of parents, Aran had spent many days alone in the land of lore, the mystical land of the Celts and the Druids. He fell in alongside Tucker and no one ever saw him or the old man again. But Whither by the Sea stayed on, becoming a community on the east coast of Eire.

Tucker had gained a set of eyes and helping hands. Aran had gained a father and a mentor.

Unknown to the pair, a far-reaching and culminating Balance in the affairs of men had begun.

Chapter One

The singular moment, the one of National Geographic quality the photojournalist had been waiting for, showed itself. They most often arrive in the early fall about the time the air begins to crisp and cool from the blistering heat of summer.

The bearded young man gazed in awe at nature's painted scenery. He had experienced many breathtaking scenes, but this was the crowning glory. He was a man who had heard his calling, and it was to capture the glory of nature's paintings on film.

A free-lance professional, it took no more than a minute for him to set up, ready to shoot. He knew from experience he couldn't capture the whole of the scene on film, not the breeze that blew gently across the deep valley below him, not the pungent scent of the pines, the earthy scent of the mountains, or the cool scent of glacier ice as it wafted over the top of the limestone Wall on the other side of the valley to the north.

The Wall in the Bob Marshall Wilderness is a natural formation of white limestone named for its similarity to the Great Wall of China and stretches almost as far. A monolith, it rises like a castle's first defense against the ravages of civilization. The light from the westering sun climbed up the face of the Wall, changing its whiteness to the color of polished gold, brighter and purer than any king's crown.

The breeze blew stronger over its top from the north, carrying the scent of primal purity across the intervening valley to the photographer. It seemed as if time suspended, the world stopped spinning, and the sun fixed itself in place allowing the perfect moment to linger as long as possible, creating a time when the soul meets nature and communes with its Maker.

To embed it all on film would be impossible.

The fullness of the scene and the glory of the moment inspired the man as he began clicking away, each snap of the shutter capturing a subtle difference from the one before, a nuance of color, a shift in the position of a branch, the hue of the sky contrasting with the changing color of the Wall.

Withdrawing his eye from the lens long enough to take in a deep breath of the high mountain air, he returned it only to stare straight down the barrel of a large bore rifle. It belched fire, its thunder booming and echoing off the face of the Wall. They say you don't hear the sound of the shot that kills you; he didn't feel any pain, so, outside of the initial shock, figured he was okay for now, and by a minor miracle, he hadn't knocked the camera off its tripod when he jerked backwards at the roar of the gun.

"Jumpin' Jesus!" he exclaimed, straightening around to face his assailant. The mountain man stood motionless and unmoving, in tune to the flow of time in the wilderness of the Rockies. He lowered his rifle, setting the butt of it on the ground. Through his bushy salt and pepper beard he said, "Look behind you."

"Wha-a-a-t?"

"Look behind you," he deadpanned.

The photographer hesitated, then turned and looked. His heart stuck in his throat at the sight. Lying on the ground, not thirty feet away, was the largest grizzly bear he'd ever laid eyes on. He swallowed hard, twice, before he could find his voice, his rubbery legs hard pressed to keep him standing.

"I . . . didn't hear a sound," he squeaked.

"Course you didn't," replied the mountain man, who had moved with the silence of the huge bear to stand beside the photographer. "That old griz didn't get to be a silvertip by tramping around noisy in these woods. Lucky for me you came along."

The photographer turned to stare in disbelief at the old codger.

"Don't you mean lucky for *me* you came along?"

"Nope, just what I said, lucky for me."

"How's that?"

"For two reasons, one, you drew that griz out so I could kill him and get him out of my hair, and two, you're the person to hear my story and get it out there before it's too late."

"Before what's too late?" he asked, his face pale, his eyes blank and staring, as if searching for the world he'd been torn from and the realization of the *almost that had happened.*

"Before it's too late to tell my story, I don't live up here 'cause I'm looking to turn into bear shit. I simply can't return to civilization . . . can't, and that's it." He paused, looked the photographer up and down, and asked, "What's your name?"

"Joseph James and what is so important about your story?"

"First off, my name is Truman Struck, and my story, true by the way, is about saving this world from the total and absolute

3

domination of evil. I can understand your doubting that, but after you here it, you will be convinced of its reality.

Where's your gear? I'll help you pack it to my cabin. It ain't far and mostly downhill. We'll be more comfortable and safe from bears and such while I tell you the entire story. It'll be dark soon anyway."

After slight hesitation, the young man agreed. "I don't have much gear, I can pack it myself," he said.

"Alright then, I'll skin the bear. You can keep its hide for a rug and as evidence of how our meeting came about, it'll add to the credibility of the story. It's hard enough for me to believe it sometimes. You don't own a rifle do you?"

"Not a gun of any kind. I'm a photojournalist and I shoot only with my camera."

"Of course," he replied, "but you might want to think about carrying one, considering that bear lying dead behind you." The younger man nodded his head in agreement. "But, good for now, nobody will think you shot that bear yourself then, will they?"

"No one that knows me anyway," he replied.

Truman gutted and skinned the bear, leaving the head on, and then made a travois out of pine limbs to haul it on.

It didn't take Joseph James more than a few minutes to pack his gear, and together the men moved single file along the downward winding path, dark shadows creeping up the base of the Wall as the leaves of the aspens above them shimmered like gold coins in the waning sun.

The photojournalist, his gear in an aluminum frame backpack, walked behind the mountain man. He noticed for the first time a fringed leather case, slung like an old time quiver across the man's back. It wasn't for his rifle; he carried that in his left hand. Before long the young man's lungs and muscles were screaming for oxygen as he tried to keep up with Truman, at least a quarter century his senior. After a mile of winding down the mountainside and just before dark, he spotted a log cabin off to the right hunkered down in a small clearing. Truman left the path and headed for it.

"There's a whole string of Forest Service cabins up here, so I never stay in one place more than a few days," quipped Truman as he stepped onto the wooden porch, pulling the hide laden travois off to one side.

Joseph James waited for him to open the wood slab door and then stepped into the one room structure behind the mountain man. The cabin's interior wasn't much; sparse, rustic, strictly functional with none of the comforts of home, except for a stone fireplace in which Truman quickly built a fire.

Outside, dark fell.

He got the fire blazing to his satisfaction and brought two cups of hot coffee to the plank table, setting one down in front of Joseph James. Before seating himself, he twisted to his right, hooked his left thumb under a shoulder strap, lifted it over his head, and removed the leather case he had slung across his shoulders and then laid it on the table. The photojournalist could tell it contained something heavy, but not Truman's rifle, that was leaning in a corner.

In a single heartbeat, dark engulfed the mountains in freezing air.

"Ever been all alone in the world, Joseph James?" the old mountain man asked the young photographer. "Sure, every time I go into a wilderness area or some other remote place to shoot," he replied.

"No, I mean *all alone*, no family, no mother, no father, no children, no friends, not one single ally. Nobody you can talk to or lean on."

"Put that way, I guess I haven't," he replied.

"No, you haven't, I have, and we'll get to that. But it's lucky for me you came along," repeated Truman, seating himself at the table. Thinking about the hide out on the porch, Joseph replied, "And lucky for me," but he couldn't help feeling uneasy. Just who was this mysterious mountain man? A psycho perhaps? He wasn't unaware of the possibility and had seated himself close to the door. He understood some apprehension would be normal for the situation, but at the same time perceived something extraordinary and non-threatening about the man, and his perceptions were seldom wrong. He dismissed the idea of a psycho.

"Got a pen and some paper?" asked Truman.

"Yeah, and a recorder, do you want me to bring it?"

"Hell . . . why not," he replied, nodding his head.

Outside the wind banged against the wooden door.

"Alright then, are we ready to start?" Joseph nodded his head, his interest absorbed by the strange man across the table.

"First, we need to go back to the land of lore where myths and legends aren't shrouded in time but are new born out of sky or water or blood and come up to slap you square in the face."

THE ALPHA SLAVER

CHAPTER TWO

LUCRETIA KNEW THEY would come, all the Celtic did, for it was written in the Prophecy.

"They're here," she whispered to the bowman at her side.

"Go, tell the others," she commanded. No sooner had her words hit the ears of the archer than he slipped away into the onshore mist, a receding shadow of disappearing substance.

The Celtic queen remained by the oak tree, watching as the ship's dragon head parted the fog, its long body following, its oars dipping like wings into the cold, gray sea.

In the bow of the silent ship stood Bukwold the Slayer, proud and unyielding and possessed by an invincible aura. The horns of his war helmet spiked toward the sky as his long blond hair blew back from underneath it.

A giant of a man, the Norse king, of all the warriors of his time, was the most feared. He never bothered to enter into a battle. They were merely for winning. He waged complete war with the vicious intent to crush his enemy and remove their memory from the face of the earth, and he engaged in his business with ice water in his veins.

Lucretia studied him, as he stood motionless in the bow of the ship, his senses probing the onshore mist for unseen danger. Herself a seasoned warrior, she knew her eyes would never see another like him, no man living or yet to be born could match his magnificence.

The ship came to a noiseless stop in knee-deep water. Bukwold raised his right index finger; the men slipped without a sound over the sides and formed a line parallel to the shore. Bukwold joined them as they moved forward, deadly shadows in a phalanx, their King at its point.

Lucretia slipped into the woods to ready her forces for the Viking onslaught.

Chapter Three

Tendrils of steam, like fingers of a ghost, rose off the hot blood dripping from Bukwold's axe. The muscles of his forearms, like tightly twisted ropes, were extensions of the handle that held the deadly singing blade.

Widening his stance, he snapped his head left to right waiting for the next attacker, his blood spattered hair whipping back and forth across his shoulders.

No enemies came at him. His vision changed and slowed, and as he focused on the stillness before him, his battle-heated blood began to cool.

He stared down at the headless corpse lying at his feet, one of thousands of others that had lain in the same place, but this one was different, it was the body of a woman. Leaning down he ripped the tunic from off her shoulders and flung the bloody rag a few feet, covering her head. She had been brave and he thus honored her in the Norse tradition.

When he first engaged her, he thought he would swat her away like an annoying pest. But she held her ground, her fiery red hair swirling like flames around her head, stinging him twice with her blade. Scattered about the battlefield were the bloodied bodies of many of these warrior women . . . too many. It was a sight he'd never seen before, not the killing field, for that was his domain, it was the women. And as he watched the ground drink the blood draining from their bodies, he realized they were now part of the enemy. The enemy. He had made everyone his enemy, and why, he asked himself? Many brothers in arms lay dead among the scattered corpses. Was it any longer worth the cost? Had it ever been? No, he answered himself, and besides, he had nothing more to gain or to prove.

Holding his axe by the end of its handle, he set the blade on the ground and leaned his massive weight against it, weariness invading his bones. Lifting his gray, tired eyes above the carnage, he noticed a solitary figure across the killing field, standing still and silent by an ancient oak tree. It could be a girl, or a boy, or a pixie, or a fairy. Bukwold had heard the stories of Celtic magic. Maybe they were true. The stories of their fighting prowess had proven to be so.

Picking up his axe and holding it by the end of its handle with the blade resting on his right shoulder, he approached the silent sprite, aware that it could be a trap.

He caught the aroma of wild roses as it mixed with the stench of death. It grew stronger as he drew nearer to the diminutive figure. She remained as still as the tree she leaned against, the breeze blowing through her copper hair, whisping its strands about her cherubic face.

Stopping within striking distance of the motionless waif, he looked into her innocent, yet fearless, violet eyes and asked, "What is your name child?"

"Lucinda," she replied. "Why did you kill my mother?"

Why, indeed, thought the Viking, as he swung his axe in a powerful down stroke, burying the blade into the heart of the oak, opposite the neck of the child. She didn't flinch, didn't twitch a muscle, but continued to stare into the blond giants' eyes that looked distant and tired, like those of a man who has seen all he wants to see of life and of death.

The Slayer turned to face the battlefield. A warrior and a king, he had no heart to kill women and children, and to conquer the Celts he would have to do just that.

Suddenly he shouted from the depths of his lungs, "Here and no further!" his voice filling the open bloody field before him, its echo dissolving into silence as it crashed against the roar of the sea.

He turned back to Lucinda and held his hand out to her. "Will ye come with me child? We will find you a mother to raise you up."

She stood as still as the tree she leaned against and said, "As you have struck to the heart of the tree, so shall your branch strike to the heart of the evil you have brought about." Her words stunned him and he was the one now silent as he watched the young girl disappear into the woods.

He turned and grabbed the handle of his axe and tugged on it with all his strength. It didn't budge. That settled it. He let go of its handle.

"Here, and no further," he proclaimed, as he turned to the aftermath of the slaughter, to the field that was to become known as "Where Bukwold Struck the Tree."

CHAPTER FOUR

THE MAN, TOSSED onto the rugged shore by the fierce storm, lay listening to fast approaching footsteps thudding on the rocks and drawing closer.

Barely able to lift his head, he peered through the fog toward the sound. Seeing shadows emerging from it, he laid his head down between rocks washed smooth by eons of ocean waves, too exhausted to fight or flee.

A pair of strong yet gentle hands turned him over on his back. His eyes, out of focus at first, spun back in to reveal a coppery mane of hair framing a woman's face, a face seasoned by the severity of life's struggles.

She was beautiful in his sight.

"What is your name," she asked the battered man.

"Patricius," he replied, the speaking exhausting his breath.

"You were on the ship with the Britons?" she asked.

"Yes."

"Why," she asked, her hand slipping to touch the hilt of her sword.

"I was to be sold into slavery."

"Are you hurt bad?"

"No, just bruised, nothing broken . . . so tired . . ."

She gave him a drink from her wine flask.

"If you are able to stand, I will help you to walk," she said. He nodded. He was light and much too weak for a man still young.

"Who . . . are you?" he asked as they half-walked, half-hobbled along, his arm over her shoulders, her arm around his waist.

"Lucinda, daughter of Lucretia, of Whither by the Sea."

"Of what people are you?" he asked.

"We are Celtic," she answered.

His bruising had gone deeper than at first thought and Patricius stayed the winter with the Celts.

Trained in the care of plants, he spent his time pruning the wild roses that grew everywhere in the woods. In the evenings he would carve the rose wood into oblong beads until he had enough to string together a loop a foot in diameter. From the strongest wood, that near the root, he carved a T shaped cross and hung it from its own small string of beads attached to the main loop.

He used them as prayer beads, a reminder to offer prayers of thankfulness for deliverance from a life of slavery. As his fingers moved slowly around the loop, stopping at each bead to pray, he heard a soft knock on his door.

"Please . . . come in," he answered.

The door flew open and slammed with cracking force against the wall. Patricius snapped his head toward the sound, the howling wind driving an arctic blast of ice pellets into his face.

As he stared through slitted eyes, the pellets congealed into the form of a woman clothed in a tattered robe the color of snow. Her long white hair blew out behind her, against the incoming wind. Set within her fleshless skull were black hollows for eyes and a mouth opened wide to reveal sharp and jagged teeth. Roars like unleashed hounds from hell issued from her throat as she launched herself, her gaping mouth aimed at his exposed neck.

On reflex, he put his hands up in defense of the apparition, with the cross at the end of the loop of beads dangling free between him and the gruesome creature.

"Blasphemy!" it shrieked in rage and halting its flight in mid-air, it hissed at Patricius, and then twisted around and flew out the door.

The young man collapsed in a heap on the floor.

"Patricius, are you hurt? I came as quickly as I could."

He looked up to see Lucinda's face and those of the people with her. She turned his head one-way and then the other examining his neck and throat.

"What was that hellish thing?" he gasped.

"We call it a Ban~She. It arrived with the Vikings when they invaded our land. In some places it is called a Vam~Pyre."

"I have heard strange stories of them in my homeland, stories I would never have believed . . . until now."

"How did you drive it away?"

"I held this up in front of it," he said, lifting up the rose wood string of beads with the cross dangling visible to her.

Patricius spent the rest of the winter carving beads of rose wood and stringing them into loops with the cross attached, making sure each family in the village had one as a means of protection against the Ban~She.

With the spring came the time of his departure. He wanted to travel, handing out bead loops and telling the story for the reason of their making as he travelled from village to village.

Lucinda kissed him lightly on his forehead. A rapid blush flooded his cheeks, causing the villagers to laugh with unmasked goodwill.

"You shouldn't use your Roman name as you travel Patricius. Some may not act too kindly toward you because of it. I think you should call yourself . . . Patrick."

"Patrick. I like it, and so I shall use it," he replied.

"What do you call your string of beads?" she asked him.

"I think . . . um, a rosary, because it is made from the wood of the rose. Here, I want you to have the first one I carved," he said, removing the rosary from around his neck and dropping it into Lucinda's hand. She looked uncertain. "Don't worry, I have another in my pocket," he said. Then he turned, and after blessing the villagers, began his westward journey across the island.

Some held smiles, some let tears roll, all had well wishing in their hearts for the robust young man.

Lucinda reached down, took her daughter's hand and said, "Come with me." Together they moved along the path leading into the woods. Not far into them they reached the ancient oak where Bukwold's axe was buried. Draping the rosary over its handle Lucinda shouted, "Here and no further. Now you, Marion," she said to her daughter. "Here and no further," spoke the child, her voice bold and defiant against the evil Bukwold had brought.

Chapter Five

"LET ME GUESS," said Joseph James, "that's the story of of St. Patrick and the seed of the idea that the crucifix repels vampires, ala Count Dracula. Come on man, I've been around the block a few times. You don't expect me to believe those tales do you?"

The mountain man eyed him long and hard and replied low and deep, "Not yet."

Clacking his coffee cup down on the wood surface of the table, Truman lifted the flap of the leather case lying at his elbow. Reaching into it, he pulled out a rolled up piece of bound leather, the thong blackened by age. He tossed the scroll to the younger man and said, "Read it." Joseph James unrolled the sheet of leather and flattened it out on the table. "I can't read this. I don't recognize any of these symbols," he said, pointing to the jumble of markings cut into the surface of the leather.

"The language is ancient Gaelic," said Truman, a serene smile accompanying his words, "Go ahead, look again."

Joseph looked down at the leather sheet. The symbols began to swim before his eyes, forming themselves into words he could read.

Across the table, Truman grinned.

The photojournalist's attention leaped from interest to astonishment in a matter of seconds. He felt as if he'd been taken out of his familiar world of natural beauty and placed in a time warp as he looked into the aged man's lively eyes. And as the gray bearded fellow spoke, it felt the closest thing to rightness Joseph James had ever known.

Of course, upon Truman's initial proposal to listen to his story, Joseph had the furtherance of his career uppermost in his mind. Their chance meeting and the circumstances in which it took place was in itself enough for a good story. He already had several embellishments in mind, like the discovery that the old geezer had taken LSD somewhere along the way, had seen God, had seen the Devil, and had decided the safest place in the world was in the wilderness.

He looked down at the scroll and back at the old man, his mouth dropped open. Finding his voice he said, "What in the blue blazes of Hell is this?"

"The land of legend and lore son," replied Truman, chuckling under his breath. "It's simply called the Prophecy. Don't ask me where it originated, 'cause I don't know.

But if you agree to hear my entire story, you'll find out how it came into my possession."

Yes, Truman could very well be a psycho. But as the younger man looked into the steel of the older man's eyes, he knew he'd met a soul tried by life and by death, feared neither, and that to listen to his story was a no-option must.

Truman leaned forward on his elbows. "Do you think I could be in the grip of madness?" he asked.

"The thought crossed my mind, but I want to hear your story, and reserve judgment until then. No offense."

"None taken, in fact I would have been worried about your qualifications if you weren't a little skeptical. But your curiosity should override your skepticism, if you're true to your calling, don't you think?"

"Yes . . . I suppose so. But why do you say my calling? Photojournalism is my profession, one that I chose at a young age."

"Let me ask you one question," said Truman.

"Shoot."

"Do you understand it when I say that the middle of nowhere is the center of everywhere?"

Pensive for a moment, he swallowed and then nodded. "As strange as it sounds, especially to me, I do understand it."

And Joseph James had been opened like a window to forever through which the story would be poured.

THE DREAM

CHAPTER SIX

"**I** CAN'T REMEMBER EXACTLY when it started, sometime just before the snow flies up along the border. They used to call this the last best place, and maybe it was, once upon a time, but that's how all fairy tales begin. This is no fairy tale, it happened, and I do not exaggerate when I tell you the continuation of the human race, or at least the delaying of its extinction, depends on the telling of this story and you getting it out there.

Ever since I discovered beer at a young age, I've liked to drink it, so much so I became an alcoholic, or, maybe I was one to begin with and those first beers triggered the disease. But that's irrelevant, what is relevant is that I drank and drove once too often and got slapped with a five year prison sentence here in Montana.

I remember with vivid clarity my first glimpse of it through the bars of the cell window. The snow was drifting down soft, like feathers swinging on invisible strings in the still and silent night. The scene launched me back to a time in my youth when Christmas was joyous and magical. But not this time, nor has

23

it been any year since, for that comforting scene held within its deceptive embrace the very fountainhead of all that is evil.

Have you ever been to the Deer Lodge valley Joseph?"

"No, I haven't. I'm from Northern California."

"I've always wanted to visit there, guess I never will, oh well. Anyway, the Deer Lodge valley sits ringed by the Rocky Mountains. The nearest and highest peaks loom off to the west. Lower and more gently sloping mountains are far off in the east. To the north, the low hills are barren and make a flat horizon so they don't stop much of the cold wind. To the south, the mountains are treeless, but higher and more jagged than their northern counterparts. Get the picture?"

Joseph nodded silently as he stood to refill his cup.

"My cell window faced south, toward the higher and more jagged peaks of the barren hills."

Joseph sat down, the wooden legs of his chair scraping against the hand hewn planks of the floor, his hands wrapped around the hot mug of coffee. After setting it down, he picked up his pen and held it poised over the paper.

"The snow had quit falling but the silence of the cold remained, and as I watched, the moon exploded from behind a cloud, casting a glow of spotlight intensity on the whitened ground. From the intensity of that light, my gaze moved up the shadowed hillside.

About a third of the way up it I saw a large, black, rectangular object. As my eyes adjusted to the shift in light, I made it out to be a simple, nondescript concrete building set into the hillside like an abandoned bunker. No lights glowed in the two smaller rectangles on the face of it, which I took for windows. It was nothing more than a no frills building squatting on the hillside for no apparent reason and with no obvious purpose. And as I gazed through the bars of the window, I wondered how I was supposed to make it through the coming aloneness of winter with my health, my sanity, or anything else in tact, and closed my eyes."

*   *   *

"I moved, feeling the serenity, through a lush green meadow, the surrounding trees were all dressed up for Fall. I think it was afternoon. The sun was high and full ablaze, but it wasn't hot. I walked along a winding path through tall grass. Scattered along the path were apple trees bearing blood red fruit. A few insects hummed nonchalantly about, not near, not far, just there. The path led into a mist enshrouded dark forest at the edge of the meadow. It looked forbidding and chilling and I felt a prickly caution before moving into it. I found it wasn't as dense as I at first thought. The sparse underbrush and the trees rustled but I felt no wind.

A sudden whooshing sound caused me to twitch. I peered into the woods that were on both sides of the path. The mist, neither thickening nor thinning, began to wrap itself around the trees like hands groping for a finger hold around a throat. The sudden whooshing sound flew by my ears, louder this time. I ducked, thinking it was the sound of a large bird winging its way south just above the treetops, but I saw nothing. Straightening, I continued my journey along the curvy path. As far as I knew, I was out for a leisurely stroll on a sunny afternoon.

Sunny? A moment ago, the fog covered the landscape and blotted out the sky.

I looked up at the exposed sky from the middle of a small clearing. The mist above had dissipated, I knew not when, and the sun had sunk down in front of me, trying to penetrate the remaining low-lying mist, causing the tiny particles of water to glow golden and shine rainbows.

The air suddenly felt dank, as if the sun could no longer radiate heat. Taking in a deep breath, I caught no scent of distant ocean air, or of the nearby pines. Instead, there was an odor like that of damp, humus earth, or the wet fur of a mongrel dog.

WHO-O-O-SH!

My curiosity pressed hard against fear. Sound is made by something of substance that produces waves in the air, and this was a large substance.

A shadow flitted across the face of the sun, causing momentary darkness, and then disappeared into the woods on my left, as a crashing came through the misted underbrush.

I heard a low growl rumble from the depths of a cavernous chest as the sound of rustling bushes, cracking twigs, and breaking tree limbs circled around to stop, hidden, in front of me. The pungent odor of dank earth, churned up by whatever was out there, assailed my nostrils and nauseated my gut. Then my apprehension crystallized into cold fear at the thunderous sound of crashing and splintering in the woods. Something alive and howling hurtled towards me and hit me with the force of a runaway train, its fetid breath hot in my face, my ribs feeling as if they had been splintered. My hands went up as I flew backwards, each one grabbing a handful of damp stinking fur, then I hit the ground hard on my back. At the same time my knees came up and, arching my back against the pain, I flipped the repulsive beast off my chest, in a flash I turned over and scrambled to my feet, ready to face the thing's next attack. But it was lying on its side across the dirt path, not far from me, its rear hooves digging at the ground, its front paws clawing at it, its jaws snapping as foam spewed from its mouth.

It was like nothing I had ever seen or imagined. I should have turned and run but the creature mesmerized me and drew me nearer to it. The sun rested on the tops of the western peaks ready to take its plunge behind the granite spires. The beast's chest and shoulders, the size of a horse's, were covered with thick gray foul smelling fur. Its hindquarters and legs were covered with pink scaly skin and sparse wiry hair. Its head and neck were of the same pink scaly skin. It had ears like a hog's that stood up instead of droop; its muzzle was like a wolf's with six-inch tusks instead of sharp canines. Its jaws snapped up and down as it raked the ground with its front paws and bellowed in fury, the guttural sound like the roaring of an enraged mountain lion.

I don't know why it didn't spring up and come at me, but I didn't waste time thinking about it. I leaped ahead, landing with my left foot on the beasts shoulder, pinning it to the ground. I could feel its muscles pulsating under my foot as it let go with a furious howl strong enough to curdle the blood of a demon. I hoped I had enough strength to keep the hellish thing down.

I managed to retain my senses and began kicking the loathsome beast in its leathery throat with the top of my right foot. Once, twice, again and again, squelching the beasts gurgling shrieks. I screamed with the effort. Sweat ran down my face, my heart hammered against my ribs, both inside and outside. Outside?

"Hey, hey man you alright up there?" the guy below me hollered as he thumped the underside of my bunk.

"I was lying on my left side and had been kicking the wall with the top of my right foot," I said.

"So it was a dream you were having?" asked Joseph James.

"What else could it be?" I replied.

"Anyway, I answered my celly—that's short for cellmate—yeah, yeah I'm alright, just dreaming I guess."

"I guess so. You were kicking hell out of the wall," he said in his gravelly voice.

"After the dream I lay there silent on my bunk, staring out at the moonlight bathed bunker crouched on the hillside, as if it were ready to strike at something, but what or how? It was a simple unpainted concrete structure and nothing more."

CHAPTER SEVEN

SOMETHING HIT THE slab wood door with a thud, followed by a haunting hypnotic howl.

"They're after the hide!" I hollered and sprung up with a swiftness that surprised me. I grabbed my rifle and Joseph James opened the door just as I got to it. Then I fired a single booming shot into the air that scattered three huge gray wolves into the blackness of the night.

"They probably hated the old silvertip more than me. He stole many a meal from that pack. Better give me a hand here Joseph, we'll have to drag the hide inside for the rest of the night, stink and all." I said.

Completing the task, we refilled our coffee cups and sat down at the table.

"Now, where were we? Oh yeah, I'd had my dream and was kicking the wall. Foot hurt like hell the next morning too.

We had our usual rude awakening when "CHOW CALL" blared over the loudspeaker, located in the ceiling, ten feet outside our door, pretty much next to our ears. Then our door, along with thirteen others in the block, slid open and clanged to a stop, vibrating the walls, jangling everyone's nerves, started the day off right, I guess. Maybe I'd get used to the sound someday, but hoped I never would. Some had, like my celly Chico. He'd been locked up for twenty years now and was over the half-century mark in age, like me.

"You going to breakfast?" I asked the semi-awake Chico.

"Fuck no. I hate that goddam sausage gravy. What were you dreaming about anyway?"

"Some kind of a dog or wolf was after me and knocked me down. I rolled it off me, pinned it to the ground with one foot, and was kicking it in the throat with the other."

"Strange dream, bro. You sure were bustin' hell out of the wall. I thought you might wake up the whole damn block. Probably the haints paid you a visit."

"The what?"

"Better go to breakfast or you'll miss it," he replied and then rolled over and fell back asleep.

I shuffled along with the crowd of other inmates. A few were lively but most were like zombies in the early morning darkness of winter. The wind blew cold out of the east, making a final stand before the sun came up to bring an illusion of warmth.

Our overcoats were olive drab in color and none too thick. They wouldn't keep a man from freezing if he was out in the winter weather too long. The walk to the chow hall was about the length of a football field, not too long.

Seat yourself, gobble it down, choke it down, wash it down, done. Grunt a few good mornings in between to some faces in blue shirts and blue stocking hats, throw on the quick freeze overcoat, and head back to the cell.

The same good morning once again.

Walking south, I moved my gaze up the mountainside. The mysterious concrete structure seemed to float on the roll of razor wire strung on top of the twelve-foot high chain link fence. Morning sunlight struck the top of the mountain, and the dawn revealed what appeared to be a long, high fence attached to the eastern side of the hunkered building, extending about thirty yards out from it. I focused on it and could see it was built of wooden planks, set horizontally, with equally spaced gaps in between to allow the wind to whistle through. Its only purpose, as near as I could figure, was that it was used for a loading chute. I made my way back to the cell.

"How was breakfast, extra shitty, shitty, or almost not bad?" asked the now awake Chico.

"Shitty," I replied to his knowing chuckle which sounded somewhere between a working gristmill and a rock crusher. I poured myself some water from his hot pot, added instant coffee to it, and sat on the blanket covered stainless steel toilet, the only chair in the house.

A few men were out in the day room chattering away. Some of us worked, some of us didn't. Chico didn't because his liver was shutting down from hepatitis-C. I worked in the afternoons as a teacher's aid, helping guys with math and reading so they could obtain their GED.

Occasionally, out in the fourteen by seventy foot day room, a scuffle would break out and somebody would end up with a black eye, then both the combatants would go to the hole. It didn't matter what or who started it. That was the extent of any violence on the low security side where we were. On the high side, it may have been different, but judging from what I'd seen so far and the stories I'd heard, prison is nothing like the movies or television make it out to be. If portrayed in reality the show would be way too boring to attract an audience.

Most of the men I'd met were easy to get along with, some I even liked, and some like Chico, I'd go to war with. But there was no need for that. Seventy-five percent of us were locked up for drinking something, or smoking something, or snorting something that one group has deemed illegal. And that group has the power to enforce their proclamation. I don't know when societal denial will come to an end and the starched collars realize that people like to feel good and get high, like from having sex for instance. It's only natural.

All the collateral damage done; robberies, rapes, murders and the like, caused by the drug's illegality, would be diminished by a whole bunch.

"Oh, sorry, Joseph James, I got carried away. Pet peeve of mine as you probably guessed."

"I sort of figured that out. But I see your point, and for the most part, agree with it," he said.

"Well, well, a man after my own heart to boot. Anyway, where was I before I got on my soapbox?"

"In your cell, after breakfast, sitting with Chico."

"Right, thanks. And so, it isn't We the People anymore, but You the Taxpayers or You the Voters, or You the Consumer . . . hallelujah!"

"Soapbox," interjected Joseph.

"Sorry. Let's see . . . so anyway, life in prison, one-oh-one.

Imagine that for all of your life you have defined yourself by what you do, by what you have, and by how fast and how far you have climbed the ladder of success, in other words, living a normal life in terms of current society. And then, in the blink of an eye, all of that doesn't amount to a gob of spit, not your education, not your profession, not your money, not where you're from, or if you ever had parents or not. Bam! You're in prison! And it's about standing on your own two feet with no family, no friends, and no support group around you."

Outside the cold wind rustled the birch leaves. The mountain man continued. "Anyway, I got back from chow, was sitting on the toilet chair, and asked Chico, "What was it you said earlier?"

"Bout what?"

"Something like aint's."

"Haints."

"Whatever," I said.

"They's spirits, reluctant—and I can't imagine why—to leave this here shit hole. This block we're in used to be the maximum-security unit. Block X, next door, was the old death row. People have hanged themselves, cut their own wrists and throats in this place."

He took a gulp of coffee and then gave me a look that said he believed what he was telling me. I did not.

"I had a nightmare, that's all," I said.

"The worst you ever had?"

"Pretty much," I replied. He didn't answer, didn't need to. As far as he was concerned, the case was closed.

"Besides, don't you mean haunts?" I asked.

"Nope, 'cause they ain't neither haunts nor saints, but somewhere in between. They'll do you good, comfort you, or scare the living bejeezus out of you. Haints.

By the way, what'd the animal in your shit kicking dream look like?"

"I'm not sure, something like a wolf, or a boar with a chest the size of a horse's."

"There you go, that makes about a dozen of you now that have described the old boarwolf," said Chico.

CHAPTER EIGHT

MEDICINE HORSE CAME around and asked me to walk the oval with him during recreation time.

"It's below freezing out there," I protested.

"Just barely," he countered.

"Don't be a wuss," chimed in Chico.

"You don't have much room to talk," I said. He chuckled. He'd get out more, all the time in fact, if he could.

Out to the oval I went.

Horse was a Lakota, a little older than me, he wore his hair to his waist and there wasn't a streak of gray in it. Barrel chested, he had the classic Native American face; chiseled, stoic, and with the high cheekbones. At the most, he was five feet tall. He got shortchanged in the legs. They looked like they were meant for a different body and somehow got stuck on his.

We braved the winter weather as we trudged around the track situated outside the gym. The sky, sapphire blue above us, was deceiving. It looked gorgeous but was deadly cold. Stocking hats pulled down over our ears, coat collars pulled up, gloves, thermal underwear, and socks on, we were the only ones on the track. The rest were in the gym, lifting weights. Big biceps garnered respect in prison, which left me out. But I could hold my own.

"Spirits walk the hallways," Horse said above the wind.

"What?"

"Spirits walk the hallways," he repeated.

"Did Chico put you up to this?" I returned as the wind bit into our faces. Medicine Horse enjoyed the feel of it, but not as much as he enjoyed my question.

"I have not spoken to Chico in a week, maybe longer," he replied.

"I don't doubt your word, but why are you telling me this?"

"Wally said to tell you."

I had never met Wally, but I knew who he was, a Lakota holy man, eighty years old, and confined to a wheelchair. Medicine Horse pushed him to meals and the infirmary when the need arose. Wally lived in the cell next to Horse over on X block.

The sky suddenly changed and snowflakes began to spin down, dry and powdery, and as they built up, they crunched under our feet every step we took.

"What's Wally got to do with it?" I asked.

"He sits on the High Hill, close to death, close to the spirit world where he will soon travel.

From the High Hill, the veil begins to part; he sees more of the next world than he does of this one. He told me to find the Ishtay Wakanka."

"The what?"

"The Ishtay Wakanka. You are the one they seek."

The wind picked up.

"What the hell are you talking about Horse?" I hollered, turning my face toward him and into the biting wind.

"The spirits seek a man such as yourself."

"And exactly how is . . . myself?"

"Have you not always searched for truth? Have you not labored to understand what lies underneath all things? Have you not tried to understand Wakan Tanka?"

The snow swirled and danced in the wind as it fell heavier around us.

"Wakan what?"

"Wakan Tanka. The Great Mystery, The Everywhere Spirit, That Which Is, in white man's words, God."

"I suppose I have tried, in a round about way, although I've never been much of a church goer."

"The spirits have seen this."

"Are you sure the first part of your name shouldn't be . . . Crazy?" I asked. He simply chuckled.

"Why would the spirits send the nightmare then?" I asked, as if I was beginning to believe what he was saying.

"To get your attention, you wouldn't have sat up so straight if angels had visited you, would you?"

"It was a dream, not a visit. But supposing it was a visit, why would the 'spirits' seek me?"

"Through you they will be able to go home more easily."

"Crazy . . . Horse," I said, shaking my head in bewilderment.

He became silent as we rounded the last turn of the oval.

Straight ahead of us was the building. It looked like it was floating—cold, dark, and empty—on top of the razor wire. I could feel the emptiness within it reaching out like tentacles to touch everything around and its touch would render loneliness desirable.

The snow stopped. The wind picked up and sang through the planks of the loading chute. Gutters, hanging loose off the building, clanked against its side in time with the wind's song, a song that called to the growing emptiness in me, and like the fabled sirens of old, it offered a subtle promise of comfort and mystery.

Horse looked at me. "Are you sure it was just a dream?" he asked.

CHAPTER NINE

HORSE AND I climbed the few steps to the entry door of the minimum-security building. I pressed a buzzer, the guard looked up through the Plexiglas and pressed a button, the door lock snapped back and in we went.

"Afternoon Homer," I said.

"Afternoon gents," the guard replied as we slipped our ID cards through the slot under the interior window.

He waved us on, didn't want to take his feet off his desk or move his ass off the soft chair he was leaning back in.

Like people everywhere, most of the guards were regular types, putting in their time, doing a minimal job, and wanting as few hassles as possible while on their shift.

I peeled off into Y block Horse continued to X block.

He never said another word to me about spirits, and didn't need to. My instincts were beginning to line up with what he'd told me.

Many men had met their death in this building by hanging themselves, or slashing their wrists, or cutting their own throats in here, so I guess it was possible restless and bewildered spirits

39

could walk the halls. I didn't rule it out; the smell of lost hope and dying dreams permeated the place.

I asked Chico if he'd put Medicine Horse up to trying to convince me the haints were real.

"No, honest bro, I didn't. Why?"

"He spent the entire rec time telling me about spirits that walk the hallways."

"Do you believe it," he asked.

"I'll keep an open mind on the subject, but that's as far as I'll go."

"Suit yourself, but you'll be convinced, sooner or later."

CHAPTER TEN

I HAD NEVER FELT such aloneness. I found some solace sitting in the day room watching snowfall from out of the white skies of day or the black skies of night. Sometimes it blanketed the land like a down comforter. Other times it pelted the ground with tiny ice particles, the wind then piling it into powdery drifts. Sometimes the moon and stars were generous in their sharing of light. Sometimes the night was so black it was palpable. But none of it could pull me out of the spiraling vortex I had fallen into. Whether the day room was crowded or not, I always felt alone, secreted somewhere deep within myself, a place I had retreated to, a silent void within my soul, which felt as frozen as the snowy scene outside. And always there was the building and its siren song calling to that empty place within me.

Chapter Eleven

Winter relented to the gentle hands of spring as they sought to get a grip on the land.

I didn't have anymore freakish nightmares or thoughts of haints. The immediate intense pull of the building subsided to almost nothing, and I paid little attention to it sitting there, always dark, on the mountainside. But during the moments when the wind would sing through the planks of the loading chute and the gutters would clank in time to the music, its drawing power pulled at me much stronger than at first, finally occupying my mind enough that I asked Chico if he knew the story behind it, if there was one.

"Used to be a slaughterhouse," he said, pouring hot water over a spoonful of instant coffee and tossing in a packet of sugar.

A slaughterhouse, I wasn't surprised, it explained the loading chute on the eastern side.

"Have a set," he said. I sat down on the blanket covered toilet seat. He sat down on his bunk.

Chico was a friend I could talk to. He had nothing to prove and nothing to lose when he spoke, nor did he care what anybody thought of him. When he did speak, it was from the heart and true with nothing wrapped around it to have to wade through. What you saw was what you got, a rough looking, short, stout, mostly Apache with tattoos up and down his arms, and 'fuck off' tattooed on his lips. Fuck on the upper, off on the lower. He always liked to say, "Read my lips," and if he ever got out of prison he wanted to get a custom T-shirt that read:

Jesus Loves Me
everybody else thinks I'm an asshole

That's how he was, one of those rare people who actually did have a heart of gold and would give you the shirt off his back.

"They shut it down about five years ago," he said. "I used to work there myself, killing, skinning, and cutting up the meat. That was how they fed us back then. We'd get steak and eggs three times a week, and real hamburgers, not like now, of course."

"Not even close," I replied with some angst. The food here was always the same, lousy.

Chico took a gulp of his coffee. "This is nasty shit, but I can't leave it alone."

"Me neither," I said, fixing myself a cup.

"Now, where were we?" he asked.

"Slaughterhouse."

"Oh, yeah, anyways, they shut it down." I asked, "Why? Doesn't the prison own the cattle around here?"

"Yeah, sure they own the cattle. But it's sold on the hoof nowadays. We used to butcher it ourselves up there to the slaughterhouse," he said.

"I know, you already told me."

"About five years ago. Did I say that already? Don't seem that long ago. Time flies when you're having fun, huh?" he chuckled and took another swallow of coffee.

"They shut down the slaughterhouse because . . . ?" I urged.

"Oh yeah, about five years ago, I s'pose you want to know the reason why."

"I'm curious, sure."

"Well . . . I've got nothing but time, as they say, whoever the hell *they* are."

CHAPTER TWELVE

"**D**ID YOU FIND the Ishtay Wakanka?" Wally asked as Medicine Horse strolled into the old man's cell.

"Yes, he is a white man."

"Bring him to me that I may see him. Then I will know for certain," said Wally. Without a word Horse disappeared into the hallway and walked on cat's paws down the thirty feet of it to Y block. Entering, he moved just as silent to cell seven. He stepped in through the open doorway, his shadow causing me to look up at him. "Wally would see you," was all he said. Chico nodded at me. "The story of the slaughterhouse can wait," he said. I nodded back and followed Horse through the dayroom and out to the main hallway.

It was the first time I'd met Wally. I'd seen Horse pushing him in his wheelchair now and then, but I had never spoken to the man. He sat in his chair, dressed in a plain gray sweatshirt and gray sweat pants. His snow-white hair was parted in the middle. He appeared frail in his body and the lines on his face were many and deep, giving it the look of saddle leather. His eyes, though tired, were still bright and strong, strong enough to see the end of his days. Of average height, he sat perfectly erect, and probably weighed no more than a hundred pounds.

He riveted my attention. He was a grandfather, an elder in the world. His presence was peace, his face was wise, and his eyes danced. He seemed as if he had come from eternity and to there he would soon return. He was gentle, yet commanding, and I approached with immediate respect, waiting for him to speak.

"What is your name?" he asked.

"Truman Struck."

"True Man Struck," Wally repeated, letting the name roll off his tongue. He smiled. His teeth weren't anywhere close to Hollywood white, but they were all his own.

"Ishtay Wakanka," he said, raising up his right hand with the palm facing me. Suddenly, the frail old man rose up from his wheelchair, his snowy hair falling to his waist. I felt a gentle hand push me forward, and after three steps, I was standing before him. Placing his right hand on the top of my head, he whispered, "Ishtay Wakanka," and then sat down.

I stepped back, expecting to bump into Medicine Horse. He wasn't there

"I must rest now," Wally said. I nodded. My mind was confused, but my heart at peace. For the first time in my life I felt like I'd been in the presence of a true holy man.

Horse walked with me back to the block and then to my cell. We didn't speak on the way, didn't need to.

He just smiled, he could see I was awestruck and that I knew what Wally said was true, though I didn't yet understand it.

CHAPTER THIRTEEN

"WHATTA YA KNOW?" asked Chico, as I plopped down on the blanket-covered toilet.

"Nothing about the slaughterhouse," I replied, then looked up to say goodbye to Medicine Horse, but he had disappeared.

"Oh yeah, the old slaughterhouse, up there on the mountain," Chico said, pointing his right thumb over his shoulder.

I glanced out the window. Centered in its frame loomed the concrete structure, a gray blotch on the otherwise pristine landscape. It sat on a natural ledge a third of the way up the mountain, two large windows—with the long sides vertical—faced us. A double sized garage door, winged by a retaining wall on each side, was underneath and centered between the darkened windows, which gave the appearance that the building had a crude face with gray, mottled skin, two black holes for eyes, and an open, gaping mouth.

I shook my head, trying to clear my vision, shuddering as I did so. I blinked and looked again. I saw a decrepit old concrete structure, looking abandoned but right at home in the gray drizzle of early spring.

"You want I should turn up the heat?" Chico chuckled. Of course, we weren't able to; they kept it at a constant sixty-five degrees in the cellblocks.

He resumed his story. "Eight of us worked there just before it was shut down. I worked on the killing floor and I liked it." He winked. "The truth be told, the other guys probably didn't have the stomach for it.

I had me a big fucking knife, I'd slit their throats, hook 'em through the hind legs between the bone and the tendon, hang 'em upside down, shove 'em over a drain and let 'em bleed out.

I had an electric winch to help out of course." He paused, gave me an amused look and asked, "Wanna hear more?"

"No."

"Next I'd slide a big plastic tub underneath the poor departed creature after it quit bleeding, then slit it open and pull out all its insides; guts, lungs, liver, heart, the whole shebang, and let the mess fall into the tub, saving out the liver of course.

If I had the time, I'd cut off the legs. I always cut off the head, used a little electric chain saw for that. Just like slicing through butter with a hot knife. Then I'd shove 'em down the line using the overhead track, minus the head and insides, and sometimes the legs if I was feeling generous."

"You already said that."

". . . to the skinners. There was two of them.

Took longer to skin the stupid critters than it did to slaughter 'em, ya see. Not a big operation as you can tell," he said, once more poking his thumb over his shoulder toward the building.

My attention drawn, I looked in that direction. The sky had darkened to the hue of gunmetal. The steady drizzle was turning the whitened ground into winter ugly slush. A sudden flash of light lit the face of the mottled gray building, with its dead black windows for eyes, and that gaping mouth that seemed to say, "Feed me."

"From the skinners, the carcasses were then pushed on down to the cutters, who'd make the whole mess into meat. Four of them there was. So altogether there was . . . lessee . . . me, Joe and Pete, the four cutters, Ray, Roy, Tuffy, and . . . hell, I can't remember the other guy's name, real quiet fellow. Makes what . . . eight of us?"

"Seven," I answered.

"Right, eight of us up there to the slaughterhouse, are you bored yet?"

"Quite."

"Well, after I'd kilt the last stupid critter, I'd go and help the cutters grind the meat into hamburger. We'd do two beeves a day was all, and then clean up the whole goddam mess each and ever day."

"Interesting."

"Stunk too."

"Fascinating."

The wind played its siren song through the blood stained planks of the loading chute, barely audible through the window glass.

"You ever heard the story of Sleepy Hollow?" he asked from somewhere west of left field.

"The one by Washington Irving?"

"That'd be it."

"Sure, I've seen a couple of movies about it."

49

"Ichabob Cain."

"Okay . . ."

"It wasn't Crane, like in the book, but Cain, like in Cain and Able."

"And . . . ?"

"That was the fourth cutters name, just remembered. Probably looked like the weird duck in the book, too."

"You're bullshitting, aren't you?"

"No, really, Ichabod Cain, that was his name. Hey, that rhymes, sort of. Anyway, we called him . . ."

"Let me guess, Icky."

"Damn you are sharp son!" replied Chico. We chuckled.

The wind song playing through the loading chute picked up, drawing my attention once again out the window to the building on the hill.

"Kind of eerie ain't it."

"What?"

"That sound, almost like music, but it ain't."

"Yeah, eerie."

"Some say it's the song of the haints."

"Come on man," I groaned.

"I ain't saying it is," he protested. "Just some say so and maybe it could be. That's all I'm saying bro, that's all. Now, where was we?"

I thought I saw a shadow flit across the face of the window. From the corner of the eye, things sometimes seen are not there, then again, sometimes they are. It's a fifty-fifty guess.

"Ichabod Cain," I answered.

"Tall, gangly fellow," he continued, "thin, but as strong as any of us. His face was thin and ghostly pale, his nose long and thin like the rest of him, and in profile, came to a definite point. His forehead, mouth, and chin slanted back from there, his forehead the most, couldn't miss the Adam's apple neither. His hair was jet black, along with his bushy eyebrows. His eyes, dark brown, almost black themselves, protruded outward with a penetrating gaze. He wasn't easy to read, always kinda secret like, intelligent I s'pose. He almost never talked, but when he did, it carried weight. He was the type who could say a lot with few words."

"How tall was he," I asked.

"Six-two, six-three, somewhere thereabouts."

"Hair . . . long, short?"

"Medium length. And ya know, if I was a movie maker, he'd of been the perfect fit for the real Ichabod Crane of the story, or, a perfect fit for old Count Dracula hisself, though he never displayed any fierceness, just a perturbing strangeness, otherworldly like. He sure would of been a good fit for the part though, put a set of fangs in his mouth and a black cloak on him and all that there."

It wasn't my blood, but the marrow in my bones that turned icy as I visualized the mesmerizing Count of old.

"Yeah, old Ichabod Cain, quite the story all on its own . . .

Chapter Fourteen

. . . Ichabod Cain lives down the lane, Ichabod Cain he's so insane," chanted the girls from across the street as the tall, gangly adolescent slogged his way up it, galoshes splashing with each step through the gray and dismal day.

He'd gotten used to the boys making fun of him; they'd done it all though elementary school so it didn't bother him anymore. He was different, and no denying it, but he liked it, and he didn't like them.

He'd thought his situation might improve, and had hoped he'd stop being teased so much now that he was starting his first year at Butte High. If anything, it had gotten worse, and it hurt worse, now that the girls had joined in.

But the girls, that was different, he liked them. He'd liked them ever since that patch of black fur had sprouted on his crotch.

"Ichabod Cain, lives down the lane, Ichabod Cain, he's so insane," continued the high-pitched chant from across the street. He wished they'd stop. He knew they wouldn't.

Down the lane is an isolated, impoverished area of Butte, known to the locals as Walkerville. No one knew how the neighborhood—on the other side of the tracks and located in the flatlands of the hilly town—got its name.

Butte became a town due to copper. An open pit mine on the edge of town needed a large workforce, and people, most of them Irish, flooded Butte. Eventually the boomtown atmosphere attracted hard drinking, two-fisted Irishmen to work the mines, brothels on every other corner with a bar between them.

Maybe there were some churches around at the time, but they weren't too prominent if there was. An unknown group had gotten a statue built right smack dab on top of the Continental Divide, just east of town. The dazzling white one hundred foot statue was visible for miles around. Named, 'Our Lady of the Mountains' she represented Mary the mother of Jesus.

Maybe it was enough to redeem Butte.

Maybe not.

And, like all towns built on a boom, the boom goes bust, but the town continues to hang on, generation after generation, sowing its wild oats on Saturday night, praying for crop failures on Sunday morning.

Such is Butte, such is Walkerville, but 'Our Lady of the Mountains' remains always smiling down on both.

Walkerville is where the shanty Irish live. The "I don't give a damn, spit in your eye," hard working class, the miners and the miner's sons, and the sons of the sons of the miners, like Ichabod Cain, son of Jubal. Except Ichabod wasn't Irish, at least half of his blood wasn't, and the gypsy half made him tall and dark and gangly with black hair and dark eyes, the gypsy blood made him different. He wasn't the least bit interested in the rough and tumble lifestyle of the shanty Irish.

". . . Ichabod Cain, he's so insane," the girls chanted behind him as he slogged on to school. In spite of the teasing he received from them, at least it was attention, and he liked that. It made him smile, curving the corners of his razor thin mouth upward as his loins heated and surged.

He wondered, no, longed to, no . . . *needed to*, know how a girl felt. Very soon he would, he assured himself. For since that black thatch had sprouted on his crotch, he'd climbed to the top of the Continental Divide every Sunday of the summer to spew his seed in offering at the feet of 'Our Lady of the Mountains' always remembering to end with ". . . and pray for us sinners, now and at the hour of our death, amen."

". . . Ichabod Cain, he's so insane," filtered up to his ears from down the hill. Whirling in his tracks, he focused his eyes with fierce intensity.

They say genie is the root word of genius, and ma**ybe** that's what happens when Celtic and Gypsy blood are mixed, or maybe it's more along the lines of magic.

Like a herky-jerky stick man walking in the shadows, Ichabod Cain disappeared over the top of the hill.

Down below, the street was silent.

*   *   *

The teasing had stopped and the boys left Ichabod alone, not because they'd matured or felt a particular amount of empathy, if any, for their fellow man. It just wasn't fun anymore.

Ichabod was a nerdy, bookworm, geek. The type who could disappear into the woodwork, and be comfortable and better off left alone there. He liked it that way, until he got in the classroom, where he was a brilliant light turned on.

He'd always sit in the front seat of the aisle against the wall. It was a strategic placement; he had a co-conspirator who would sit diagonally across from him at the back of the room.

That way, he would have a reason to turn and check with his friend about something, and at the same time maybe get a glimpse up some girls skirt without being too conspicuous about it. Or, if some other classmate should ask him a question, he'd have to turn to answer it and maybe get a look that way.

It seemed strange to him to be captivated by need rather than overrun by curiosity. Yet, it didn't matter to Ichabod if he was darkening or his soul was twisting into tightly convoluted knots.

"Ew-w-w, I'm not touching that thing."

The jocks in class snickered at Jenny Lee's reaction as the biology teacher placed a formaldehyde soaked piglet in the stainless steel pan on her desk.

"The pig I mean," she quipped. "It's so icky."

"What?" Ichabod asked looking up from the piglet he'd sliced open, holding the gleaming scalpel in his right hand.

Jenny Lee's face reddened. "I mean the pig, it's so pink and icky and it looks almost like a baby . . ."

". . . pig," finished Ichabod as he reached over with his left hand, picked up Jenny Lee's scalpel, and deftly slit her specimen open with a single perfect incision. "See, it's not so bad. In fact, the internal organs of a pig are quite similar to those of a human, and are placed in the body cavity in the same location."

"How do you know?" she asked.

He pinned her with an intense look. She froze and was as still as the frightened butterflies he had pinned before making them a part of his collection.

"Books," he answered, "on the comparative anatomy of mammals, homosapiens being in that class. I'm going to become a doctor you know."

"Homo, homo," someone whispered from the back, another someone snickered. The teacher looked up from his desk, quieting the room.

Ichabod released her mind from his and placed the scalpel in her hand. Taking his own, he told her, "Now watch me." He flicked his wrist twice, severing the little piglet's heart.

"And I'll huff and I'll puff and I'll blow your house down," he whispered lifting the heart from out of the piglet's chest and showing it to Jenny Lee.

"Thanks, I guess," she meekly responded.

The thin line that served as Ichabod's mouth twitched at the corners in what amounted to a smile.

* * *

Officer Ed Mallory pulled to an unhurried stop in front of Tom and Edna Lewis's home. Pausing long enough to take a deep breath and then slowly exhaling, he opened the door of the cruiser and got out, his stiffening joints not making it easy, his reluctance making it harder still.

Just up the hill a ways from Walkerville, the Lewis's had lived in the same house for twenty years, the same amount of time Ed Mallory had been a cop.

Slumped over more from the twisting in his guts than the wind driven drizzle, he trod up the four steps to the porch, crossed it, and then knocked softly on the door. Tom Lewis answered. Recognizing Ed, the haggard lines recently gouged into his face softened for a moment by the glimmer of hope. He stepped aside, allowing Ed to enter, and then closed the door against the late October weather.

"Any news?" asked Tom. His hope died, for he saw a depth of sorrow in Officer Mallory's eyes he had never seen in a human being before this night, and he was a professional counselor. Fighting back his tears, Ed nodded his head once in affirmation. "We'd better go sit down," he said, gently taking Tom's arm, guiding him to the sofa in the front room. Edna stared beyond the fire in the fireplace, its offered comfort not felt as she sat with hands folded neatly in her lap, her hair up in a bun, her housedress plain but fresh and clean. She was always the lady. Tom sat next to her. Ed seated himself on an easy chair opposite them.

The fire crackled, sparked, and then flared.

"We found Jenny Lee," he said, his voice barely above a whisper, but it echoed and then hung heavy in the room.

"She . . . she . . ."

"Oh dear God . . . no," whispered Edna, trying to stand, but her legs betrayed her.

"She's dead . . . murdered," said the officer, nearly choking on the words, as they resonated like a freight train around the normally cheery and hope filled room.

His twin sister Edna slumped on the sofa, escaping the gritty horror of the news by falling into the oblivion of a faint.

*　*　*

Down in the dimly lit basement of the dimly lit unpainted house in the poorly lit flat part of town, Ichabod Cain sat at his highly polished, ultra clean workbench.

"And I'll huff and I'll puff and I'll blow your house down," he said under his breath while he sliced the heart in half. His mouth twitched at the corners as he placed one-half in a stainless steel pan and tossed the other half on the cold concrete of the basement floor. Hessian, his huge Rottweiler, trotted over from the bottom of the stairs and gobbled down the morsel with a single swallow.

Hessian's gangly master, preferring his part of the delicacy medium rare, held it with a two pronged meat fork over the blue flame of the Bunsen burner, his dark eyes protruding and ablaze with anticipation. Hessian whined, he wanted more, his dripping saliva coagulating into a puddle on the unforgiving floor.

"Go lay down," said Ichabod. Without a sound, the beast of a creature returned to his post at the bottom of the darkened and well-worn wooden stairs. From there, he could and he would, warn away any intruders, including Ichabod's old man, Jubal.

Hessian had learned when he was just a pup, to never disobey his master.

In the ecstasy that can be known only by the mad, Ichabod bit into the soft richness of the young woman's heart. Only the ecstasy he experienced earlier could possibly exceed it. His curiosity to know about young women no longer overran him, his burning need momentarily satisfied. He had experienced 'it', and he found the use of 'it' a much better way to spew his seed.

Upstairs, the doorbell clanged. He heard his lazy drunk of a father get up and open the creaking barrier of a door barely able to keep the world at bay.

"Trick or Treat!" squealed the Walkerville urchins, their high-pitched voices filtering down the stairwell. Hessian growled low in his chest. Trick or treat indeed, thought Ichabod Cain, as the knots in his soul twisted tighter.

"And pray for us sinners now and at the hour of our death, amen," he whispered as he sank his teeth once again into the still dripping morsel.

At the foot of the stairwell, Hessian whimpered, the power of his longing almost exceeding his power to keep it in check, but keep it in check he did.

*   *   *

The lights in the auditorium dimmed. A spotlight flared, hitting a single podium at center stage. On top of it was a microphone.

A short, pink skinned, bald headed man approached the podium from its right and, after adjusting his wire rimmed spectacles and bow tie, spoke to an audience he could not see.

"And now, I'd like to present the valedictorian of the Butte High School graduating class of one thousand six hundred and sixty-six," he announced with surprising enthusiasm.

The auditorium remained silent.

"Oh, I beg your pardon," the pink skin of the man's bald head darkening from the flush of embarrassment.

"I mean the graduating class of one thousand nine hundred and sixty-six . . . Ichabod Jubal Cain."

Icky smiled at the apparent slip in speech. How right you are Mr. Principal, he thought as he left his front row seat to approach the podium. A smattering of obligatory applause followed him, but at least they didn't chant, "Ichabod Cain, he's so insane."

He won the honor of valedictorian by default. His academic record demanded it, and left no room for other consideration.

No one, besides himself, had graduated from Butte High with a straight A average from start to finish. And that included physical education. Though pale and thin, he possessed enormous strength, equal to that of any strutting jock that entered the gym.

Not an athlete by any stretch of the imagination, he always responded to the question, "How do you manage to stay so strong?" with the same answer, "It's all about heart," he'd say, with a twitch at the corners of his mouth.

The jocks often heard their coaches talk about having heart, so they accepted Icky's answer as a valid one.

Dodge ball was his game, his rail thin body nearly impossible to hit. He'd give a little tuck here, a tiny twist there, and *zip*, the ball would shoot by him and smack against the wall. It was like trying to hit a ghost, they'd say.

Once in a while, the quarterback of the football team, or a starting pitcher on the baseball team would throw at him. All bets were on the thrower, so sure were they that Ichabod would get tagged. But the ball would mysteriously swerve away from his body just before impact.

Ichabod could throw with fearsome intensity, his lanky body a tightly wound spring that uncoiled with merciless force, his arm a vicious whip, and often the ball would swerve off course to smack somebody in the face or in the genitals, as if it had been willed to do so.

He'd led the Bulldogs to the state basketball championship during his senior year, just to prove he could. His coach marveled at his ability to take over a game, seeming to will shot after shot to drop through the net. When asked about it, Icky would always reply, "It's all about heart, coach" and then smile. And Oh Lordy did he have a charming smile when he displayed it. In fact, so much so that he'd stolen the hearts of many young women whenever the Bulldogs were playing in another town. And it was likely he'd stolen their virginity also. He just had a mesmerizing way about him.

A member of the winning state debate team, winner of the regional science fair, Ichabod Cain was the perfect product of the American Dream and voted most likely to succeed, although everyone knew success for him wasn't likely, it was a sure thing.

Yet, in the face of all that, Ichabod wasn't popular, but that was his choice. They said he was aloof, even cold, but that was his business and the right of genius.

He took the podium, the light applause quickly dying to silence.

"Ladies and gentlemen, esteemed faculty, and class of nineteen sixty-six," The kids erupted in cheers. Goofy bunch, he thought.

"Life before us is full of opportunities," he began,

"and the public education system has taught me not only to see them but also how to take full advantage of them. For that I'd like to thank the town of Butte, and in particularly, Butte High School." There was an explosion of cheers, this time from the entire audience. "And that is what we, the graduating class of nineteen hundred and sixty-six, need to recognize, that there are myriads of opportunities in front of us. And who can tell what the future will bring? The future will bring what we take to the future." The loud applause died down at the wave of Ichabod's hand. "And who knows what greatness lies in the hearts of men and of women." And oh how well he knew the hearts of women.

"To paraphrase a famous author, the future could be the best of times or the worst of times. It could hold the temple of wisdom, or the ruins of foolishness. It may prove to be a spring of hope, or a winter of despair, a time of dazzling brightness or of suffocating darkness. And we, the graduating class of nineteen sixty-six, will play a major part in the shaping of what the future brings if we seize the opportunities that lie before us."

The auditorium erupted into wild applause.

"I, as many of you know, have decided to pursue a career in medicine, as a doctor. Unfortunately, there isn't a medical school in Montana, and so with a heavy heart, I will be leaving this fine state. But who in their right mind would turn down a full academic scholarship? And so I have made the effort, throughout my High School years, to take advantage of the opportunities and have studied any and all sciences remotely related to the study of medicine and my career goals. And because of that, I have learned one thing beyond the dimmest shadow of a doubt…"he paused, holding the crowd breathlessly silent, "…if God decided the world needed an enema…Butte is where he'd stick it! Fuck you very much."

The audience sat in stunned and absolute silence.

Ichabod Cain strode off the stage to his left wearing the largest and most charming grin anyone had ever seen on his hatchet thin face. And as he went he chanted, "Ichabod Cain lives down the lane. Ichabod Cain he's so insane," and then shot his right arm straight up in the air with the middle finger fully extended just before disappearing through the door marked EXIT.

Jubal Cain slowly and without rhythm clapped his hands together, the only member of the audience to do so. He was much too drunk to have understood a single word his son had spoken.

On a late summer Sunday morning, Ichabod decided he should pay a visit to Our Lady of the Mountains one more time before leaving for the east coast.

He hadn't been up to see her since the beginning of the summer past. His visits had naturally been less frequent since he'd discovered what '*it*' was like. He never waited for a free will offer. He always imposed his will and took '*it*' whenever he wanted.

*   *   *

The climb seemed steeper than he remembered and the path more strewn with boulders and other debris. Scattered dead pine trees on the upper end of the trail stood like bleached skeletons, but the scent of pine was still pungent as it came off the face of the near mountains. He paused to breathe the wild air deep into his lungs.

The old excitement stirred in him, for he would soon be worshiping at her feet. It had been a long time. He feared she may be angry, supposing him to be lax in his devotion.

The temperature dropped, but no cloud had sailed between him and the warming rays of the sun. No shadow fell across the path in front of him as he walked slowly along. He glanced up at the sky. It was just as bright and as blue as it had been when he started his climb. How long ago he wondered, holding a bare wrist up to his face, forgetting he'd left the watch at home. Maybe he'd started an hour ago, maybe two hours. It didn't matter. Maybe he'd spend the night asleep at her feet. He had a packsack with some granola bars, some water, and a warm jacket, and also a couple of tabs of lysergic acid diethylamide, better known as LSD, a new and still experimental mind expanding drug. He wanted to be one of the first in the country to try it. He'd figured out the formula and manufactured it in his private lab.

Imagine he, Ichabod Cain, a pioneer of mind expanding, enlightenment bestowing, and life enhancing chemical compounds. He shivered with excitement at the thought.

It was valid research in terms of the medical field. And if he was going to be a doctor, he needed to understand all he could about the workings of the body and of the mind. He envisioned himself being in the forefront of a new social order, one that he would create in his own image.

Hail Ichabod Cain!

He sucked the thin air into his lungs, making up for the oxygen debt he'd incurred during the climb. It was always an exhilarating experience, gazing down on the tiny burg of Butte, the huge open pit mine on its eastern edge begging to receive God's enema. He threw back his head and laughed, remembering his stunning valedictorian speech, the staccato bursts of his laughter echoing off the mountains.

What a glorious day!

The sheep had been shorn, he'd had his fun, and now it was time to move on.

Seated on a large granite boulder, he slipped the packsack off his back and set it on the ground by his feet. Reaching into it he pulled out the jacket and put it on against the fall feeling mid-morning air. The journey down the mountain would take about a third of the time it took to climb it, about an hour, plenty of time before dark fall.

He looked up in adoration at Our Lady of the Mountains, her pure white covering shining brilliant in the sun. His breathing returning to normal, he drew in another deep breath, filling his lungs, and then slowly, like the Zen practitioners, exhaled through his mouth. It was good to be alive, to be able to do what he chose. His future looked as bright as the sun reflecting off the statue of Our Lady, she whom he revered.

Reaching into the pocket of his long sleeved flannel shirt, he pulled out a small piece of folded tin foil, removed two tiny tablets, opened his canteen, and with a swig of water, swallowed them down.

The experiment begins.

He waited . . . nothing.

Ichabod stood up, walked slowly over to her and standing at her feet began preparing himself for worship.

He'd always heard her sweet voice as it whispered softly inside his head. But now, looking up into her face, her eyes came to life! This was beyond hope, beyond imagining! He stepped back, enabling himself to look fully into her face, the top of her head one hundred feet above the ground on which he stood.

Oh, those lovely eyes, they matched the heavens! Oh the bliss! His enraptured heart thumped against his ribs, expressing his adoration, resonating like a xylophone within him. Xylophone? Yes! He could hear the music, like a thousand wind chimes in him and around him, playing a harmonious song to his Lady.

He stared into her face, now tilted down toward him, not facing out over that horrible little town below. She had not blessed it, oh no. She reserved her blessings for Ichabod and him alone. He looked up into the divine blue of her eyes, eyes that looked serenely back at him. Then . . . she spoke. Her mouth moved with celestial grace. He could not contain his rapture. He began swaying back and forth, rocking from one foot to the other in rhythm to the wind chimes within him. Surely, they rang out into the valley below him, carried on the wings of unseen angels. For the first time in his life, Ichabod wanted to share something with the world, the bliss that filled him within and without and was more than he could contain.

The sun rested on the top of her head, shining like a golden crown against the divine blue of the sky.

"Ichabod," she spoke with the same soft soothing voice he heard inside the confines of his head, the same voice that directed his thoughts, piqued his interests, inflamed his desires; the same voice that had chosen the objects of his explorations and the fulfillment of his desires. This same voice had directed his comings and goings and he now heard it with his ears as he watched her beautiful lips move to form the words. He feared he would not be able to contain the pure glory of it all, but would gladly give up his life in the trying.

"You are a fool," she said.

"Wha . . . ?"

"Did you think there would not be a price to pay for what you have received?" she hissed. He cowered and dropped his eyes in the way of the reverent when they have been shamed. After a moment, he raised them in supplication to her face.

The sun lifted off her head, leaving a billion tiny stars spinning beneath it. Then it dropped behind her, relinquishing the light to the domain of darkness.

She glowed and pulsated, her whitened surface writhed as he looked into her eyes. No longer filled with soft kindness, but now were hard, cold, and as ancient as a glacier, throwing malevolent beams of light on him, in him, and through him. He was naked before her in the truest sense for she looked into the very depths of his soul, and she liked what she saw.

He dropped to his knees, transfixed as the shell around her began to crack and fall apart. Chunks of thick plaster and concrete thudded all around him but he was unable to move, feeling like he was made of stone. His previous rapture quickly dissolved into cold fear.

"... and pray for us sinners now and at the hour ..."

"Do not blaspheme before me!" she hissed. Like Medusa of legend, dozens of snakes sprouted from her head, born out of her mind, and writhing in time with the rest of her swaying body.

Her body? Ichabod stared in open mouthed wonder.

With the shell of plaster and concrete removed, it had morphed into a shimmering mass of light. Dirty red blood pumped through transparent veins and arteries as electric current sparked and ran alongside the conduits of blood. Her magnificent heart pumped the fluid with the power of a locomotive.

"Would you make me your master? Would you serve me and do my bidding? Would you be mine forever?" she asked.

"Yes, oh yes . . . please let me serve you," he replied and then rose to his feet, his legs shaky and almost unable to hold him up.

A tiara of stars spun around her head replacing the snakes. Her face held the fierceness of a ravenous beast. Her eyes spun from ice blue, to deep purple, to blood red, until they settled into a dull amber color that glowed with tempered fury.

"Who are you?" he squeaked.

Remaining silent, she scratched her pulsating heart with her thumbnail. Dirty red blood trickled out. "Come. For your reward, you may drink from the heart of all hearts."

With no effort he floated up to her breast-less chest and placed his tongue on the trickle of her nectar for a taste. It was oh so sweet, and he began to suck; thirstily, greedily, drinking in all the desires, fulfilled and yet to be filled, that coursed through her veins.

Spinning in his head were visions of ancient cultures and nations, empires and kingdoms, and all the glory of them marching swiftly across time, wading through the knee deep blood needed to set them up, and needed again to tear them down.

She pulled him away from the heart of all hearts, the fountain of the world. He whimpered like a lost child as she set him on his feet before her.

Fingers of mist closed slowly around her, like lovers hands caressing her from head to toe, her eyes never leaving his. The mist engulfed her, forming a swirling robe that sparkled like countless diamonds.

"Let me see you," she whispered.

Ichabod disrobed before her.

"Now look at me," she ordered. He looked, and again her eyes penetrated to the depths of his soul.

A freestanding mirror materialized in front of him. He could see his body glow and shimmer and fade. He could see his veins and arteries, and then his heart as it pumped dirty red blood with sparks accompanying the fluid on its journey through his translucent body. And underneath it all was a twisting black mass of darkness, an insatiable serpentine coil that wrapped itself around his spine, and then, as he watched in wonder, encircled his heart, where it nestled and settled and took up permanent residence.

She had completed her work and his soul was hers.

"Do you like what you see?" she asked in her sweet and comforting voice, the voice he had known for so long, the one, only moments ago, he feared he had lost forever.

"Yes, oh yes, very much, oh thank you my Lady!"

"And I also like what I see. Do you belong to me then?"

"Oh yes . . . always," he proclaimed.

"And so you do, and so you will. Turn around and behold," she said. He turned slowly to look down into the valley below. The town didn't twinkle in the darkness like normal, but instead it glowed, and its streets ran red with blood and reeked with the stench of fear and resonated with howls of despair.

To the east of the seething town, the mouth of the huge open pit mine became the mouth of a gargantuan serpent and the glut of tainted blood spilled into its thirsting jaws.

"Turn toward me my pet."

As one hypnotized he tore his eyes off the scene below and turned to face her. She stood as still as silence, robed in mist. Her majestic heart, now the color of a faint pink rose, pulsed calmly within her chest.

"You have learned very well my pet," she said, and graced him with a smile. "Curl now, like the dog you are, and sleep at my feet," she commanded and laid her right hand gently on the top of his head. Flooded with warmth, sleepiness quickly overtook him, like a drug injected into his veins. "Who are you?" he asked before succumbing to it.

"I Live," she replied, gracing him with another smile.

I Live. Of course, he thought as he fell into a deep and dreamless sleep.

* * *

The rays of dawn stabbed his eyes. Snapping them closed, he waited a moment before opening first the right one, and then the left.

He tried to move, but couldn't. He tried to remember, but there were only fragments of images drifting like ghosts out of reach.

My Lady! His mind shrieked in panic as her image focused to clarity. He struggled to stand, his joints stiff and achy in spite of his youth. Disoriented, it took a moment to get his bearings. Butte below, the light of dawn painting it in an inviting light, began to come alive and would soon drive away that light. He turned his head left and then right, but didn't find what he was looking for.

Where was she?

The same familiar voice whispered inside his head, telling him to turn around. He did, and his reward was laying his eyes on the object of his panicky search. The morning sun had transformed her gleaming white surface to gold. With her serene face looking out over the valley, Our Lady of the Mountains blessed the coming day, as she had always done.

He stepped back, the morning breeze ruffling his jacket, his mind ruffling the memories of the night before.

Something clicked in his mind. Expecting to see himself naked, he looked down at his fully clothed body. He stepped forward and touched the hem of Our Lady's robe. It was solid. But what did he expect? Oh yes, mist, a robe of heavy mist. Confusion ran through his head like the pounding hooves of stampeding horses.

He stepped back, giving himself room to look up into her face. Her eyes blazed blue. Beams of light shot out of them and burned into his soul. Ichabod dropped to his knees. It hadn't been just a dream after all.

"Your soul is mine now," said the voice.

"Yes."

"Go your way Ichabod. I will always be near you, if you ever need me, just call my name."

"I Live," he whispered.

"Yes my pet. You are my beloved."

Oh the bliss! The utter rapture!

Tears of gratitude streamed down his face to fall on the feet of the whitened statue bathed in golden glory.

RETURN TO THE DREAM

CHAPTER FIFTEEN

"No siree . . . ain't no forgetting that boy Ichabod," said Chico. "Well, he wasn't no boy, just a figure of speech, of course."

"Of course," I replied.

"Icky was a Butte boy born and raised just forty miles to the east. Some said he was a genius and he probably was in a real warped sort of way. But one thing was certain, once he left Butte, young women stopped getting killed."

"Murdered?"

"Yeah, and not just a good, clean, quick one either. They'd all had their hearts cut out after they'd been raped."

"My God, what happened to the hearts?"

"Nobody ever found a single one cause he ate em."

The wind picked up and played its song through the slaughterhouse death chutes, the sound barely audible through the barred window as ice pellets like bony fingers tapped against the glass.

"Was Icky ever suspected?" I asked.

"Why sure, but not until he was long gone back east somewhere, all wrapped up in an Ivy League school and eventually he became a bona fide doctor."

"A doctor?"

"Yeah, you know, the guy that looks down your throat, sticks needles in your butt cheeks, sets your busted bones, tells you to turn your head and cough. You know . . . a doctor, and a heart specialist to boot."

"How'd he end up here in prison?" I asked.

"Well, being from Butte, maybe he got homesick or believed that bullshit about this being the last best place and decided to check it out."

"Right. Come here on vacation, leave here on probation."

"Now you're getting it," Chico said. "Anyhow, old Icky, he goes back to Butte, but it wasn't the same, of course. He'd been gone close to thirty years and nobody knew him and he didn't know anybody either. His pa died a long time ago before he returned."

"What about his mom?"

"I was getting to that. She died right after he was born. Beautiful woman too I hear. Gypsy they say, whatever that means. Anyhow, Icky graduated at the top of his class.

He was the valedictorian, and the story goes he gave the whole frikkin' auditorium the old bird finger that night, I sure would have liked to seen that.

Near genius some said, and I tend to believe it, 'cause not only was he a doctor, but somewhat of a rocket scientist too, I reckon."

He stopped to chuckle at the thought, which brought on a violent coughing spell. He wiped the flecks of blood from his mouth and went on.

"Yes siree, a genuine rocket scientist."

"How's that?" I asked.

"Well, see, he climbed up to the top of the Divide, up over Butte, to where a huge white statue stood looking out over the valley. It'd been there as long as most folks could remember. Our Lady of the Mountains, she was called. Anyways, somehow Icky managed to climb up there with enough powder and such to send that Lady a flying through the night sky on July the third with sparks a'blowin out behind her. She made a perfect swan dive and landed right smack dab in the middle of what was once an open pit mine but had filled with water. For fun, the locals call it Acid Lake.

I sure woulda liked to have seen that sight ... *whoosh*, an arc of sparks flyin' through the air, that there revered statue splashin' down in Acid Lake. Yes siree ... I sure woulda liked to have seen that." Now he laughed hard enough to cause wheezing. The wheezing turned to a full blown coughing spasm. When finished, he wiped the flecks of blood off his mouth. There was more this time.

"And so Icky was arrested for ... ?" I asked.

"They claim it was for destruction of public property, with a criminal endangerment kicker thrown in on top of that. You don't send a hundred foot, twenty ton statue flyin' through the air without a chance of it hurting someone I suppose."

The bony fingers of winter thrummed fierce against the window glass. Chico continued his tale, his face a shade of gray from the burst of coughing.

"Anyway, the first worst place is what this is and anybody who comes here for any length of time knows it. But be that as it may, old Ichabod returned and then came to prison.

I think I already told you he started working up there to the slaughterhouse."

"Yeah, you told me," I replied. "One day I was too sick to come in to work, so the boss asked Icky if he'd do the killin' that day," explained Chico. "Took to it like a duck to water. I went to work the following day and the boss moved me to the cuttin' floor and left Icky on the killin' floor. None of which hurt my feelings any, ya see."

I nodded.

"Come along my beauties the psycho would say to them poor dumb critters and then he'd slit their throats and let out a warped little shriek.

Pretty soon, he wasn't wearing gloves and he'd let the hot blood wash over his hands while he waded in it up to his ankles and his eyes a blazin' with the twisted glee of a maniac. We all knew Icky was a little off. This was a small glimpse of just how far.

He wasn't satisfied no more with slittin' their throats and then cuttin' off their heads. So one day he talked the boss into getting him a heavy double bitted axe, so he could lop off their heads with one swing. More efficient that way he said. *WHOOSH*, he'd swing the axe down and *WHACK* off'd go their heads. Then he'd laugh like a frikkin' maniac, scary at times."

"Sounds like a man who loved his work," I said.

"He even talked the boss into having a ramp built so's the heads would roll about fifteen feet and then drop off the dock into a dumpster. Each time one would roll down into it and land with a thud, he'd holler *Score* and then shoot his fist up in the air.

We gave the looney bird plenty of room and got to callin' him Icky Odd. Most of 'em did it behind his back. I'd call him that to his face. He'd just smile at me like he didn't give a fiddlers diddler that he was odd."

"To say the least," I interjected.

Chico suddenly dropped his head and looked down at his hands clasped between his knees. He could have been considering his next words or contemplating the meaning of life. Only Chico knew.

"You need a breather, Chico?" I asked.

"Nah . . . I'm alright. Give me a minute and we'll finish this long winded tale." He took a shot of his asthma inhaler and then continued. "So after awhile and a lot of hemmin' and hawin' Icky talked the head supervisor into letting him stay in a room down in the basement seven days a week and be the caretaker of the place. That boy was one persuasive bastard."

"He stayed there?" I asked.

"Yup, right up there under the slaughterhouse. Hell, he loved it I guess. He even planted flowers and such around the place. Watered the grass, mowed it on the weekends, painted the inside of it and all that there kind of stuff. Made it all real homey he did.

Shortly after he got moved in up there escapes increased, becoming more and more frequent like."

"How frequent?"

"About four a year over a span of three years, twelve of 'em altogether, never found hide nor hair of 'em neither, until they got to number twelve."

"What happened then?"

"The supervisor had to take a trip up there to check on something late on a Saturday. Well . . . he walks out on the killin' floor and there's this twelfth runner's head setting on a metal table in the middle of a circle of lit candles, Old Icky, who was naked as a jay bird, had the rest of the runner hung by the heels, like any old carcass, and was busy stripping the hide off'n the guy as he was munching on the dudes heart like it was candy."

My stomach lurched.

"You okay boy?" asked Chico.

I nodded that I was.

"Well, when Icky seen that Larry the supervisor had him dead to rights, he dropped everything and bolted down the stairs to the basement screaming, "I Live, I Live." Course Larry chased after him. He says Icky ran in to his cubbyhole of a room and just *poof* . . . disappeared. Larry seen him go in, and when he went in after him he was gone. Nobody's found him or any parts of him since."

"So he killed twelve escapees?"

"Yup, they found an old abandoned and forgotten tunnel that ran out from the basement to a potato cellar to the east of the slaughterhouse. The runners would make there way to the cellar, and from there, underground through a different tunnel to the basement."

"Didn't anybody know about the tunnels?" I asked.

"Oh sure, but like I said, it had been forgotten. And since nobody had been caught, they assumed that, like most runners, these would try to get as far away from the prison as they could and take the least amount of time in doing it.

Yup, old Icky had hisself a barbecue and a smokehouse up there and was feasting on them boys all the frikkin' time."

My gorge rose in my throat.

"Well, ever since then the old slaughterhouse has been shut down. And that's it, the story of Ichabod Cain."

"Sounds like a tall tale to me Chico, something along the lines of Sleepy Hollow itself, made up by guys that have been locked up way too long."

"Suit yourself bro, but you asked." With that he rolled over and within a few seconds was fast asleep.

The icy fingers of the winter storm tapped at the window with the fury of a frenzied predator. I shivered as if they'd gotten through and were tapping on my bones.

Chapter Sixteen

I forgot all about haints and the boarwolf and Ishtay and Ichabod but never the mottled gray building squatting on the hillside and its siren song playing through the death chute. Sometimes when I walked around the oval it would seem far away and distant as I mulled its secrets over and over in my mind not sure what I was trying to discover. It was when I ignored it that it seemed to come alive and draw me. At times so powerful I would stop in my tracks to stare up at it even in the most severe weather.

Medicine Horse would watch me from a distance, his face like granite, his arms folded across his chest.

I didn't talk to him much these days because I thought he was crazy. Or then again maybe he was right. But he was always around, watching me as I walked, or he was sitting nearby in the chow hall, watching me as I ate, never letting me out of his sight as best he could. I'd make it a point to walk by him to grunt and say, "How," just for fun. Every now and then he'd almost smile.

CHAPTER SEVENTEEN

My JOB AS a teacher's aid helped to keep me somewhere near sanity, whatever it is, but I believed I hadn't lost it . . . yet. Working for Laura was more of a pleasure than it was a job and was always the bright spot of my day.

Some guy in class was babbling on about something one day, and after politely listening, Laura ended with, "We all have our fantasies to help get us by," referring to those of us incarcerated. But everyone else is alright upstairs, right? Her statement caused me to think about all the weird stories I'd heard around the place and so I concluded, yeah, that's what they are, what they must be, fantasies, built up over the years of isolation and loneliness, of deprivation and regret. So maybe it was a good thing after getting classified, categorized, dehumanized, and finally altogether forgotten, to have our fantasies. It at least made the pursuit of happiness available, though it had to be tempered by the confines of the prison.

My main job was to help the guys with the math part of their GED requirement, mostly by drilling the multiplication tables into their heads.

Getting their GED was often a stipulation by the court in order to be considered for parole. That was the carrot. Dragging them through the drudgery of pursuing it after their enthusiasm wore off was my challenge. The guys ranged in age anywhere from twenty to sixty years.

On first meeting her, I thought Laura was quite plain, but the more I was around her I discovered she was intelligent and witty and honest and courageous. When she smiled, her entire being lit up, the beauty inside transforming any small lack on the outside, and she would sparkle. Unpretentious, she made no attempt to be charming and yet she was very much that way, a woman of strong internal substance.

So I enjoyed myself and Laura and felt like I was useful. Class time was always a good time until the day Jesse Largo walked through the door. A Navajo man from New Mexico, Largo was around thirty, six feet tall, two hundred pounds if an ounce. He wore his jet black hair cropped close to his head. Younger, taller, and heavier than me, he was a veteran of several state prisons and he had an air about him that spoke one word—trouble.

Largo was friendly enough at first, bright enough to obtain his GED except he didn't want to work at it, but Laura made him work, and he seethed over it.

He lived in the same block as I did, just down the 'street' from me. I was in cell seven he was in cell fourteen.

He'd rail on about Laura every chance he got. I made it a point to avoid the guy but sometimes I couldn't, us being neighbors and all.

Ever been around someone who just immediately pissed you off, whether they'd done anything to you or not? Largo had that effect on me.

He topped it off one day while we were playing a game of chess in the dayroom. Looking across the table at me, gloating because he'd captured my queen, he said, "If this was a real prison, Laura would have been raped by now." His eyes narrowed and glinted with an evil light. I didn't blink. "Not with me in the room she wouldn't," I said.

His mouth dropped open and his eyes widened for an instant but then returned to their usual narrow slits in less than a second. He stared in disbelief at me over the top of the chess pieces. I held his gaze until he finally lowered his eyes. After mumbling something under his breath, he gave me one of those bluffy hard ass looks and then got up and walked away.

"Don't try me Largo," I said. He kept walking without looking back.

My blood was boiling. I despise bullies. They're cowards, and rapists are the worst of the lot. Besides, I liked Laura and enjoyed being around her. Hearing her voice and musical laughter sustained me far more than I ever let on. I couldn't. One, I was in prison, and two, I was twenty years older than her.

But for some strange reason, I felt protective of her.

CHAPTER EIGHTEEN

LAURA GLOWED WITH an unusual brightness as we walked through the falling snow on the way to class. Up ahead loomed the education building, just a two story concrete structure built strictly for function, form be damned.

A couple of the students walked a little ways in front of us, a couple more a little ways behind us, but Largo stayed far behind as we made our way to the second story classroom.

Walking down the linoleum-tiled hallway, I felt compelled to warn Laura of possible danger. Taking her aside I told her that if ever a fight broke out in the classroom; don't do anything except get out of there as fast as she could.

"Oh, we've been trained to do just that," she replied. "In fact, we've been cautioned that what looks like a fight could be staged and used for a set up." She didn't need to say any more, all her bases were covered.

She smiled at me with genuine appreciation for my concern, and it was, but I was also trying to impress her, which I didn't. I hadn't thought about a staged fight until she mentioned it. Quite impressive, but then, she was always that.

We settled into class, me in my customary place at the back of the room, Laura up front in the typical student teacher fashion.

The discussion centered around religion and the topic turned to Wicca, better known as witchcraft, as a religion. As such, the prison allowed it and a few people were practitioners, including Largo. During a lull in the conversation one of the guys told Laura he needed to use the restroom. She said "okay", and after getting his ID card from her, he disappeared out the door.

Two fellows off to my right got into a more heated discussion about the differences between Wicca and Christianity, and it was escalating fast, too fast.

I spotted Largo, he'd gotten to his feet two rows down and directly in front of me and was standing at the front of Laura's desk. Another inmate, down low and off to the right, stood up and headed toward the door.

I don't know where they are or how they work, but I know when they go off, and my alarm bells right now were blasting away loud and clear.

The arguing came to a sudden halt. Largo turned and grinned at me like a wolf in a sheepfold.

Then I knew.

The two arguers stood up at the same time I did and started moving toward me. I skirted around the left side of my table, putting two tables between them and me.

Laura felt it too and stood up. I yelled at her, "It's a set up, get out of here!" Largo moved into a position to block her escape. I went for him first. He turned his face toward me just enough so I could hit him between the eyes over the top of his nose. His knees buckled, he was out. Grabbing the left shoulder of his shirt, I flung him back out of the way and into the path of the oncoming arguers, who moved with less enthusiasm toward us.

I sprang for the door and ripped it open, pinning the guy standing by it against the wall. Placing my foot against the bottom of it, I grabbed Laura's outstretched hand, pulled her through the open door and into the hallway. She ran down it with me following close behind.

I'd forgotten about the one who'd gone off to the restroom. He leaned up against the wall with his hands hanging loose at his sides. Laura hesitated just long enough to allow me to get by her. I didn't think he was going to try anything but I chopped him in the throat with my left hand just in case. Besides, he had it coming for being involved.

I escorted Laura down the hallway to safety. She'd be alright from there. I turned to leave, but felt a firm but gentle hand grip my upper arm, stopping me. "Where are you going?" she asked in a voice that did not quiver, her hand did not tremble. "Back to make sure those guys get what's coming to them," I answered, and started down the hall. "Truman wait! If you go back now, you'll get locked up as well as them. Do you want that?"

"No, of course I don't. I'll wait here while you go and get the guards, alright?"

"Alright," she said and took my hands in hers. Looking at me with a sincerity born of Eden she said, "Thank you," and topped it off with the brightness of her smile.

I forgot all about wanting to hurt someone as I hung out in the hallway outside the classroom door. Nobody came out as I waited for the guards to show up, which they soon did. They went in, cuffed the boys, and then escorted that parade of fools down the hall with Largo in the lead.

The sergeant stopped in front of me. "Laura Whitherby laid the story out for us Struck. No further questioning will be needed, but you'll have to return to your unit immediately."

"Sure sarge," I replied and fell in behind the parade.

Laura was waiting out in the small lobby and handed me my ID card. Her hand was steady, her smile bright enough to challenge the sun. It was a good day.

News always travels fast through the grapevine and the prison was no exception to the rule. Although nobody in Y block said a word, I couldn't help but notice a subtle change as I entered. The bad guys gave me a wider berth; the other guys were quieter than before, and all looked at me with something like genuine interest.

Chico was reclined and snoring away on the bottom bunk when I entered our cell, I tried to be quiet as I removed my coat and stocking hat.

"What the hell kind of trouble you causing now Struck?" he growled from behind me. I took a seat on the house chair.

"None," I protested mildly. "Why?"

"Out there saving damsels in distress," he chortled. "I didn't know you had it in you."

"I didn't either, to tell you the truth. Something just clicked inside me and I went off." I didn't tell him I'd gotten a black belt in karate a decade back. What surprised me was how quickly it surfaced when I needed it. Muscle memory? Maybe. Some say there is a spiritual aspect to the martial arts, could be true. I hadn't felt at all rusty and had seen what I needed to do and how to do it with surprising clarity.

"Well . . . maybe that Willy Wonka stuff had something to do with it," said Chico.

"Willy Wonka?"

"Something like that. You know, what Medicine Horse and Wally were talking to you about."

"Ishtay Wakanka I think is what you meant. I'd forgotten all about that until right now," I said.

"Yeah, that's it, Ishtay Wakanka. What's it mean anyway?"

"Damn if I know, most likely nothing."

Chico probably butchered the words on purpose to get my mind going in that direction. I had a strong feeling he knew a lot more than he ever let on.

"Well looky here, Jeopardy is on," he said, turning his attention to the TV. "That stupid fucker don't know how many continents there are in this God forsaken world," he blurted. Then to the TV, "Seven ya dumb fuck! Although I still think Australia is a island." The woman on TV gave her answer, five. Chico hit the roof. "What kinda goddam idiots are we raising these days?"

He didn't do much anymore except lie on his bunk and amuse himself with his TV. Somewhere, somehow he had contracted hepatitis-C and it was catching up to him. He couldn't pinpoint exactly when or how he'd gotten it, either probably from a needle, shooting drugs, or from getting a tattoo, or it could have come from one of the many loose women he claimed he'd tightened up in his day. His liver was shutting down, and fast.

"I was thinking," he said, "they oughta have a category on Jeopardy called Prison Terminology. I could just see it, "Prison Terminology for two hundred Alex."

"A son of a buck snort, ball bustin' bull-dyke bitch."

"What is a . . . Guard?"

"Right you are, for two hundred!"

"It'd be funnier than hell," he said, chortling, I burst out laughing. Then the cough reached out and grabbed him as Medicine Horse suddenly darkened the open doorway of our cell. He stood there looking at Chico for a long while, kind of distant and wistful like, but stoic as always. Chico's cough died down.

"Horse, come on in," I said.

He stepped inside but remained standing and greeted us with, "Hoka—Hey."

"Hoka what?" I asked.

"Hoka-Hey," he said. "It is good day to die."

So, he was still crazy.

Chico swung his legs over the side of the bunk, sat up and patted the spot next to him. "Whyn't you sit here Struck, so's our guest don't have to stand up." I sat where he indicated. Horse sat on the house chair, his expression unchanged. We waited for him to speak.

"Wallace Red Eagle dropped his robe last night. Hoka-Hey. The last thing he said to me was to be a brother to the Ishtay Wakanka and so I will. But tomorrow I move to A unit because I am no longer needed in X block, so I will watch you from afar," he said to me.

Through the window, off in the distance, the siren song played through the loading chute. Ice pellets kept rhythm as they pinged against the glass.

The air split, cracked open for a heartbeat by a sizzling boom so powerful it rattled the window. We could feel the shockwave in our bones.

"What the hell was that?" I asked.

"Thunder," replied Horse, still expressionless.

Chico coughed and said, "Strange things happen up here in the first worst place. Maybe the beast is awake and its belly is rumbling with hunger."

"Thunder in the middle of a winter snow storm? Chico's kidding, right," I turned and said to Horse.

"Mebbe so, mebbe no. You have seen the boarwolf and heard the haints? Could be it was the belly of the beast rumbling. Could be Wally's spirit went to awaken it."

At that moment thunder clapped louder than before. I nearly jumped out of my skin.

Horse stood up and I followed him through the dayroom toward the exit door of my block.

Before we reached it he turned to me and said, "Wally waited for you Ishtay, now the beast is awake and . . . you will battle it. For this you have been chosen."

He turned and was gone.

Boarwolfs, Icky Odd, Starving Beasts, and the Mysterious Haints, I didn't need further convincing, these guys had been locked up way too long, or they knew of a reality I didn't, and for some reason it was being shown to me.

That thought slapped me square in the face.

CHAPTER NINETEEN

BESIDES MY JOB, my other refuge was the library. It was well
stocked with every kind of book imaginable; snob literature,
classical, pulp and popular fiction of every genre, educational
books, technical books, how to books, law books, and a good
selection of magazines, no skin allowed.

Up there one evening, taking my time browsing, I came to
the Native American section. Scanning the books as I passed
by, a hardcover titled "Hanta Yo" caught my eye. Curious, I
pulled it down and sat at one of the long tables to thumb
through it and get the gist of the story. Finished, I took it up to
the counter and checked it out to take back to my cell.

It's a story based on the pre-history of the Lakota nation,
better known as the Sioux. Pre-history meaning before Crazy
Horse and Sitting Bull damn near whipped the U.S. Army.

As far as I know, I don't have a drop of native blood in
me. A Norwegian, I'm about as honky as honky can get, but
most of my friends are Native American. I'm not sure why, I
think it's because I like being around people that express their
hearts with no games attached. And they know how to make

the most out of a bad situation. They're used to it. As a people they've been at it for a couple hundred years, give or take.

I returned to my cell with the book and said hi to Chico. He grunted something in return, lost in a TV show.

Crawling onto the top bunk I began reading at page one.

Though interesting the story had me frustrated. Lakota words were scattered throughout the text and I had no clue what they meant. There had to be to be an appendix, right?

Below me Chico finished his hot chocolate and belched.

Checking the back of the book I sure enough found an appendix. The Lakota words listed along with their translation into English. I found 'Ishtay' it meant 'true or good', then 'Wakanka' which meant philosopher or seer, a true philosopher, big deal. I was hoping for something like 'mighty warrior'. But, come to think of it, I have always had trouble letting go of rhetorical or other similar questions. Still, just how the hell was I supposed to battle this 'beast' of Wally's as a philosopher? More than ever I was convinced these guys were way gone in their own fantasy world.

"Gym and yard," a bored voice blared over the loudspeaker.

"Coming down," I warned Chico as I swung my legs over the side of the bunk. He either didn't hear me or he ignored me, probably the latter.

I flung on my coat, pulled on my stocking cap, and headed to the cage, where the guards were, to sign out. I always had my thermals on. Sixty-five degrees ain't that warm.

It was cloudy with a good chance of snow. It seemed there was always a chance of snow up here along the border.

I stopped at the first curve around the oval, hoping to spot Medicine Horse and tell him I'd found out the meaning of the name Ishtay Wakanka. He wouldn't be hard to spot, even among all of us dressed in our ugly green coats and blue stocking caps.

I scanned the men as they walked, some with purpose, some with hope, some just walking, but all waiting for release either from prison or from this life.

I didn't find Horse so I started on my daily two mile walk. One lap, the temperature fell. Two laps, the snow began. On the third lap, the wind picked up, and on the fourth lap it was whistling through the planks of the loading chute up at the slaughterhouse, with the gutters clanging in time to the whistling. The music was strange, mesmerizing, and pulled me to it. The building, mottled and gray, appeared to be grinning at me. I stopped to stare at it but couldn't focus right away through the snowfall. My vision cleared and the old concrete building looked the same, except for one difference, a dingy yellow light glowed in one of the windows. The scene riveted me to the spot. I rubbed my eyes with the backs of my gloved hands, thinking they were playing tricks on me. Opening them I saw the same sickly yellow light as before.

Medicine Horse showed up and watched me as I trudged around the oval, head down and shoulders stooped as if the weight of the world rested on them, and right now, it felt like it did. He joined me as I passed by him, appearing like a ghost from out of nowhere.

"Ishtay," he said.

"My name's Truman," I replied, my voice sharp enough to cut through the ears of the deaf.

"True~Man," he responded with a grin, "what troubles you?"

"Everything," I replied.

"That," I said, pointing up at the useless block of concrete hunkered into the hillside. "This place," I said, making a sweeping motion with my arm, indicating the whole of the prison, including the evil that takes place in the administrative offices.

"You and Wally and Chico, and all your goddam stories about Ichabod Cain and the slaughterhouse, about spirits and haints, and whatever other spooky shit you guys have dreamed up because you've been locked up so fucking long you can't separate reality from your own goddam fantasies! That's what's bothering me."

"Good, Ishtay," said Medicine Horse, putting a hand on my shoulder, stopping me from leaving.

"Don't call me that!" I snapped and jerked my shoulder away from his grip, surprised that he didn't turn and walk away. Instead, he grinned. "Good, True~Man. Now you are where the reality of this place can start to sink in."

"Fuck!" I exclaimed walking away from Horse and his patient, knowing grin.

CHAPTER TWENTY

I COULDN'T BUNK WITH Chico any longer. He had passed on to the spirit world. They moved me out of Y block into better living quarters.

There were about half the number of men living in the same amount of space, all of them near my age, plus or minus a decade. After fifty, it becomes irrelevant, maybe after thirty, hard for me to remember anymore. Especially since Medicine Horse pointed out that the reality of this place *was* setting in. Hell, it was closing in and starting to suffocate me with a palpable heaviness as depression steadily chipped away at any former brightness, or hope, or remembrance of life.

*   *   *

"As my mind became more clouded, it felt like my soul was becoming lost. My heart was darkening and I was starting a journey down the dark side that would lead to a point where death looked more preferable than life.

The only bright spot was my job and seeing Laura. She was about five-four and maybe one twenty. Her eyes tended toward gray, but when she smiled, they glowed blue. Her hair was auburn. She moved with the litheness and grace of a natural athlete; smooth, silky, and rhythmic. Her voice was musical, like the ringing of silver bells, and when I heard them they would diminish to nothing the siren song of the slaughterhouse.

I don't think she knew how she affected me, and I doubt I had any similar affect on her. But, there's always fantasy. And isn't it our fantasies and dreams that keep us moving forward, looking for a better life.

So what's wrong with the here and now? I guess reality, as we perceive it, sucks. And therein lay my biggest problem, I could no longer define reality. What was my reality? If it hadn't changed, it had severely shifted to the side of bizarre. I perceived that mottled gray building on the mountainside to be alive and waiting for me.

How I knew it, or why it would be, I had no idea. Was it a gut feeling, a premonition, perhaps a mischievous imp whispering dour something's in my ear, or was I simply crazy?

I heard the sound of silver bells . . . what the . . . ?

"Truman, earth to Truman," she called. I blinked twice and turned my gaze from the window and the silent gray beast on the other side of it to look into the face of my daydreams.

What was that song? "When Irish eyes are smiling," it could have been about her blue beauties.

"Laura, I must've been daydreaming," I replied.

"You were somewhere else for sure. Here's some card stock, will you make flash cards out of it please?"

"Of course," I answered my mind still somewhat over there, and not quite all here. She gave me a puzzled look, but I didn't dare tell her about the slaughterhouse, she'd think I was crazy. Maybe she thought that already. Maybe I was.

"That used to be a slaughterhouse," she said, pointing out the window. Did she read my mind?

"Oh . . . uh, what cards do you need?"

"All of them, ones through twelve's, for my class on the high side."

"Alright, how's things over there?"

"Fine, no trouble," she said.

Why was I concerned for her safety? She was one of *them* and I was one of *those*. Oh well, when it comes right down to it, we can't help how we feel. We're just damn good at keeping it hidden or bottled up, but that's humanity I guess. Some of us explode and get locked up, and some of us shrivel and slowly die inside, held captive by bars forged from our own fears. God bless us, everyone.

"Mr. Struck?" she said.

"Oh, yeah, on my way," I took the heavy card stock and headed out the door.

I moved down the polished hallway gazing out the row of windows as I passed them one by one. In the frame of each was the slaughterhouse, first, gray and mottled; next, covered by a cloud shadow; next, falling snow creating a ghostly pall; last, a dirty yellow light in one of the out facing windows.

Behind me, down the hall, Laura shrieked. I heard the scraping of chairs across the floor, and then a thud as one of them slammed into a wall. I sprinted back toward the classroom, skidded to a stop and twisted through the open doorway, expecting what, I wasn't sure, some sort of bad scene. At the very least I knew Laura had been frightened and could be in danger.

"There! Over there!" one of the guys exclaimed, pointing to the back wall. Everybody else was standing, faced in that direction.

I glanced at Laura, saw she wasn't in any danger, and then looked at the back wall. A mouse was running along the base of it, trying to find a way out.

Laura looked at me very calmly, "I'm fine, Truman. I think I can handle this situation. It just startled me a little, that's all," she said with a tiny sheepish grin, as one of the guys caught the little critter and put it in a cardboard box.

We broke out in laughter, the silver bells of her voice turning hers into a full symphony.

I turned, left the room, and on my way down the hall stopped to pick up the card stock and proceeded to accomplish my task, making one hundred and forty-four flash cards, one's through twelve's.

CHAPTER TWENTY-ONE

WINTER RELINQUISHED ITS grip and gave way to the renewing of spring. Tulips would be in bloom one day and buried under snow the next. Then the snow got washed away by the night rains.

All the paradoxes of spring wrapped themselves around me and time passed both slowly and quickly. Each day would drudge by, but when I stopped to look back I'd wonder where they'd gone. A month, a year, a season would come and go until winter once again sank its fangs deep into the Montana landscape.

I couldn't help but think of Chico buried down by the sewer pond. Him and old Wally, and there were others I'd known only by face buried there. People came and went, left and returned, the place was a revolving door, the system was set up to make you fail, according to the old timers. Most of them didn't want to leave after being down for twenty plus years. They could see the world was changing too fast and becoming too furious, and at what, itself probably, for societal denial and man's inhumanity to man.

CHAPTER TWENTY-TWO

A PRESENCE SLIPPED IN alongside me and locked in place. It felt like a long gone missing piece came back. I don't know why but I wasn't surprised to turn and see Laura at my side. It felt good, natural, and right as rain.

She smiled her brightening smile, lighting up the misted glen we found ourselves in, then she drifted off and we were distant, but not apart. We'd been joined, how or why, I don't know, but I embraced it, like the fulfillment of a dream, or a wish come true.

The mouth of a dark cave, opened wide in a perpetual yawn, was on the other side of the glen. Neither ominous nor inviting it was just there. Then the mist swirled and thickened as darkness drew near and Laura was once again at my side.

The air became heavy and stormy and charged with electricity straining to become bolts of lightning that would strike with predatory purpose. Prompted by that, we took shelter in the maw of the cave.

The interior opened to a barrel-vaulted ceiling much like a cathedral minus the stained glass windows and rows of pews.

The floor was a single slab of gray marble smooth and polished. On the far side of the cavern stood a white marble altar raised to waist height. An alcove receded into darkness behind it, the arch ten feet off the ground. Two man-sized tunnels veered off on both sides of the alcove, the darkness stygian at the mouth of each. Lichen growing on the cave walls gave off a faint odor of incense. The heavy still air held a comfortable temperature.

Laura nudged my arm in urgency and directed my attention straight ahead to the white altar; a medieval executioner's axe had appeared from nowhere and lay across the top of it.

The lichen threw off pulsating spikes of pale green light focused on the mouth of the alcove.

"Do you hear that?" Laura asked. I cocked my head first right then left. The ancient incense teased my nostrils but no sound hit my ears. "You don't hear that?" she asked with increased concern. *"Ichabod Cain lives down the lane,"* drifted softly from one or both of the tunnels or from the alcove itself. It was hard to tell. I focused my hearing in on it.

"Do you hear it now?" she asked, her concern spilling over into urgent. *"Ichabod Cain lives down the lane,"* came louder through the heavy air and I nodded yes. We continued forward.

A strong draft blew a stench like rotting flesh covered with roses out of the alcove. It wasn't foul enough to make us gag but enough to make our stomachs churn.

". . . he's so insane."

The light emanating from the lichen focused into a single beam and illuminated a man standing behind the altar. Tall and ghastly pale in the greenish light his protruding eyes bored steadily into Laura's. A sardonic smile was frozen on his face exposing sharp and prominent teeth.

The stench turned putrid.

I tried to hold tight to Laura as she drifted closer to the mesmerizing . . . what, I wasn't sure, only that it looked like a man and he was drawing her to him.

"Come to me dear heart," he spoke, the words coming from somewhere ancient and evil deep inside his chest, were soothing and comforting, masking their intent. Hurt and kill, I thought, as he reached for the axe on the altar, drawing Laura ever closer to his merciless intention.

"Laura, stop!" I shouted my voice echoing off the walls. She turned dreamily toward me her demeanor like one who is lost. I reached out, got hold of her arm, and pulled her close beside me.

I looked close at the man. He had to be Ichabod Cain, real or symbolized, and he was exactly as I had imagined him. He hissed in frustration and laid the axe down.

"Who are you?" I asked, keeping a solid grip on Laura's upper arm.

"I Live," he proclaimed and then the light flickered and he and the axe and the stench of rotting flesh vanished.

"*. . . Ichabod Cain lives down the lane,*" a mocking, sing-song voice uttered out of the mouth of the alcove.

We turned our attention to the tunnel on the left. Wafting on a breeze blowing out of it was the odor of ancient incense. Coupled with the siren song of the slaughterhouse it drew me toward that black void.

This time I was the dreamy lost one and Laura stopped us.

Then a new noise, not voices, started up, drifting and whispering at first and then growing louder, the bellowing of cattle, then *thwak*, the sound of something thudding into soft flesh.

". . . lives down the lane, he's so insane . . . Headless Horsema-a-an . . . The blood curdling screams of tortured young women followed, "True Ma-a-a-n," then a loud hiss, and all the while, the stench of rotting flesh mingled with roses assaulted us.

". . . *dear heart, dear heart,*" sang a mocking voice.

A grunting, a howling . . . I recognized the sound, it was the boarwolf, and it made me quiver.

"*HE'S SO INSANE!*"

Then the voices screeched to a stop and the slaughterhouse siren song, played through the loading chute, overtook the insane medley. A glance at Laura confirmed that she heard it. Accompanying the soft and eerie music was a softer voice singing, "*I live, I live, I live down the lane.*"

The drawing toward the tunnel increased, the music pulling me, the singsong voice pulling her. We strained against its magnetism with all the strength we could muster, causing beads of sweat to run down my forehead and Laura's face to contort into a grimace as we fought against it. After an exhausting struggle, we snapped free and instantly everything stopped, the music, the voices, the singing, and the stench. We turned and looked at each other and smiled, amazed at our absence of fear, and strolled out of the cavern with our senses skewed off center.

Outside, the mist had lifted, and the fern covered glen was bathed in light. Above, the cloudless sky sparkled blue. We threw our arms around each other and embraced, sharing our relief at having escaped the cavern and the intensity of the drawing and the evil that dwelt in its darkness.

Laura looked up into my eyes, hers so beautiful and a blue that matched the sky. She tilted her face up toward mine, inviting a kiss . . .

The goddam alarm clock went off.

The troubling dream went deep, being so real, so clear and undistorted and at the same time so beyond belief. Worse yet, it felt close to home, too close. But the most disturbing part was Laura, how did she fit in, if at all? But I was certain of one thing; she'd be in some sort of danger if she were near me.

CHAPTER TWENTY-THREE

My new celly was a white haired devout religious man who did the computer programming at the library. A quiet person, he read his bible every day, and tried to adhere to its tenets. He never pushed his beliefs on me; in fact he seldom spoke to anyone at all.

Tall and slender of build, the normally unobtrusive gentleman asked if something was troubling me beyond the normal chagrin of prison.

"Why?" I asked as I mixed my cup of instant coffee.

"You tossed and turned last night and cried out a few times. Bad dream?"

It wasn't like Corky to pry and I didn't feel as though he was. I told him the highlights of the dream and the cavern as I remembered it. He thoughtfully rubbed his chin as he sipped his morning tea, and after some contemplation said, "I don't put much stock in dreams myself. But once in awhile they can have meaning. God has, at times, spoken to people through dreams, says so in the bible."

"I suppose it could be," I nodded. I figured God could do whatever he wanted; otherwise, he wouldn't be God, would he?

"Is the woman in your dream someone you know? Someone you're close to?"

"I know her, yes. She's the teacher for the GED program and I'm her aid. We're not real close, friends maybe."

"H-m-m, was anything else in the dream familiar?"

"Yeah, the boarwolf, and it was in a previous dream. Chico, did you know him?" he nodded, "told me the story of Ichabod Cain, whom I'm sure was symbolized as the man in the dream. And an old medicine man told me, prior to the dream that I was going to do battle with some unknown but powerful evil beast. Crazy shit. Pardon my French."

Corky just smiled, unoffended. I imagine he'd heard about everything there was to hear by now. He'd been locked up for twenty-five years. I didn't ask him why and he never offered to tell me. The story I heard was the classical "he came home and found his wife in bed with another man," and killed them both in a jealous rage. So he copped a life sentence because of the betrayal and unfaithfulness of a woman. Justice? It's a slippery word at best. The irony of it was the other man was the honorable judge John Langthon out of Ravalli county, a drunken buffoon and totally without honor. But he was one of the good old boys.

"Well," Corky continued, "the dream may mean something, but likely not. Could be a result of all the stuff rattling around in your head from the stories you've heard, and it sounds to me they are just that . . . stories. Except for Ichabod Cain, he was real and he did what he did, and then . . . poof . . . disappeared, just like Chico probably told you."

"And they've never found any trace of him?"

Corky shook his head no.

"Got any advice?" I asked.

"Like I said, there may or may not be anything to the dream, except, I think there's a good possibility of some type of danger ahead for you . . . and the young woman if she's with you."

I'd never mentioned that Laura was young.

". . . and you should do what you can, now, to keep her out of harm's way, along with yourself. That's how I see it."

"Wouldn't hurt I guess, and thanks," I replied.

"Anytime," he said.

So now what? What was I to do about Laura?

CHAPTER TWENTY-FOUR

I DIDN'T MARK A calendar like some. I got up each day and went about my business or pursued my interests. Time passed easier that way.

The initial blast of weirdness from the slaughterhouse had subsided to almost nothing and along with it the threat of potential danger.

Medicine Horse had been absent from my life for quite awhile when he popped back in as though materializing out of thin air, appearing beside me as I walked the oval.

"Horse, good to see you," I said.

"Soon, spring will be here."

"Yeah . . . and . . . ?"

"And it is time for you to prepare yourself, Ishtay."

"For what?" I asked, playing along, not reminding him Ishtay was not my name.

"For the right to live," he pronounced.

The right to live, what the hell, I wasn't under a death sentence as far as I knew but I suppose they could figure out a way to burn me at the stake if they wanted to bad enough.

"What the do you mean by that?" I asked Horse. Never in a hurry, we walked a ways before he answered.

"Two winters ago you were told you would battle the awakened beast."

I had forgotten that one. "Thank you very much for reminding me," I said. He ignored my sarcasm.

"Spring will be here soon," he repeated, "and then you will see."

As far as I could tell, winter still had a good strong grip on the land. The sky turned a deeper gray as the north wind picked up cold and began its siren song through the death chutes of the slaughterhouse. My attention drawn, I looked up at the gray, dead looking structure. It looked harmless, but in my gut, I knew it wasn't. It had only been hibernating, and Medicine Horse had given me a wake up call.

I turned to Horse to ask what, exactly, he was talking about, but he was gone, as if taken by the wind.

It occurred to me that I might consider his mumbo-jumbo as serious. If it was, my association with Laura would sooner or later put her in danger, and if so, how could I remove her from it?

I wrestled with these questions for a week, first saying none of it was real and then saying that all of it was real, and ended up telling myself I was a fool for giving any credence to the situation.

In spite of that I decided there was too much evidence to eliminate the possibility that there *could* be some substance to it and Laura *could* be in danger.

The next day I told her I was quitting my job as soon as she could find a replacement for me.

"Why? Don't you like it?" she asked.

Woops, I hadn't thought of giving her a reason why, lame or otherwise. I couldn't very well tell her I'd had dreams that told of danger for her, or that a couple of crazy Indians had said I was going to battle some mysterious beast lurking around the prison. Maybe I could tell her my new job was to rid the place of its presence. Uh-huh, lame.

She'd think I was a total lunatic if I told her the reasons why and maybe call the psych ward for real.

"I like your work and I think we get along well don't you?" she asked.

That started a meltdown. "Sure . . . it's . . . it's just that I've decided to try something else."

"Like what?" She wasn't going to let me off the hook.

"Working in the furniture shop," I blurted. "I've always wanted to learn woodworking."

"Well . . . okay, I'll miss you, but if your mind is made up it's made up."

My melt down heated up. This was damn hard, especially since my decision was based on, *"the possibility of."*

"I'll miss it here too, and thanks for the opportunity to work for you, I've enjoyed it."

"Well, you're not done yet. It'll take awhile to find someone to replace you. You're not in a great hurry to leave are you?"

"No, and actually, I have to contact the furniture shop yet." I was in no hurry at all.

Second-guessing myself for a time afterwards, I settled on the idea that I'd done the right thing by taking Laura out of harms . . . *potential* . . . harms way. Err on the side of caution; better safe than sorry, and that's all the clichés I can think of.

Chapter Twenty-Five

The Chinook wind blew warm overnight and melted much of the snow. Spring followed, coming a month early just as Medicine Horse had predicted, which made me wonder if all the other things he'd spoken were believable, which in turn made me apprehensive.

I had convinced myself that I'd done right by Laura. My replacement was starting Monday, two days from now. I'd see her around from time to time, but never long enough to say anything more than "Hi", and that only in passing.

But my head still went around in circles as I walked the elliptical outdoor path.

I heard an unfamiliar rumbling and looked up. A flat bed truck, loaded with industrial equipment, was rolling by on the gravel road just outside the fences. I watched as it ground up the southern mountains and came to a stop at the slaughterhouse. It backed toward a double sized door, which rolled up, and then a man emerged, directing the truck back to a precise spot. A few more men appeared and the place got busy for the first time in five years or so.

The truck stopped, a forklift appeared, and the men went to work unloading the equipment.

I put in my two miles around the oval track and returned to my cell. Corky looked up from his reading.

"Hey Corky, I saw a flatbed of equipment being unloaded at the slaughterhouse. Any idea what's going on?"

"They're converting the old butcher shop into a small cannery," was all he said.

"Are there going to be jobs for inmates up there?" I asked.

"I hear there is. You interested?"

"I'm quite interested now that I'm unemployed."

"Keep your eye on the bulletin boards. If they're looking to hire, it'll be posted on them."

THE DREAM MANIFEST

CHAPTER TWENTY-SIX

THREE WEEKS LATER and without fanfare, the cannery opened. I got hired as one of eight men to work it and once up there I volunteered to be the swamper. That way I'd be out of the loop of bickering and politicking and all that nonsense sure to happen once the novelty wore off.

I kept vigilant and on the alert as I went about my business thinking maybe I'd get lucky and catch a glimpse of something . . . anything . . . that may give credibility to all I'd seen and heard and felt about the place. But as far as I could tell, it was nothing but a simple functional building, used for industry, and the only thing unique about it was its age.

A wide dim lit stairwell led down to the basement. Over the stairwell, the walls and ceiling were high, giving it the feel of descending into a vault. Wooden handrails attached to the walls ran the length of the stairs on each, side and I made sure to scrub them once a week. The stairs I'd mop every day as part of my routine, but as an inmate I was forbidden to go any further than the bottom stair without my supervisor's permission and so I kept off the four-foot square landing at the bottom of the them. The entrance to the main basement was just an opening in the wall off to the right of the landing.

"Hey Struck," Larry said as he approached.

"What's up?"

"Need you go into the basement and get a special barrel. It's a fifty-five gallon plastic one with a spigot screwed in near the bottom."

"Sure, right away," I said and turned to head down the stairwell and into the vault of the main basement, my stomach knotting up as I went.

Butterflies swirling around in my stomach brought it awake remembering the stories I'd heard and the dreams I'd had about the mysterious Ichabod Cain, and part of me held back as I descended the stairs. It was odd, I thought, stepping down from one stair to the other, that I hadn't really thought about the stories of the old slaughterhouse and all that they implied since I'd begun working here. And as far as I'd noticed, all the haints had either left or been laid to rest. Descending the darkened stairs brought severe doubt.

I reached the bottom landing, stopped to draw a deep breath, and stepped through the open doorway off to the right, my heart thumping against my ribs. Dank musty air assailed my nostrils, causing me to turn my head to the side. A single dim light bulb hung down in the middle of the empty main room. I took in another deep breath, the air still dank and musty like any old basement. But underneath the ordinary I detected the faint aroma of incense, probably from an old bag of potpourri stashed in a corner. The scent was distantly familiar, but I couldn't place from where.

With my eyes fully adjusted to the dim light, I surveyed the forty by forty foot room. Along the far wall in front of me were six fifty-five gallon plastic barrels, the one with the spigot on the far right up against a door set in a wall built out perpendicular to the foundation wall.

A door to where?

In the middle of the perpendicular wall and built out from it I saw the room where Ichabod Cain had lived. Made of plywood and two by fours, the single centered window had an interior curtain pulled closed over it. I assumed the door would be locked.

I stared in awe at the place where legend had been born. Eerie and silent, I wondered what gruesome deeds, what diabolical, maniacal plans had been dreamed up in that room and why. But I really didn't want to know as the stories and the nightmares about it flashed rapidly through my mind. The back of my neck tingled, raising the hairs on it.

I ran my eyes further along the far right wall, past Ichabod's door, and towards me. Another door was on the right of his former room leading to what, another room, or could it be a tunnel?

This door had a window about a foot square and set dead center at head height in it.

I felt compelled to look through it. Crossing the forty feet to get there lasted forever. What little light penetrated through the window revealed a tunnel on the other side, but I couldn't see far enough to determine its length.

I tried the door, it was locked. I peered again through the window as the faint odor of incense increased, making my head spin slightly. Then, about thirty yards down the tunnel, a sickly yellow light flashed and stabbed my eyes hard enough to make them hurt.

Jerking my head away from the window and rubbing my eyes with the backs of my hands, I again looked through the window. This time I saw nothing. Turning, and with much caution, I walked slowly to Ichabod's former room to peek through the window in the locked door. All I could see was a couple of stacks of cardboard boxes in the center of it. The room was twelve by twenty feet, enough to sleep and cook in, and God only knew how many bodies were cooked and eaten in that dingy room. I shuddered at the thought and moved on, catching the faint scent of . . . roses.

I continued down the wooden wall toward the plastic barrels until I reached the first door I had noticed. Peering through its window, I could see it was another tunnel, but where it led to, I couldn't tell. So I had a small room with a tunnel on each side along with the faint aroma of incense and roses, but what meaning did it have.

Then it clicked . . . the dream. The cavern, the alcove with a tunnel on each side, here it was, right in front of me.

Was it my battleground? Had Medicine Horse been right? He'd been right before, but this was just too bizarre.

I shuddered.

"Hey, Struck! Did you fall asleep down there?" Larry hollered from the top of the stair.

Chapter Twenty-Seven

Spring turned to a hot and sultry summer. Returning from a six-month check up at the infirmary, my path converged with Laura's and we fell in beside each other.

"Is everything thing going okay in the classroom?" I asked.

"Yes . . . they're alright, fine actually. Well, no, not really fine."

I hadn't heard of any trouble at the school and the prison grapevine was lightning quick. "What's been going on? There's no trouble is there?" I had to ask.

"Oh no, it's just that you were hard to replace, and now my job is much more time consuming and difficult."

With those few words, she made feel like I was walking on air and floating across the sidewalk.

"And I wanted to ask you . . ." She stopped, looked earnestly into my eyes, and said, "What was the *real* reason you quit me?" Her look said nothing but the truth would suffice.

The dam broke and the truth spilled out as I told her about Wally and Medicine Horse, Chico and the dream of the boarwolf, the slaughterhouse, and Ichabod Cain, the dream of her and me in the cave, and ended with Corky's advice to remove her from possible danger. She probably thought I was crazy, but there it was, all of it, out in the open, for better or for worse.

"But you still haven't told me why you quit," she pressed.

"It was the last dream," I said.

"The dream where we entered a cave and the interior was like a cathedral?"

"Yes."

"You quit because of a silly dream?"

"I thought you could be in danger," I said.

"Because of a dream," she stated and shook her head at the incredibility of the action based on it.

"I gave it quite a bit of thought, and yeah it occurred to me I was being foolish. But since I've gone to work at the cannery, I believe I made the right decision."

"How's that," she asked.

"There is danger up there, unseen and unknown, but definite, dark, and deep." I replied.

"Aren't you being a little dramatic?"

"No, I don't think so. But even if I am, you're out of harm's way, and that's the point right now. Besides, I went down into the basement for the first time yesterday and the room Cain lived in is set out from a wall with a door on each side. Both the doors lead to a tunnel."

"Like the dream."

"Like the dream," I echoed.

Locked into our conversation, we hadn't noticed the sky darken. Lightning exploded from it, sizzled down and struck the metal flag pole in the center of the grass courtyard. The

Montana state flag burst into flame, the United States flag flying above it did not.

With mouths dropped open, we watched the state flag flash and burn and the wind blow away its ashes.

The United States flag remained untouched by the flames underneath it. Now *that* was dramatic.

"My God!" exclaimed Laura.

"God Bless America!" some old timer across the courtyard hollered, taking off his blue hat and placing it over his heart. Another inmate raised his right arm high in the air, extended his middle finger and shouted, "Yeah . . . fuck you, Montana!" I laughed and had to agree with that. Rain cut loose and entered the drama, coming down in sheets, causing us to hustle into the foyer of the education building. Laura turned to me, touched my arm, and asked, "How do you know I'm not *supposed* to be with you?"

"I guess I just assumed that to be the case."

"Because . . . ?"

"You're a woman. I'm supposed to keep you out of harm's way if I can."

"I'm a big girl, Truman. I can take care of myself . . . but I do appreciate your concern."

"Sure."

I had to return to my unit and got a soaking on the way.

At least it wasn't cold, it wouldn't have been anyway, Laura always made me feel warm on the inside.

Laura stood in the foyer watching the strange man hurry through the downpour. She thought chivalry had died out centuries ago. It wasn't a bad thing and she sort of liked it, although she would never admit it.

Chapter Twenty-Eight

I DIDN'T GO INTO slaughterhouse basement for several months. Then, from somewhere out of the blue, my boss asked me if I wanted to live there, down in the basement, fixed up cozy in what was now a storeroom but without much effort could be made into a livable room. That way, he told me, I could keep an eye on everything; cut the grass, shovel the snow, and wander around a little. "At least," he said, "you'll be out of general population. No guards and you can do your own cooking, steaks or whatever you want. We'll supply the food, a TV, hell; it'll be just like being at home. What do you say?"

"Plus swamp five days a week?"

"Of course, but you'll be paid for seven if you take the offer."

"And if I don't?"

"I'm sorry, Struck, but Caretaker is a new position, one the administration dreamed up, and we have to fill it. So, if you don't take it . . ."

"Someone else will," I added.

"That's the long and the short of it. So what do you say? I think it's a damn good opportunity and I'd like to see you take it."

"I'll think about it. Didn't the last person that lived down there end up going crazy?"

"Old Ichabod, nah, he was crazy to begin with. I'm sure you'd be all right. Let me know in a couple of days, will ya?"

"Alright, a couple of days," I replied as my head spun round and round at the prospect set before me.

*   *   *

The day was cooling from the blistering heat as evening approached. The natural colors brightened and intensified as the suns rays turned golden and friendly instead of deadly.

My mind swirled as I walked the oval. Should I? Shouldn't I? What if? Why? Why not? Because. It felt like a championship tennis match playing in my head, without the love. I walked and wrestled with myself until my legs ached and my head felt like it was going to explode. Where were my advisors now? I looked around, no Medicine Horse, no Wally, no Chico. Laura would be on her way home, fifteen miles away in Anaconda. Meeting her now was only the gift of chance anyway.

And always the slaughterhouse, nestled smug on the hillside. Though now a cannery it hadn't changed a damn bit. It was still a crouching beast hunkered against the barren hillside, a patient, hungry beast waiting . . . for what? Me?

"Yard in!" the guard bellowed over the outside loudspeaker.

I turned and started for A unit. I hadn't taken two steps when I heard the siren song whistle through the loading chutes behind me, the rain gutter tapping time against the side of the concrete cannery.

No wind was moving, not even a slight breeze. Maybe there was one up on the hillside. Maybe it was waiting for me and was mocking me. Maybe I was losing my mind.

"Yard in!" the guard bellowed again. Behind me, someone yelled, "Bite me!" Yeah, bite me, or what seemed more likely, devour me.

Tonight I needed a good long deep sleep.

*　　*　　*

Returning to my cell, Corky asked if I'd like some tea.

"Sure," I said and grabbed my cup. He filled it with hot water and then handed me a bag of chamomile tea, the calming stuff. "Thanks," I said as I dunked the bag in the hot water.

Our cell had a wooden dresser for each of us with three drawers and a slide out table for writing or typing on. Above the table were two close together shelves and then a third with more space above it.

The bunk beds had two by fours at the corners with a sheet of plywood placed on ledgers. We placed our inch and a half thick mattresses on the plywood.

The bars on the windows were outside and we could open them from the inside. For seating, we had dinette style chairs, fashioned of bare wood.

The floors were plain concrete, the walls of sheetrock painted white. The solid wood door had a small glassless window in it so the guards to peek into the room.

Overall, it wasn't bad Corky said. And he had a basis of comparison, having been shipped to Texas and then Tennessee, courtesy of the state. They'd contracted with the Corrections Corporation of America for more bed space because the prison was so overcrowded. I don't know if there were actually more criminals or if it was due to the passage of more silly laws. A legislature could make spitting on the sidewalk a felony if they wanted to.

Anyway, Corky sat at his table and I sat at mine as we drank our tea. It was sundown and I hit the wall switch to turn on the overhead light.

Corky was never very talkative. It wasn't that he was a timid soul or had nothing to say. I think he was wise, and when he did say something, it carried weight.

He reached up to his top shelf, pulled down a book and began to read in silence. The chamomile hadn't started working yet and I was still wound up. "What ya reading?" I asked out of curiosity.

"My Bible, want to hear what it says?"

"Okay," I replied. Why not? Maybe it could help; it certainly couldn't hurt the situation. He began. "They sat in darkness, and in the shadow of death, bound in afflictions and irons, and there was none to help," he read aloud. "That's from Psalm one oh seven," he said.

"What does it mean?"

"It means I'll be seeing you Truman and my prayers will be with you," he stated as if it were a matter of fact.

"Do you believe, Truman?" he asked.

"Believe what?"

"That Jesus of Nazareth was crucified, was buried, and then rose from the dead?"

"He rose from the dead? No, sorry Corky, but that's something I just can't convince myself of. Death is final and in the end rules all."

"Well, you don't have to convince yourself, something else will."

I wished these people would leave me alone and suddenly the idea of moving into my own place—alone and quiet—might give me the chance to get some resolution to the possibility of this or the possibility of that, of life, of death, of life after death, of angels, of demons, of maniacs, of murder, and of mayhem.

Whether I was like St. George off to slay a dragon or Don Quixote off to tilt at windmills or Sherlock Holmes off to solve a mystery, I didn't care. All I wanted was some peace and quiet and for the clanging voices of confusion inside my head to shut the hell up.

I crawled up on the top bunk and began questioning my sanity. But what is it anyway, has it ever been defined? Maybe I never had it to begin with. Did it matter? No. I was just me, Truman Struck, and right now my head spun and ached, and I was in desperate need of sleep.

The chamomile did its work and I drifted off to sleep wondering if I'd ever been sane or not, whatever being sane meant.

CHAPTER TWENTY-NINE

THE NEXT DAY I accepted the Caretaker position at the cannery, proving to myself that I was insane. Oh well. I had to, I had to find out what it was that kept drawing and pushing me toward the slaughterhouse, and why. I could no longer deny what had been happening, it kept coming at me from all directions. And I knew deep down in my gut it wouldn't let me go, not until I decided to find out the truth about this . . . madness.

"Good!" Larry exclaimed after hearing my decision. "It'll take about a week to finish the paperwork and get the place set up so it's livable."

A week later he handed me a key to the door.

"Go on down and take a look around if you want," he said.

I took it, watching my hand closely to see if it was shaking. It wasn't, so far so good.

"Thanks," I said. He tore off on some other mission. I flicked on the bare light bulb over the stairs and began a slow descent. The single bulb in the main room shed enough light to see but not enough to chase away the shadows in the corners. The six cardboard boxes I'd seen in my room were stacked in the middle of the warehousing space. I crossed the concrete floor to my room. The key slid easily into the door lock, I twisted it to the right and it just as easily unlocked. Opening it, I felt along the wall for a light switch, found it, flipped it up and an overhead fluorescent fuzzed on. The room wasn't anything special and much cleaner than I thought it would be, no dust or mold or skeletons. It had a wooden dresser the same as the ones in our cells. A single bed with a thicker than I was used to mattress, and an overstuffed easy chair with armrests, much better than the bare wood I sat on in my cell. A sink, shower, and toilet in its own partitioned area comprised the bathroom, located near the foundation wall. A blue-gray industrial grade carpet covered the concrete floor.

The entry door had a foot square window in it, like the tunnel doors on each side of the room. A two-foot square window centered in the middle of the outer wall looked out at the main and the never changing basement. A dishwashing sink had a small refrigerator next to it, a microwave sat on a shelf next to that. The nightstand by the single bed had a reading lamp on it, and a small dinette table also with a lamp on it and a one padded chair completed the furnishings.

After adding a few things and some personal touches, I'd have all the comforts of home. You betcha. But it seemed like an accommodating place and felt okay.

Some of the old timers called their cell their 'house' after awhile, and in a sense I could see how that could be.

The overhead light flickered, went out for a few seconds, and then came back on, startling me enough to make me twitch.

I'd suppressed all thoughts of possible danger lurking behind the concrete wall between the doors to the tunnels, but I found out right away it didn't take much of a jolt to make them resurface. Oh-boy.

Nothing changed after the light flickered except my state of mind and the air, it stank. After scrutinizing the room, I discovered the reason for the foul odor. In the farthest corner from the door lay the body of a large rat. I wondered how they'd missed it when they cleaned the place. I wondered why I hadn't smelled it at first. Oh well, it was here now, and I had to deal with it.

On the shelf by the microwave I noticed, for the first time, a clear glass jar containing a potpourri of aromatic herbs and flowers. Though the odor was faint, I could tell it was roses and shaking the jar increased the potency of the aroma, yup, roses for sure.

And I got it, rot and roses, the dream manifesting. Strange and spooky, but what was I to do, run?

After scooping the body of the rat into a plastic garbage bag with a shovel, ready to take it to the dumpster, I glanced around the room one more time before flicking off the light. I noticed, again for the first time, a calendar hanging on the interior concrete wall, I hadn't looked at that wall before now, that's what I told myself anyway. I had to wonder what lay behind the mysterious wall, in the space between the tunnels.

Setting the bagged rat and the shovel out in the main room, I returned to take a closer look at the wall calendar. Was it there before? I wasn't sure one-way or the other. Even with the overhead fluorescent switched on it was still a dim room.

The calendar was eight years old, turned to the month of July, with the third day of the month circled in red. The top half of the calendar was once a glossy picture of a white statue gleaming brilliant on top of a high mountain and against the deep blue of a crystal clear sky.

"Our Lady of the Mountains" the caption said. Underneath it someone had written, "YANK MY NOODLE IT'S A DANDY" and underneath that they had scrawled, "It doesn't take a rocket scientist to understand that, DOES IT?"

The calendar and its hand written message had to have been Ichabod Cain's before he disappeared. Where had he gone? No one knew, or no one would tell.

But it didn't matter now.

Angry, I tore it off the wall, took it out of the room, tossed it in the bag with the dead rat, closed and locked the door and started for the stairwell as ". . . *he's so insane*" rattled around inside my head . . . at least I thought it was in my head. And as I ascended the dim stairway, the plastic bag felt slippery, wetted from the sweat pouring out of my palms.

Chapter Thirty

Sometimes wishes do come true and my path coincided with Laura's on the next day.

"Laura, I'm glad I got a chance to see you before I leave," I said.

"Before you leave? Did you get a parole or something? Where are you going?"

"Not far, just up to live at the cannery, underneath it actually, in the basement. I'll be the caretaker up there seven days a week. It's a newly created position according to my boss."

She was slow in responding. Either she didn't know what to say or she was being careful in choosing her words.

"You're going to face them, aren't you?" she asked, seeing below the surface of the situation. She had pinpointed the truth of the matter before I admitted it to myself.

I couldn't look into the beauty and earnestness of her blue eyes and not give an honest answer. She brought that out in me. I wasn't sure how but I think it had something to do with her purity—not in the sense of moral values—but in her person.

She was who she was without pretense, guile, or games. She was all woman and all natural.

"Face them? Who?"

"Either your own demons or the ones up there," she said pointing her thumb over the top of her shoulder toward the cannery.

"Maybe you're right," I said.

"You know I am Truman. I have to teach a class in a few minutes. You be careful," she said, hastily writing something on a scrap of paper and handing it to me, she turned, took a few steps away, and then turned back to me and said, "Send me a note if you need to see me or talk to me," and continued on her way. I watched her walk. I loved to watch her walk, and started thinking if only . . . if only I was twenty years younger, if only we'd met under different circumstances. But I caught myself. If only doesn't count. The question "what if" might, as in what if I'm living under the slaughterhouse and some goddam monster eats me alive or I run into the ghost of Ichabod Cain, or what if I go *POOF* and disappear, nothing but a swirling mist blown away by the slightest of breezes.

What if demons, mine or somebody else's are for real? Maybe I should have taken Demonology 101 in college, except I don't remember the course ever being a part of any curriculum.

In a week I moved into the basement room at the cannery.

All I had to do was put away my personal effects like toiletries, books, and clothes, and the place would be homey, almost.

I made up the bed, put away most of my stuff, looked around with some satisfaction, and, not bothering to lock the door, headed out the room and up the stairs not whistling in the dark . . . yet.

The instant I topped the stairs a white flash like a lightning bolt without the sizzle and the heat, but with the force, hit me square in the chest and passed through me. The constricting pain caused me to grab the handrail to keep from falling backwards down the stairs. I twisted around and looked down the brilliant lit stairwell to watch the light carom off the walls until it disappeared through the open doorway and into the basement.

I clutched at the pain inside my chest as my heart pounded double time against my ribs. Through watery eyes I scanned the walls and high ceiling for scorch marks. None. I descended the stairs in pursuit of the strange, mysterious flash of light.

A soft pulsating glow emanated from the main basement out to the bottom landing, like a fluorescent light struggling to turn on. By the time I reached the bottom landing my legs felt like rubber. Stopping for a moment, I drew in a deep breath and then stepped into the basement.

In the center of the room, suspended in the air, floated an apparition of such exquisite beauty my breath was drawn from my body, and I stood transfixed in open-mouthed wonder, unable to draw in another.

Translucent, a mist of pure white silk, and yet solid in appearance, she looked at me with kaleidoscope eyes that sparkled like multi-colored stars. They were large and I knew she could look all around me, and in me, and through me. "Lucy in the Sky with Diamonds", it had to be her.

I say she only because the robe, which glittered like a thousand polished diamonds, flowed down and around her to stop just above the tiniest of feet shod in sandals made of spun gold. Her pure white hair, crowned with a gold tiara ringed with blood red rubies, hung down below her waist. Her face was more beautiful than any ever made of flesh. Neither old nor young, it spoke of wisdom and deep unconditional love.

I felt like a child in the presence of this being of light. I wanted to drop to one knee and proclaim her, "My Lady, My Queen," giving some token of my acknowledgment that she was as far above me as the stars above the earth.

For in that single fraction of a second when she passed through me, she knew me in a way so intimate it was beyond mortal knowledge. She didn't condemn me, or revile me, or recoil from my presence.

Instead, she looked at me with a beauty celestial, a peace unshakable, and a love eternal.

Not from this world, she had to be an angel.

She raised one hand, palm out, her elbow remaining stationary at her waist. Her sleeve, large and loose, folded into the main part of her robe, losing any distinction from it.

Would she speak? Oh please beautiful One, grace me with the sound of your voice! Every ounce of my being, every nerve, every cell, every bone, every muscle, every pulse of my heart and every spark in my brain was at attention, focused on the angelic apparition that floated, clothed in misty white silk, in front of me.

And in a single heartbeat life as I'd known it lost all its allure and meaning. To live forever in the presence of this . . . this manifest love, was now my only longing, my only desire, my only . . . need.

"Truman," she whispered, her voice surrounding, soothing, and caressing me. Tears rolled from my eyes. I could not stop their flow.

The rapture! It held me transfixed in place. I could not step forward, could not kneel, could not collapse in a heap.

I had been relieved of all that had gone before in my life, relieved of all the toxins that had become parasites of my soul. She was . . . purity, and she had spoken to me.

"Y . . . yes, m . . . my Lady," I barely whispered, afraid my tainted voice might drive her away.

"Welcome," she said, and my soul was flooded with peace. My impurity could not drive her away, this I knew.

"Who . . . who are you?" I asked with trembling lips.

"I Live, Truman, and I would have you belong to me."

I would gladly shed my blood for her, lay down my life for her, but before I could say the words, a powerful voice behind me thundered one word, *"NO!"* Its power knocked me to my knees as My Lady dissipated into vapor mist before my eyes, and I was released from her spell.

A dream, yes, it had to have been, I thought, as I picked myself up off the concrete floor. Sleep walking? Perhaps, but I'd never done it before that I remembered. If a dream, why wasn't I on my bed?

I turned around and looked up the stairwell, nothing there, except the single light bulb feebly trying to drive away the shadows.

I proceeded into the main basement room, my emotions swishing back and forth between utter loneliness and deep twisting sorrow, like those of a child who has suffered abandonment.

I felt lost, alone, and empty, but I wasn't afraid, and underneath the initial onslaught of emotion, I felt relieved.

In some supernatural way I had been rescued, but from what exactly, I couldn't say.

Where had that voice come from that chased her away? Larry my supervisor? No, it was Saturday. God? I couldn't believe God would take any interest in my life. But on the other hand a lot of strange, puzzling, and spooky things had happened that I would never have believed possible.

I felt drained, like my soul had been almost sucked out of me, and with my body resisting it, I was exhausted. Butterflies swirled around in my stomach as I recalled the stories I'd heard and the dreams I'd had about the mysterious Ichabod Cain. It was odd that I hadn't really thought about the stories of the old slaughterhouse and all that they implied since I'd begun working here. And as far as I'd noticed, all the haints had either left or been laid to rest.

Shuffling into my room, I flicked on the overhead but the light was too much. It reminded me of I Live. I'd heard that name before but was too tired to recall. Switching off the overhead, I walked on rubbery legs to the nightstand and flicked on the reading lamp, straightening; I turned to my right and looked directly at the spot where Ichabod's calendar had hung for eight years. The unfaded patch of green had marks in it, etched into the concrete. It read REVELATION 13. *Who gives a fiddler's diddler,* I thought and lay on the bed.

My hands locked behind my head, I stared at the ceiling, letting my mind drift, knowing I had no chance of sorting out the reasons for the series of strange events, but still, to my amazement, I felt calm despite being dead tired. Revelation, I'd heard that before, somewhere . . . sometime . . . long ago, even if it was yesterday. Oh well, Thy will be done, whoever Thy is. Very strange place, this.

Well, onward creaky knights in rusty armor.

Now *that* was amusing.

In A unit, alone in his cell, white haired Corky rose from prayer.

CHAPTER THIRTY-ONE

I AWOKE DISORIENTED. THERE was nothing to indicate whether it was day, night, rainy, sunny, or whether the world continued to exist at all. No natural light ever entered the basement.

It became clear that my previous perceptions of the world were shredded and my new ones were oh so very real, at least to me, and last time I looked, nobody else walked in my shoes.

The how was irrelevant at this point. The why was crucial for me to know.

The only certainty I knew is that I was stuck in a room once occupied by a madman underneath what once was a slaughterhouse where blood flowed every day, animal and human. My empty stomach lurched at the thought.

Dreams, dialogues, visions, and events of unexplainable strangeness had brought me here. I felt like a board piece in an unknown game, and I was desperate to find out what the game was.

I flipped the table-reading lamp on, added coffee to a cup of hot water, and plopped down in my easy chair to drink it as I stared into nothingness.

Not sure what I felt at this point, besides a pawn in a game, I did know it was just me against whatever it was out there, or perhaps in here, I thought, glancing at the back wall. I felt like a man in the middle of a maelstrom with one rubbery leg to stand on. Fear didn't get a grip on me. Though perplexed and confused, I had a strange curiosity. The grisly ghouls, the mutated beasts, the heavenly angels, *had* to fit like the proverbial pieces of the puzzle, or the other pieces of the game. Otherwise, they were just manifestations of my fractured mind and projections of it. Scary thought, and now I did feel afraid, not of boogeymen with fangs, or of monsters hiding under my bed, but of what I might find at the end of this strange quest, and that was the question, the why of it.

The clock on the nightstand read 4:00, it could be AM or PM, I had no idea how long I slept.

I pulled back the window curtain and peered out at the basement room. The view and the light would never change unless I decided to turn off the one-lit light bulb or it burned out or the power went out or some otherworldly being that shone in and of itself paid me a visit; it happened before.

But if the light did go out, I'd be caught in pitch black darkness, so I thought it a good idea to get myself some candles and some matches and some extra light bulbs.

Finishing my coffee, I decided I'd better see if it was day or night. After setting down my cup, I glanced at the unfaded patch of green on the back wall. Blank. Nothing, no writing, no REVELATION 13 etched into the concrete.

Of course, it had been a dream, hadn't it? I couldn't tell anymore. Maybe life was a dream within a dream like someone once said, Poe or Shakespeare or maybe Walt Disney.

Upstairs revealed that it was late afternoon and the day was winding down into evening.

The cannery was eerie when the machinery was stilled and no one was around, not ominous, which speaks of danger, but eerie, which speaks of edgy.

A lot of death had taken place here. Countless cattle and twelve human beings gleefully slaughtered and here I was, living amongst the butchery etched in the ether.

If nothing else, the story of Ichabod Cain was true. What had turned his wheels remained a mystery. Chalk it up to a mental defect, the shrinks had said. Of course, what else would it be?

A sociopath at the least, but more likely a psychopath at the far end of the spectrum, just a thin line away from being locked forever in his own padded cell. Somehow, he managed to fool everyone along the way.

He'd literally been caught red handed butchering the body of the twelfth escapee, and it was a good assumption that the previous eleven met the same end and for the same reasons. Their remains never did pop up.

That Cain was a genius there was no doubt, as far as measuring intelligence goes, but there's no way of measuring what's in our hearts, where we live. Some keep them open, some keep them closed, most of us guard them so close we may as well not feel at all, and some run rampant down the dark side of theirs, following a bloody path from which there is no returning.

Of such was Ichabod Cain. Yes, he was a genius, but he was also clever enough not to let his heart be known, which was as cold and as hard as the nine-tenths of an ice burg that lies hidden beneath the surface of the water. Perhaps he knew his heart was as black as the end of the world night and that could be the reason he always ate the heart of his victims . . . hoping on some primal level to change his own into something approaching human. The trouble was his twisted soul had so intertwined with his heart he wouldn't be comfortable any other way.

There is no returning.

In any event, they never did find him after he ran down the stairwell screaming . . . I Live . . . I Live!

That's where I'd heard the name the angel of light had said was hers, in Chico's telling me the story of Ichabod. That was for damn sure ominous.

Alone amidst the silent machinery the phone rang in the storage room. I double timed it across the process area and took it off the hook.

"Cannery, this is Struck," I answered, figuring it must be a sergeant or someone of that ilk calling to check on me. The whole prison had to know by now I was living up here as the Caretaker.

No answer.

"Cannery, Struck," I repeated.

After a brief silence a tentative voice asked, "Truman?"

"Yes . . . ?"

"It's Laura."

"Laura! I didn't recognize your voice over the phone. What's going on?"

"I thought you might call but you didn't, so I called to see if you're okay. Is everything all right over there?"

"Call you? How?" I didn't understand her. "Wait a second," I said, and reached into my jeans pocket pulling out the scrap of paper she'd handed me yesterday. Sure enough, there was her phone number written on it.

"Your phone number, I just now found it, crumpled up in my pocket."

"Of course. Is everything all right? I've been thinking very strongly about you."

"I'm still alive anyway."

"Did something happen?" she asked, the concern level in her voice going up a notch.

I told her about the apparition of the angel and the spell it had me under. I told her about the powerful voice that had broken it and chased it away. "I think it was just another dream," I ended.

"But afterward why did you go into your room, lie down and go to sleep instead of waking up on your bed in the first place? It doesn't fit the pattern of dreaming at all."

I couldn't argue with that, and if I did use the argument of a dream within a dream, we would be getting on a metaphysical merry-go-round and neither of us had time for that nonsense.

"I could have been sleepwalking," I said.

"Do you have a history of it?"

"No," I replied. "Okay, none of it fits the normal patterns, but there are always deviations from the norm and exceptions to the rule, you know."

"Yes, I know, but flimsy explanations just don't feel right, know what I mean?"

"I know exactly what you mean," I said, and right now I wished with all my heart I could hold her for awhile.

"I wish I could see you," she blurted as if she could feel my longing reach out to her and she wanted to respond.

Now *that* would truly be unbelievable.

"I know what," she said. "I'll talk to the Security Major and see if I can get clearance to come and visit you up there."

"How can you do that? Get clearance I mean."

"Well, let's see, I am on staff and a teacher, you were my aid, and we need to finish discussing a new curriculum we were starting before you quit. How does that sound for starters?"

"Sounds like a plan that could work."

"It will work. And also, you know the gravel road that intersects the one going up there from the prison?"

"Sure, we crossed it every morning going to work. I often wondered where it came from."

"Well, if you go east on it, it'll take you right to Anaconda.

"That's where you live?"

"Yes, so you can see how easy it would be for me to come by the cannery. Anyway, if I can't work it out so that I can come up there and see you, I'll work it so you can come in and see me, okay?"

"Yeah, uh, fine," was all I could say, thinking it was a good thing she couldn't see me right now, because I was probably floating on air, like old what's her name down in the basement.

"And Truman, remember, I'm as intrigued by what's happening to you as you are. And even though my involvement has only been in your dreams so far, I feel like we are in this—whatever *this* is-together, you know?"

"Yeah, I know." The woman definitely had heart and it was the open kind.

"Oh, I nearly forgot," I said. "Do you know anything about the word revelation?"

"I know the definition of it. It means to understand something previously hidden, like a light that suddenly shines in the dark, sort of. Is that it?"

"Maybe, but the version of it I saw was spelled out in capital letters and the number thirteen followed it."

"It must be a reference to the last book in the Bible, the thirteenth chapter. Was there a colon after the number?"

"I don't remember, but I don't think so," I replied.

"Why are you asking anyway?"

"It was a part of this afternoon I forgot to mention to you. I removed an old calendar off the wall of my room. Later I looked at the place it had been, an unfaded patch of green paint, and I swear the word and the number were etched into the concrete and a short while later, it was gone."

"Truman, we need to talk. Call me anytime. You still have my number don't you?"

"Right here in my hand."

"Be sure to put it in a safe place, will you please?"

"I will, and thanks for calling." Now that was an understatement. Thanks for caring. Thanks for easing my mind. Thanks for soothing my soul. Thanks for giving me hope.

"Bye, bye Truman. I'll be in touch. Take care and don't hesitate to call . . . promise?"

"Promise, and thanks again."

"Bye bye," she said and the phone fell silent.

The wind must have picked up, I could hear the gutter clanking against the side of the building. I had some daylight left so I decided to take care of the problem.

It wasn't hot out, but pleasant, the sun well on its way to disappearing behind the high western peaks.

The clanking gutter hung loose on the east side of the cannery, bent in the middle and each side hanging down at a forty-five degree angle with the ends almost touching the ground.

The wind came up stronger and began to whistle through the planks of the loading chutes behind me.

I grabbed one end of the gutter and yanked hard. It didn't budge. I gave it another quick, powerful jerk. Still no give. Looking up at the angle in the center, I saw the twist of wires holding it in place. I was going to need a pair of pliers, or better yet, wire cutters.

In the main room of the basement was a freestanding tool closet. I unlocked it and found what I needed, wire cutters.

After climbing up on the roof and cutting the gutter loose, I dragged it to the west side of the building and laid it out full length along the foundation wall.

The main prison nestled still and silent a couple hundred feet below me. All seemed quiet and peaceful in the waning sunlight. It felt good to stand there outside the walls and chain link fences of the prison. It was another degree of freedom and I was glad I'd decided to take the opportunity allowing me to enjoy it.

The east wind curled gently around the corner of the building to where I stood on the western side. I breathed deep of the cooling air. All in all things weren't that bad being semi-retired up here on the mountainside.

Stepping around the corner of the building, the wind out of the east hit me full in the face, not hard, just enough to make me take note of it. Then, turning right around the next corner, I was once again on the east side of the building where the gutter had been dangling from that twist of wire.

Chapter Thirty-One

Mission accomplished.

I felt a strong sense of satisfaction as I turned the next corner and was on the south side of the cannery.

As I approached the entry door, the wind picked up and began playing its siren song through the loading chutes, I could hear the gutter tapping against the side of the eastern wall, keeping perfect time.

Yes indeed, a strong sense of satisfaction I thought, as I opened the door and entered the former slaughterhouse.

Back in the basement, I returned the wire cutters to the toolbox, locked the cabinet and went upstairs to watch what promised to be a glorious sunset. Some were breathtaking when they painted the underbellies of the thunderheads with the colors of fire.

The pangs of hunger got a solid grip on my stomach and I headed down to my room to get something to eat. I placed my hand on the railing and held it there as I descended the stairs. At the bottom of the railing I felt a thread brush against my hand. Caught there on the last support bracket was a tuft of white thread. I worked it loose and brought it to my eye. It wasn't thread, but strands of long white hair. They hadn't been there the last time I cleaned the handrails. No, they hadn't been there. I was sure of it.

I didn't know anyone who had long white hair, except of course the angel, I Live. Real angel hair, well, I'll keep it around for Christmas, none of that phony store bought stuff this year, no siree.

I went into my room and opened the drawer of my nightstand. I took pains to fold the angel hair and laid it out on the bottom of it. I noticed a book tucked away at the back of the drawer. I grasped it by its spine and pulled it out. On the front cover, printed in gold block letters was, GIDEON'S BIBLE.

"Why, just like any fine hotel room," I chuckled to myself and set the book on the dining table, it's golden letters beautifully offset by the deep green of it's cover.

I glanced over at the unfaded patch of green on the concrete wall, expecting to see ... I don't know what ... maybe, *Hallelujah to ya Truman,* but it was blank.

Pulling a frozen pizza out of the fridge, I stuffed it in the microwave, popped open a can of cold Coke, pulled the pizza out of the oven, sat in my easy chair and began to eat. The frozen pizza was far better than any I'd had over at the trough, also known as the chow hall.

My sense of satisfaction remained in place. Maybe because my life had taken a turn for the better, I thought, as I enjoyed my dinner, listening to the wind outside whistling its siren song through the loading chutes as the gutter clanked against the building, keeping perfect time.

Thunder clapped, applauding the lightning. The boom reverberated through the basement walls and down into my bones.

The power didn't go out, but just the same I thought I'd see if I could round up some candles and matches. I went out to the main room and took down the top cardboard box, leaving five stacked. I quickly went through it and found nothing but clean rags. They'd be useful anyway.

I removed the other four boxes and set them aside, stacked one atop the other, leaving only the last box in the stack. I was a graduate student of Murphy's Law and I knew how these things worked. No fooling old Truman, no siree.

I opened the bottom box, which used to be the top box when they were stacked six high in my room. Inside of it I found some old eating utensils, a couple of plastic cups, and an unopened package of six votive candles. Beside them was a box of old fashioned strike anywhere matches.

Taking the box and its contents into my room, I put the extra utensils, no doubt used by Icky, in the garbage, and the coffee cups in the sink to wash later. Opening the box of candles, I placed one on a small plate, along with a few matches, and set it on the table. The rest of the matches I put in my nightstand drawer with the angel hair.

Was it really angel hair? How could I be certain, take it to a lab for testing? Why not?

Well . . . it sounded good to me and I knew what I was talking about and it would mean the beautiful apparition I had seen was real and that was most important of all, that she was real, and so I had really seen her and with all that was within me I longed to bask in her presence once again and stay there forever, thank you.

Intending to put the cardboard box back out in the main room, something inside of it rattled when I picked it up. I opened it, looked, and found a small plastic statuette, the kind people used to stick on the metal dashboards of their cars.

I don't care if it rains or freezes, long as I got my plastic Jesus riding on the dashboard of my car.

It was a replica of Our Lady of the Mountains, about six inches tall and she fit into the palm of my hand. I didn't have anything against Our Lady, it was Ichabod Cain's outdated calendar with the bathroom message scribbled on it that I didn't want in my room. It was too bad he had to go and blow her up, but it did get him put in prison. I was convinced the man had committed a lot more bloody murders than just the twelfth prison runner that got him caught. Well, they didn't really catch him, they never found him, he just disappeared, maybe in this very room. *I don't care if it rains or freezes . . .*

Chapter Thirty-Two

THE UPSTAIRS PHONE rang, I ran past the foot square window in the north tunnel door toward the stairs, not noticing the eyes that watched me and that had watched me. Eyes fragmented into multiple lenses and multiple colors.

I would have recognized those eyes as they changed from red to orange to amber to yellow to green to blue to purple and back to red as they spun and tumbled randomly around a central elliptical pupil devoid of light, as black as deep space and just as cold, kaleidoscope eyes spinning and tumbling around that black slit until all the fragments folded into a dull, washed out yellow color, as if it were diffused through frosted glass.

The eyes of a used to be angel receded from the window into the recesses of the dark, and with a nova burst of sickly yellow light, disappeared.

Chapter Thirty-Three

I ALMOST TORE THE wall-mounted phone off its bracket.

"Laura?"

Only silence, was I too late?

I did have her number, I could try to call her, but the line was the noise of silence, the kind the dead would listen to while in their graves.

But someone *was* there, I knew it, I could feel it.

"Tru-u-uman," a muffled voice spoke, sounding like it came from somewhere beyond the grave.

"Tru-u-uman."

"Y . . . yes-s-s."

"Would you belong to me?" the voice whispered.

"Who are you?" I asked.

"You know me Truman, and I know you very well. I have been waiting a long time for you to come to me."

"Who are you?" I asked again.

"You know me Truman, you know me very well, and I have been waiting."

I knew that voice; there was only one like it in the world. "I Live," I whispered.

"Yes, it is I, Truman my dearest and would you belong to me?"

"I . . . I . . ." My heart was divided, part of me, the bigger part, wanted to shout "YES!" Another part of me fought to keep the word from coming out.

"Well . . ." she said, as if knowing my struggle and was trying to coax an agreement out of me. I hesitated and the line went static and garbled and fell back into dead silence.

Outside, the thunder clapped again, applauding another lightning strike, and I trembled at the sound.

I now, at least, understood that who or what was calling itself I Live wanted me for reasons I didn't understand, and that whoever or whatever this entity was, it was powerful and cunning and had gotten a grip on my soul, or at least a part of it, and I didn't know how.

The receiver rattled against the cradle as I hung it up with a trembling hand. Feeling like I was mired in the muck of a deep swamp without the strength to free myself, and if I couldn't, I would perish in that quagmire of uncleanness with which I had been touched.

I wanted to scream my guts out.

Managing to pick up the phone, I debated calling Laura. But what would I say?

"Hi Laura, its Truman."

"Are you alright?"

"Pretty much, but you see, there's this ghost or demon or evil angel out here and I was wondering if you'd like to help me chase it away before it steals my soul?" I decided not to call. It sounded crazy the more I thought about it, and besides, I was

certain the guards monitored the phone. Monitored? All of a sudden it dawned on me. The guards must have heard the conversation. I could picture it all now. "Hey, Struck's got hisself a hot girlfriend on the line. Oh man, she wants him real bad like, come on guys, listen in," then the speaker phone, then the heavy breathing, the sweaty foreheads, the beady eyes, and the pork bellies, the kind of people that usually get locked up, but instead work as guards.

Not a good idea to get Laura all caught up in this. Why would she want to anyway, for cripes sake, well . . . no fool like an old fool as they say, whoever *they* are.

I needed some fresh air.

The lightning strike hadn't knocked the power out so I could see clear enough to make it to the exit door.

The sun appeared to be resting atop the mountain peaks, recuperating from a hard day's journey across the sky. It cast pure golden light, causing the colors to shine brilliant and at the same time mellow and fuzzy edged. The green of the grass, the crystal blue of the sky, the gold on the far eastern mountains, the purple on the near ones, affirmed life within me. And if it was worth having, it was worth fighting for. A row of daisies danced and nodded as if giving their agreement and saying, "Yes!"

I felt a whole lot better. Though not completely free of the swamp, I was free of the muck, and felt strengthened to face what may lie ahead.

And the light dispelled the darkness.

A lone figure stopped on the oval track down at the prison and waved up at me. Despite the distance I could tell it was Medicine Horse. I waved back.

"Hoka-Hey," he hollered, his voice echoing off the nearby purple hued mountains. It is a Good Day to Die, and yes, dying is a part of life, life worth living for and worth dying for.

The daisies nodded their heads in agreement one more time as Medicine Horse resumed his walk. That was like him though, always there with the right words at the right time.

A Coincidence? I no longer believed in them.

I sat down on the torn fabric of an old aluminum frame lawn chair and watched the remainder of the sun fade away, the colors of landscape and sky changing hue and darkening as the light lessened.

It was understandable to me how ancient peoples had worshiped the sun, Ra and all that.

Was it born from the fear of the unknown, or of darkness, or of death? Is that what religion is all about, hoping to be okay in the unknown darkness of death? Or maybe they looked at the sun as the giver and sustainer of life.

Hoka-Hey! Yes! For dying is our fate from the moment we get slapped on the ass right out of the comfort of the womb. Hello cruel world.

"So live!" I told myself, even though deep inside I knew I feared the dark in this place, down in the basement, under the slaughterhouse. It was unknown.

I shuddered as I stood to my feet in the cool night air, the moon and stars seeming near enough to touch. A meteorite flamed to extinction across the sky. Hoka-hey.

Despite a feeling of dread, I set my will to return to my room. My room, it had a nice ring to it, but it wasn't truly mine and I knew I wasn't alone . . . down there.

What had I gotten into, I asked myself one more time, although it didn't make a bit of difference now. I'd signed a six-month commitment saying I'd stay on this job, and besides, what would I say, I don't want to stay because ghosts and goblins are bothering me. They'd have a bed waiting for me at the state mental hospital in Warm Springs a few miles down the road.

I went back into the sonofabitching place, stopping at the top of the stairs, peering down into the dim eeriness. The hair on the back of my neck stood up as I began my descent, not knowing what I might find down there.

At the bottom I stopped and scanned the main room. Nothing visible had changed. The single bare light bulb was hanging still as death, its twisted cord looking like a hangman's rope in the shadow above it. Deep shadows inhabited the corners of the room, as always.

I flicked on the overhead as I entered my room. Everything was in its place, the candle, the statuette, and the Bible on the table. The two cups were in the sink and still needed washing. The bed was as crisp as a military cot.

I crossed the tiny space, switched on the lamp by my bed, and then recrossed the tiny space to flip off the fluorescent, getting ready to settle in for the night and do some reading. No point in doing any thinking, I'd only be going around in circles with it until I gave myself a headache. Instead, I'd let things sort themselves out and come to me, and sooner or later they would, I had no doubt of that.

The only book I had to read was Gideon's Bible, but I had no idea where to start. I knew a little about the Bible of course, everybody does to one degree or another, Adam and Eve, Moses and the Ten Commandments, Jesus the Son of God and the Son of Man, angels and the devil and all that.

I also knew it was a controversial book, I don't know why exactly, only that a lot of different religions and denominations revolve around it. Many atrocities had been committed in the name of the book. The hypocrites and the acts they committed marching together in an endless parade.

Personally, I couldn't see that its followers had done much good. TV evangelists did find a way to get rich off it though, telling people they needed to give ten percent of their income to God. I can't fathom any reason why God would need money.

But what about old Gideon and his Bible? I still had no idea where to start so I sat down and just opened it. My eyes fell on Psalm 107 where I read, "They sat in darkness and the shadow of death, bound in afflictions and irons—and there was none to help." I'd heard that before. I stretched my mind backwards, forwards, and sideways, searching. It had to be there somewhere among the many voices, but not Laura's, not Chico's, not Horse's, and not that angelic freak, I Live. Finally I landed. It was Corky, my last cellmate. The old white haired gentleman had read it to me the night before I moved here, only a short while ago, yet like an eternity past.

That voice behind me, that thunderous *NO* that drove away I Live, was that God? Was He-She-It on my side? Had I been sent to help? Was I insane? Was I responsible for being that way if I was?

I settled on the last option, I'm not responsible for being insane. It seemed like the safest choice.

What *was* that word etched in the wall?

I looked up at the unfaded green spot on the wall expecting to see . . . what, a happy face smiling at me, or the words nyuk-nyuk-nyuk, underneath a picture of the Three Stooges?

Nothing was there, surprise, surprise.

What *was* that word?

Search. Click. Whir. And after awhile I found it—REVELATION. I looked it up in Gideon's Bible, it's the very last book in the Book. Turning to the thirteenth chapter I read, "Who is like unto the beast? Who is able to make war with him?"

Chapter Thirty-Four

WITHOUT A WHISPER of sound, the thing in the tunnel withdrew from the foot square window centered in the north tunnel door. Nothing more than a dark shimmer, it moved across the concrete floor, a fleeting substance of shadow.

Possessed with the patience of a viper, driven by the hunger of a lion, it is the perfect predator, but it does not crave flesh dripping hot with fear-laced blood. It possesses no razor sharp teeth or elongated fangs with which to rend and tear flesh, or powerful jaws to crush and crunch bones. No nightmarish face to freeze in terror those it intends to devour.

It feeds on souls.

The father of shape shifters, it inspires the legends of vampires and werewolves, of witches and warlocks, and of monsters alien and human, the fountain of Hitler's inspiration, Caesar's madness, and Pontius Pilate's guilt. The harbinger of death and the destroyer of life, from it spring all things dark and dreary, dank and dismal, dead and decaying; all things puzzling and perplexing, hateful and hurtful, terrifying and horrifying; living nightmares and dying dreams; broken promises, broken homes, and broken hearts; all decadence, debauchery, depravity, and despair, all the sorrows and lost tomorrows; all blood spilled and all men killed, all souls lost and all the damned; it obscures the hopes of Heaven and gilds the desires of Hell. The thing in the tunnel is the Fountainhead of Evil. Its hunger is for souls and its hunger is ravenous.

CHAPTER THIRTY-FIVE

CORKY WAS SOFT spoken and gentle, harmless, unassuming, and never contentious with others. He was as mild a mannered man as could be found anywhere. But behind the mantle of meekness, dwelt a powerful faith.

Kneeling down on creaky knees beside his bunk in the classic pose of prayer, he began to intercede for the safety of Truman Struck's soul as he had done every day since Truman moved.

*　*　*

Outside, Medicine Horse stood in the grassy center of the oval track, observing the gathering of ravens. The westering sun glinted silver off their feathered black bodies as their harsh, grating cries reverberated off the purple mountains, their raucous noise threatening to tear a hole in the darkening sky.

*　*　*

A sudden urge to pray the rosary struck Laura as she relaxed outdoors on her patio.

The sunset was beautiful, the buzzing insects minimal, and the iced tea perfect as she sipped the cooling drink and gazed wistfully across the narrow valley below.

Born into a family of Irish Catholic descent, she had adopted that faith as a young girl and had kept it in varying degrees of fervor since that time, graduating from one of two Catholic universities in the state.

But her faith wasn't blind and neither was she, having studied comparative religions as part of her curriculum at the university. She retained an open mind concerning spirituality and had done a term paper on Wicca, a modern day religion having ancient roots. She got a C on the paper, even though it was technically perfect, but the instructor didn't like the subject matter. Oh well, we all have feelings and beliefs that, when they're perceived to be threatened, we ourselves feel threatened.

The *urge* Laura felt was now so strong she could no longer ignore it.

Rising with the empty glass in her hand, she went inside her bungalow. Her house wasn't stylish in the sense that the décor and furnishings blended in perfect style, nor did they need to. An eclectic woman, her home reflected her tastes.

Passing under the archway from the living room into the dining room, she approached her most treasured possession.

The story surrounding the old buffet never wavered. A long forgotten Celtic artisan crafted it from the native wood of Ireland. That it had crossed the Atlantic aboard a wooden sailing ship, there was no doubt. That it had survived for centuries was nothing short of miraculous. The story also said that the oak buffet had crossed the states, beginning with her great-great-grandparents in Boston, where it first arrived. From there it made stops in Chicago, Minneapolis, Billings, and finally to the sleepy little burg of Anaconda and into Laura's dining room.

Once in awhile Laura wondered if there wasn't something magical or sacred about the old buffet. It didn't have a scratch or gouge on it anywhere, although she had noticed there was a small cut in the middle of the rear left leg. Other than that, she imagined the piece looked just as it had when the craftsman stood back to take an admiring look at the work of his hands, leaving him with a sense of lasting satisfaction.

She inhaled a deep breath of the pure mountain air wafting gently but fully through the open patio door. Letting it out slow, her fingertips lightly touched the top of the buffet and then moved in a gentle caress out from the center, each hand going in its own direction, right to right and left to left.

She wondered what tales the heavy piece of furniture could tell were it able to speak. What voices had it heard? What magic had it seen? Maybe it remembered the time it was a mighty oak in the Emerald Isle before becoming a buffet under a master's hands.

To Laura, it was a mystery, a treasure, and an anchor in her life.

Removing her hands from off the piece, she pulled open the middle top drawer, flanked by one on each side of it. All were set in a curve, the arcs of the curves were equal but opposite. The two outer drawers curved inward, the middle drawer curved outward. A backboard with the same alternating curvature on the top of it ran straight along the full length of the back. On it was a tree with an axe on one side of it and a rose on the other side, both carved in high relief.

In the shallow middle drawer lay the rosary. It had been with the buffet ever since Laura could remember. It could have been a part of the buffet except it was fashioned from rosewood and the buffet from oak. Its survival was another miracle.

Handed down from generation to generation dating back to the Emerald Isle, Laura wasn't sure how it had come to be, and had only sketchy legends to go on. One story, and the most prevailing of them, was that St. Patrick himself had carved it. That was the one she liked to believe and hoped was true.

Regardless, the hand carved string of beads was an object of veneration to her, more because of its longevity in the family than for any other reason.

But . . . there was that tiny spark of possibility that often ignites the flame of hope.

Sudden hesitation stayed her hand as she reached for the sacred artifact. Fear as a product of guilt had prompted it. She hadn't been to the confessional booth or taken communion for a long time. Maybe years by now, and she wasn't sure where she stood in God's eyes, God being defined by the church.

But the urge to pray the rosary took over, dispelling her fears, both great and small. With a whispered "thank you", she picked up the sacred object.

Sudden strength shot up her arms and into her shoulders. From there, it converged and traveled lightning quick down her spine, continuing through her hips and into each leg. Her skull tingled from the infusion of energy that permeated her being from head to foot leaving her feeling as if her bones were unbreakable and her faith unshakable.

She didn't know the source of the strength she felt, but had no doubt it came from the rosary. Maybe all the prayers that had been said using it, maybe all the faith that had been poured into those prayers, maybe all the holiness transferred by the touch of hundreds of fingertips had somehow congealed and focused into a single point, a point of gathering from the ancient to the now, a point Laura had touched in her time of need.

Kneeling by the wing backed chair that flanked the buffet, she kissed the alpha and the omega of the rosary, the crucifix, and began, "Hail Mary full of grace, all I see is Truman's face. Our Father who art in Heaven, help the man whose face I see, strengthen him I pray of thee."

Finishing, she arose, surprised that she was so bold as to pray beyond the boundaries of her childhood upbringing. But along with the previous infusion of strength, an undeniable and gentle feeling of peace had drifted down to settle on her heart.

After whispering another thank you she returned the rosary to its resting place in the top middle drawer of the buffet. She went back out on the patio and reclined once again on the chaise lounge. Below, the lights of Anaconda twinkled and danced.

The peaceful feeling remained and she soon drifted off into a sleep.

Inside the middle drawer of the buffet, the rosary many believed St. Patrick himself had carved emanated a light of its own.

CHAPTER THIRTY-SIX

T<small>HE</small> G<small>ATHERING OF</small> Ravens darken the sky, the beating of thousands of wings create a wind like the sound of thunder, and the harsh calls pierce the senses like the screams of demons intent on cracking the sky.

* * *

My heart pounds a thunderous rhythm; it feels as if it may burst. Please! Make them stop! I put my hands over my ears, hoping to shut out the hellish symphony of those black as the dead of night demons.

Suddenly it is still.

Out of the chaos the huge birds fly away in all directions. The sun glints off their black feathers, causing them to appear wet and shiny. Their synchronized flight is like a sunburst shooting out in a large circle with the edge expanding uniformly out, out, out until they are nothing but black dots against the light blue of the sky.

I take my hands from off my ears, silence, blessed silence, but only for a moment. They return, not as forceful or as raucous, in the shape of a heart against the sky. It begins to move slowly, elongating at the bottom until it forms the shape of a huge, black arrow shimmering in the sun. And then as if shot from an unseen bow, it bursts forward at lightning speed and strikes the slaughterhouse, penetrating the wall and disappearing within, stilling the noise of a thousand beating wings and the pounding of my heart.

Laura opened her eyes with a gasp. Disoriented, she needed a moment to remember she is reclined in the chaise lounge on her patio. Looking down at the reassuring lights of Anaconda, she realizes that she has not *had* a dream, but that she has *been in* a dream.

* * *

Seated on a grassy slope above the oval track, Medicine Horse watches the ravens continue to gather. Coming from all directions, they settle on the tops of light poles and buildings and on tabletops scattered here and there in the yard. Some swoop down to land on the high fences. The huge birds are hushed and still . . . waiting. That is what it is, thinks Horse. They are being patient, with no fidgeting, just still and silent, these black as night birds, these ravens the size of eagles.

Most had come for the gathering from the southwest. Medicine Horse had heard stories from that direction, stories told by his red brothers and their belief that the huge black birds were harbingers of evil, and were perhaps evil themselves, but he did not know.

The gathering ceased, as did the breeze. The air hung still and heavy. Then with unbelievable swiftness, the ravens lifted up as one, the noise from their throats like the screams of the damned. They made a huge black cloud blotting out the sun as they rose ever higher. Then, like a cloudburst, the ravens went flying in all directions, first forming a perfect circle, then a perfect heart, and then the heart formed into an arrow. It shot forward, hit the slaughterhouse, and instead of splattering against its side, went through the wall, thousands of ravens disappearing into the building.

Medicine Horse blinked his eyes and looked around him. People shuffled slowly along on the oval track. A guard stood nonchalantly at the upper end of it. No one else was stopped dead in their tracks, looking up at the sky or out at the slaughterhouse.

The elders had told him they had seen the Gathering of Ravens many times. They said they were the embodied souls of evil ones, those who had died on death rows across the land, and those who hadn't died on death row but met their end some other way, they were all the souls of those who murdered for the thrill of it or had delighted in afflicting all manner of torture.

Chapter Thirty-Seven

The thing in the tunnel didn't need to travel to feed his lust for souls. His will and cunning dwelt underneath the general clutter, clamor, and confusion in the world, and he would send it to first entice and mesmerize and then affect the total surrender of one's soul to himself.

One at a time or in groups—it was so easy to establish group think—groups maniacal or organized or sanctified. Whatever suited his desire he could have by imposing his will on mankind, who offered little resistance.

But he had a need to satisfy, and he drooled over the thought of those diseased and demented souls.

"Come to me, my minions of the lost, come to me," he whispered, sending out his will. It wasn't telepathy in the common understanding of the word. It was far more subtle than that, for he touched the Empty, that place inside us whether large or small, caused by lost dreams, or lost love, or the betrayal of trust. That place where hope has died. That place in our hearts where once was something cherished, but now are only bitter thorns. But we plod on in the hope that what we once knew, we might know again, and what had once filled the Empty might fill it again.

This is where the thing in the tunnel sends his will, like silken fingers to touch and soothe the Empty, offering false promises and inspiring false hope, until the poor and beaten down souls turn themselves over to him. Then he reaps the reward of his efforts and his joy begins, and he can turn the Empty inside a person into a bottomless pit of insatiable desires, created in his own image.

THE NIGHTMARE

Chapter Thirty-Eight

A DREAM WITHIN A dream, I thought, alone and sitting in the well-worn easy chair. The table lamp cast a comforting glow across the room. I lit the candle and turned off the light. Inhaling deeply, I reached over to pick up Gideon's Bible, hoping it might bring some direction to the puzzling maze that had become my life.

So why was I asking myself about a dream within a dream? Did the idea or the questions it brought matter, not a bit.

What was is and will be. What is was and will be again, and what will be once was and I have lost my mind. Perhaps, but the real question I now faced was . . . where did I stand in life? Dream or no dream, real or imagined, the philosophizing didn't matter, not any more, and my shift in reality was completed.

Maybe Gideon's Bible would help me figure it out, I thought, when as sudden as a summer storm the sound of thousands of screeching voices, the screams of the damned that are and that will be, pounded into my ears, hitting with gale force and pinning me to the chair.

Breaking free, I leaped from the chair to the door of my room, opening it in time to see thousands of ravens, hurtling full speed down the stairwell, smash the window of the north tunnel door off to my left and fly through it. The noise of their frenzied flight was deafening, the weight of it dropped me to my knees on the concrete floor. I covered my ears with my hands, and screamed . . . but it was lost in the hellish symphony as the ravens kept coming, a black tornado emptying itself into the tunnel.

As sudden as it had begun, the tumult stopped, the silence almost as deafening as the screams of the ravens.

I looked at my hands; both were spattered with flecks of blood from my ears. I thought I might be deaf. Maybe the force of the beating wings and the howling shrieks had shattered my eardrums, along with the rest of my senses.

I stood up from the concrete floor, my legs wobbly, my bones like water. Any senses I had left were reeling, overpowered and knocked off kilter by what I had just seen and heard.

I took a tentative step forward, and then another, stronger step, all right, my legs were back. Easing over to the broken out window, I half expected to see the beastly body of thousands of ravens come flying at me, beaks aimed for my eyes and throat.

But there was nothing, only stillness and silence. The interior was pitch black, the dim light not penetrating beyond the length of a man's body into the tunnel.

Still, there was no reflection of light off shiny black bodies nor any malevolent light reflected in open unblinking eyes.

My legs returned to rubber and what senses I had left reeled crazily as my mind pounded with visions of some huge beast crunching down on the bones of my hand and arm as I reached through the window frame. The boarwolf? I was about to find out.

I found the doorknob, gave it a twist and the push button lock released. I turned the outer doorknob and pushed. It didn't budge. Reaching through the window frame again I found a dead bolt in place, slid it back, and the door opened.

I could not see a thing in the darkness.

I found a light switch and flipped it up. A series of six bare lights about twenty feet apart flashed on at once. By instinct I ducked down, squatting on my shaky haunches.

What was I expecting? Something . . . but nothing was there, no onrush of ravens, no crouching beast from out of my nightmares, not even a scurrying rat.

Where had the birds gone?

Relief washed over me because of their absence. At the same time I felt a sense of having been let down. I wanted the confrontation so I would know where I stood in life, other than in this empty tunnel.

I looked back. Shards and jagged pieces of glass were lying on the floor. A large black feather got stuck in the window frame.

I turned and looked down the tunnel. A few wet spots were pooled here and there on the floor, courtesy of different sizes and colors of overhead leaky pipes. The equipment that ran the coolers and freezer upstairs hummed along, so I knew I wasn't deaf.

I walked down the tunnel, slow and alert for any sound, searching up and down and side to side for an opening the black cloud of ravens might have escaped out of and back into the day . . . night? I couldn't tell, my sense of time had been obliterated.

I stopped midway. Off to the right was a more recent concrete block wall, about ten feet wide and ceiling height, the same dimensions as the tunnel. My guess was it had been another tunnel that they'd sealed up. It led north, toward the main prison, and I figured Ichabod Cain used it to get escapees up here. Maybe he had stored them in the closed up tunnel, and their skeletons remained there.

Maybe he tortured them in there before the butchering.

The thought made me shudder.

"Tru-u-ma-a-n," a haunting voice called, but that could not be possible, no one lived here, and ravens don't talk. "Tru-u-ma-a-n," called the tinkling voice of a little girl. "Hee-hee-hee," she laughed, sounding as if she had just played a harmless trick on someone, and was in the throes of delight because of it.

This place was a universe away from harmless.

No point in asking who was there, I already knew, and my blood ran hot. "Show yourself," I hollered as I continued down the tunnel, the pipes overhead continuing to drip into the pools below them. Emboldened by the anger raging through my veins, I moved forward, striding with purpose as my boot heels echoed off the tunnel walls.

"Show yourself!" I screamed.

"Hee-hee-hee, come see me."

I expected the tunnel to dead end but it didn't, instead it curved off to the left into absolute darkness.

The dim light behind me was enough to show a light switch on the wall. I flipped it up and again a string of six bare bulbs flashed on at once, revealing a curved tunnel, bending out of sight to the left. I walked through it. After the curve, the tunnel straightened out and I was facing east toward the main basement. Ahead of me lay another stretch of darkness; again, I found a light switch that turned on six bulbs. This part of the tunnel ran straight back toward the main basement. That meant this tunnel was shaped like a horseshoe. Maybe a lucky one and maybe pigs will fly some day.

"Hee-hee-hee," came from far down the tunnel as the stench of rot and roses made me cough and gag.

"Show yourself, damn you!" I shouted at the top of my lungs, my anger at its peak.

Like a blink in a dream, the boarwolf came flying at my throat, snarling, fangs bared, saliva drooling down both sides of its snout, its eyes glowing with a sickly yellow light. I threw up my arms and dropped to my haunches. Then, nothing . . . it vanished with the same suddenness as it had appeared.

"Hee-hee-hee, I Live, Truman, but you won't, oh no you won't."

"Show yourself to me you coward!"

"Kaw—Kaw—Kaw," answered from the end of the tunnel. A single raven stood on the floor watching me. The black thing started forward, making short hopping motions as it moved along the shadowed corridor. Then without warning, it turned away and took flight, its wings laboring to beat the air into submission, and disappeared through the window of the south tunnel door and into the basement.

Trotting to the end of the elongated tomb, I went to stick my hand through the window, but there was a problem, the glass was intact and stopped it. I turned and looked behind me down the tunnel, no raven. I didn't bother trying the tunnel door behind me and started back the way I had come.

Moving with extreme deliberation I looked everywhere along the way for the body of a dead rat, but found nothing, no reason for the gagging stench of rot covered with roses that permeated this unholy sepulcher.

I switched off the bare bulbs in the south tunnel, did the same in the curved part, and when I got to the end of the north tunnel and the broken glass from the window, I turned and looked back before switching off the six bulbs. Six, six, six, yeah right. Give me a break.

I turned the lights off and went to my room, the sweat of tense, anxious fear on my forehead and the palms of my hands.

I noticed the candle I'd left burning had barely begun to form a puddle of wax. Judging from the amount, I'd been gone only a few minutes in real time. But then, what was real anymore? It had seemed a lifetime in the tunnel, walking edgy on the line between life and death. But I knew where I stood in life.

I had to make my stand. I had no other choice.

"I Live, but you won't, oh no, you won't," taunted me from outside or inside my head. Time and space were no longer real dimensions from where I stood.

Chapter Thirty-Nine

Upstairs, the phone rang. Now what? I took my time getting there, figuring it was I Live playing more games.

"Hello. Slaughterhouse," I answered, with unmistakable annoyance.

"Truman?" a hesitant female voice asked. It sounded to me on the verge of mocking. I wasn't in the mood.

"Yes, of course, who else would it be?"

"It's Laura, are you all right up there?"

"Define all right," I said.

"Don't play games with me please," she said, and she was right.

"Sorry," I said. "I've just had a few thousand ravens come flying through here is all." Bite my tongue, that sounded crazier than hell.

She gasped at the other end of the line.

"Oh, no, they didn't attack me ala the Hitchcock movie. They just . . . mocked me. Yeah, that's the word, they mocked me."

"You weren't dreaming?"

"I did think that was a possibility, for awhile. I mean, they flew down the stairs, turned, broke out the window in the north tunnel door, flew into the tunnel—the tunnel is shaped like a horseshoe—and then apparently exited through the south tunnel door except the window of that door wasn't broken."

"They just disappeared?"

"Yeah, except I saw one raven actually fly through the unbroken window. Other than that, they just disappeared, like Ichabod Cain."

"It had to have been a dream, Truman," she stated.

"I'd be inclined to think so myself, except I found a huge black feather stuck in the frame of the broken out window. A keepsake for me I guess."

"We need to talk," she said.

"I thought we were."

"I mean face to face. I have clearance to have you brought here so we can discuss curriculum. Can you be ready in fifteen minutes?"

"Sure. I'll put on my finest prison blues."

"All right, I'll call the guard tower and have someone come out and get you. See you in a few."

"Okay, in a few it is."

Chapter Forty

THE THING IN the tunnel is as ancient as creation itself. Invisibility for a cloak, it's manifestations to human eyes can take any form he wishes, from angel to demon and everything imaginable in between. More than that, he can project images into the minds and onto the hearts of mankind, whom he creates in his own image, Man-unkind.

And oh what joy it brings to it!

Working on minds was easy, working on hearts more difficult.

But oh, the rewards . . . so delicious!

Watching hearts of young lovers break into pieces!

Watching hearts full of hope crumble to dust!

Watching hearts fall to the ground without a spark of passion for living!

These . . . yes these are the savory rewards and his delight, sweet, sweet morsels of despair!

The master illusionist, he deals in false ideas, false hopes, and false reality, sending out spokes to turn an endless wheel of which he is the hub, fattening up hordes of people, preparing them for slaughter, the death of kingdom after kingdom and nation after nation, which he sets up for that very purpose.

Oh, the savory feast of filling the Empty in men with greed and lust and deceit, dangling false hope before them, obscuring their deepest needs in the deepest recesses of their hearts, first poisoning their souls with pain and hatred and murder, and then crushing them and drinking them down through a strainer, savoring every drop of the anguish and fear and hatred he creates in them.

He is the wisdom of Babylon and Egypt and Rome, the creator of the Dark Ages, the Renaissance, the Age of Reason, and all history.

Oh the Glory of Gettysburg! How sweet it was to wade in that blood and gore, in that banquet of agony and confusion, a feast of sanctified murder!

Overfed, he flew to his sanctuary, his solitude in the far western mountains. Slow and sluggish from his gluttony, he could not obtain his normal speed.

Satiated with souls, he drifted slowly over the tops of the granite peaks, so pleased and contented with himself he didn't notice the thunderheads gathered up ahead. He floated beneath their pregnant bellies filled with rain and crackling with electricity.

A bolt sizzled out of that roiling mass of black sky and drove him onto one of the peaks, pinning him to it.

Another bolt cracked open the peak and drove him deep into the granite, the crack slamming closed behind him, trapping him.

Twisting and squirming, shrieking and snapping at the sudden agony of his situation, he soon discovered he could move freely in the veins of metal in the granite and into anything anchored to it, like that silly statue up on the mountain. But he could not escape, not without an opening.

It had been easy capturing Ichabod Cain. All it took was a little twist on his already twisted soul. And almost he'd gained his freedom when he'd had him blow that silly statue off its base, but it wasn't enough, it didn't create the opening he needed.

Despite his entrapment, he could send out his will to captivate and manipulate, but it took much greater effort, and after creating two world wars, he was lean and hungry. The morsels the ravens brought to him barely sustained his strength. But he would feed, and soon, as soon as some mortal would ask to see his face.

Was there a God? He didn't know. He only knew he'd been around since time began, since before this world—this playground of his—had come into existence. He only knew he lived, and that was his favorite game, playing I Live, and for all he knew, he was God.

He had gotten trapped once before while curled up and resting in an oak tree. A strange man bit his axe into the heartwood, pinning his tail. Mere metal would not have done it, that axe head was something different.

The blood on the strange axe head mingled with the heartwood and like magic the tree grew into the mightiest of oaks in the land, its trunk engulfing the axe and the odd set of beads wrapped around its handle, keeping both safe.

Not long after, a faller, without knowing, loosed the trapped creature for the Time When.

And the Time When was now.

Chapter Forty-One

Outside, a car horn honked. I almost tripped over a table bench getting to the door, not that I was spooked or jumpy, I was past that, I was anxious to see Laura.

What did she want? *Guess I'll find out* I thought as I eased into the cab of the pickup, a guard acting as my chauffeur. Without speaking a word he dropped me off at the change house where another guard patted me down, making sure I wasn't bringing anything into the prison. He checked my inmate ID card and then asked me where I was headed. I told him and he sent me on my way.

Once past the other two locked gates I had to restrain myself from jogging and settled for a brisk walking pace, not understanding my anxiety. Or was it anticipation? I've never been much good at sorting out my emotions.

The education building, painted a cream color now peeling here and there, exposed the gray concrete block underneath. The windows on the lower floor were fashioned of glass block, the thick stuff that lets light in but you can't see through.

Inside, and straight ahead of the main entry, was the chow hall. To my immediate right was a flight of stairs. I climbed them, turned left on the landing, and climbed a shorter flight of stairs, which put me in an upstairs hallway. To my right was the closed library and to my left were the classrooms and offices.

The fifty-year-old building housed the administration, but they'd gotten a new one built and had handed this one down. It's funny how it works that way everywhere and always, the administration first, but why not, the big shots call the shots.

But just for a moment imagine a world without toilet paper or flushing toilets or no sewers or how about no garbage men or janitors?

It's a smelly world after all.

How'd I get on that side road? I wonder what emotion caused it, anxiety, anticipation, the synapses in my brain firing out of sequence or not firing at all.

I was beginning to wonder about myself, but not too much, I never had the time for that sort of thing. I'd probably just be spinning my wheels anyway, or end up in an asylum somewhere.

"Truman!" The shout snapped me out of it. Laura was coming toward me down the left hallway at an excited pace. Dressed in blue jeans, a loose fitting white cotton blouse with no sleeves, her hair in a ponytail, she looked gorgeous and for a moment I forgot our age difference and why we were here.

She gave no indication that her focus had wavered from the business at hand, whatever it might be. I didn't know yet.

"We need to talk," she said. I thought that was the reason we were meeting, but didn't say so.

"Okay . . . about what?"

"Come on, I have access to the library. We can work in there." With that, she unlocked the sliding gate, I slid it back, she flipped a wall switch, and the overheads boomed on.

The glaring lights revealed an entire wall of law books on the far left. To the right of those was a row of long tables set end to end for reading or study, but mostly the guys gathered there to bullshit, making the place more like a pool hall than a library.

In the middle of the single large room were four free standing shelves, about thirty feet long and eight feet high. Books of all kinds lined both sides of each shelf offering an abundance of good reading if a person wanted to take the time, which most of us had plenty of.

"Here, sit here," said Laura pulling a chair out from in front of one of the two computer screens to our right.

"There's no Internet, but there is Encarta," she buzzed. "But before we start, we need to talk."

Again? Okay. I nodded my head, hoping I'd be able to keep up with her. Her adrenaline pumped but I had no clue about what.

"When I talked to you on the phone and asked you what's up, you said thousands of ravens had just flown through the tunnels of the slaughterhouse, right?"

"Why, don't you believe me?"

"Of course, the question is . . . will you believe me? Just before I called I you I had been asleep out on my patio and I dreamt . . . let me tell you all about it."

"Sure," I said. There wasn't any stopping her even if I'd wanted to, which I didn't.

"I was on the prison yard when suddenly thousands of ravens coming from all directions descended on the place. They darkened the sky before landing everywhere, on buildings, on fences, lampposts, the grass, the bleachers at the softball field … even a few landed on the razor wire. They were everywhere I looked.

Then, as one, they flew up, a great ominous black cloud in the sky. From there, they formed an open circle with sky showing through the middle. Then, from out of the circle, they formed into a giant heart with the bottom tip pointed at the slaughterhouse. The heart then elongated and formed into an arrow that shot forward as if out of a medieval long bow.

Anyway, this huge arrow made of ravens rocketed toward the slaughterhouse, hit the wall and then disappeared into it! Just disappeared. Gone. Kaput. No mas."

"And when exactly was this?" I asked.

"Just before I called you."

"Was it right after your dream?" I asked.

"Well no, not *right* after the dream. When I first awoke, I had this strange powerful urge to … say some prayers for you. I am Catholic, yes, but certainly not devout in the traditional sense of the word. But it was so strange … so compelling, that I went over to the buffet, pulled out the family rosary and prayed it for you right then and there. You do know what a rosary is, right?"

"Right. Did you bring it with you?"

"Bring what? Oh, the rosary, no I forgot. I'll bring it next time, okay?"

"Sure. So you dreamed, or possibly envisioned, what I experienced at approximately the same time. Got any ideas?"

"I don't know, a coincidence? It doesn't seem likely due to the time convergence."

"Easy with the big words," I quipped.

She smiled. Beautiful.

"So somehow, someway, we're connected in this, this thing, whatever it is," she said.

"Maybe. But then again maybe I've just gone insane."

. . . *he's so insane.*

"I don't think you are, because if you were, you'd be all on your own, without me," she explained.

I had to laugh at that logic and she'd get no argument from me. I felt the tension ease up and then dissipate into nothing, funny how laughter can do that. Funny how we laugh less and less, or perhaps more reasons to laugh erode away. Slow but constant it seems, we're taught how not to be people.

We the people, oh well, dreams die all the time.

"In it together," I echoed what she'd said, sort of.

"So . . . where do we start?" she asked, rather nonchalant I thought, considering she could be in danger of the mortal type. She'd either taken the news lightly or had already accepted it as fact.

"If I'm in it with you, then I'm *in it* with you, and there's nothing we can do about it," she said.

I tried not to let my mouth drop open. It was obvious she accepted it as fact, but did she read my mind also.

"I have no idea where to start, hell, how about with the ravens?" I offered.

"I vaguely remember something about them when I did my term paper on Wicca. I don't practice it. I just thought it would be fun and sort of . . . uh . . ."

"Rebellious," I finished for her.

"Well, let's say adventurous, to put Wicca in the category of religion for illustrating Comparative Religions at a Catholic university. A few hundred years ago I'd have been burned at the stake."

"They have a different kind of witch hunt now," I said. She looked at me and then continued. "Let me think. The raven was one of many animal spirit guides, and I think I mentioned before that a southwest Native student of mine said they believed ravens were, not necessarily evil, but portents of evil, the carriers of souls or of evil spirits. I'm not saying there's anything to it. It sounds a lot like superstition."

"At this point I don't think we should confine ourselves with the traditions of modernism," I said.

"Easy with the big words," she replied, and then tickled my ears with her musical laugh.

"How about I search raven and you search Wicca," I said. She was already at the Encarta site and had typed it in.

Now *that* was spooky.

I got the standard dictionary definition of the black bird. Laura got an entirely different take. "Here it is, raven, under animal spirit guides. I'll read what it says, "Raven—the raven is a shamanic bird traveling between the worlds. Those with this medicine learn to be comfortable in the dark and with the dead." She paused and looked at me. "Is that you?" she asked, point blank. I shook my head no. She continued. "The dark feathers of the raven hold the mystery of magic and the Underworld—that's with a capital U. The dark is like the void before creation and after destruction.

The raven was sacred to the Celtic Bran and had many aspects of the war goddess Morrigan. Two ravens, named Hugin and Mugin were familiars of Odin—you know about him, right?"

"He was the big honcho of Norse mythology, like Zeus in the Greek." I replied.

"Odin would send them out into the nine worlds to see and know all and then report back to him. End quote. What do you make of it?" she asked.

"I find it strange that the two cultures mentioned are the Celts and the Norsemen, and that ravens served both in some capacity connected with war."

"Two quite different cultures, that's for certain."

"It says here," I said, referring to the dictionary, "that ravens feed primarily on carrion."

"Yeah . . . and . . . ?"

"Probably nothing except carrion is dead and rotting flesh, and there's one other thing I've been reluctant to tell you."

"We're in this thing together, remember?" she said.

"Alright, I've heard voices."

"I'm not at all surprised. What did they say?"

"In the tunnel, when I followed the ravens, one was like a little girl's, mocking me and saying, "I live, but you won't, oh no you won't." And another time an apparition like an angel appeared in the main part of the basement, right outside my room. She was so beautiful and pure! She spoke my name and I was captivated. And at that moment I wanted nothing more in the world than for her to reach out a gentle hand and touch me on the top of my head. I asked her name and she said, "I Live." Later I found a few strands of her long white hair caught in the stairwell handrail. I have them in the drawer of my nightstand."

"I'd like to see them," she said.

"You will."

"Is there anything else that you remember?"

"Yes . . . whisperings about Ichabod Cain being so insane, both in the dream about the cavern and down in the basement."

"I don't know what to make of it," she said with a hint of frustration.

"You're Irish, or mostly of Irish descent, aren't you?"

"Yes . . . why?"

"Well . . . going way back, that would make your roots Celtic, right?"

"Uh . . . I suppose so," she replied looking puzzled. She wasn't sure where I was going with this. Hell, I wasn't sure where I was going with it.

"As far as I know, I'm of Norwegian descent," I said.

"And . . . ?"

"And, sorry to say I'm not sure, just something about what you read. Would you read it again, please?"

She did.

"So the raven is tied to both Celtic and Norse mythology or tradition, and I'm not discounting that there's something to it. And maybe—and I know there's a very slim chance—there's some kind of connection there."

"There very well could be. I'll start researching at home on the Internet. We can't access it here of course."

"Research what?" I asked.

"How the raven fits in the Celtic and Norse mythology and in the mythology of many other cultures. And also, genealogy, yours and mine. What was your father's name?"

"Herald."

"Grandfather's?"

"Thorvald."

"His father's?"

"Gunnar."

"Any further?"

"No," I answered.

"Actually that's a good start." She paused, looked intently at me, put her left hand on my right arm and said, "Truman . . . be very careful," she whispered.

"Of course I will," I managed to squeak. Man, she had an affect on me like no other I'd ever met. "And you be careful yourself."

"I will. We'd better go."

"One more thing, were the ravens in your dream . . . normal?"

"Yes, in every respect except for one. They were huge, the size of eagles."

CHAPTER FORTY-TWO

THE SHARP WESTERN peaks wounded the sun as it crashed blood red behind them. The midsummer air turned toward cool as I headed to the change house. I stopped, turned, and glanced up at the education building. Laura stood there looking down at me from an open window, I waved, she waved back.

If only.

But I couldn't think about it, not for a single transient moment. It would be better to think in terms of what if, which speaks of possibility.

"Truman," spoke a deep soft voice from out of the shadows. The moon was three-quarters, low in the night sky, and I couldn't make out who, if anyone, was there.

"Ishtay."

"Horse," I replied, "step out where I can see you."

"No Truman, I do not want the guards to see me. I'm supposed to be on my way to the infirmary, but I needed to speak with you first."

"Is something wrong with you?"

"No, but listen, because I must hurry." My eyes adjusted to the light and I could make out the shadowy features behind the words, and it was the granite face of Medicine Horse.

"The ravens," he continued, "they gathered, rose like a dark cloud, made a circle, then a heart and then formed themselves into an arrow that pierced the slaughterhouse, disappearing into it. Did you see them?"

"Yes, I did, and Laura dreamed of them at the same time." No doubt now that we were in this together.

"I will keep an eye on her for you," he said.

"Thanks, Horse. We'd better be on our ways."

"Hoka-Hey," he returned and drifted off into the shadows.

*   *   *

Joe Tindle, one of the few guards that was still human and saw others that way, was on duty at the change house.

"Hey Truman, how's it going?" he greeted.

"Going alright Joe considering where I'm at," I replied as I turned my back to him, held my arms straight out, and spread my legs. He gave me a cursory pat down so he could say he had just in case.

"How's things with you?" I asked as I turned to face him. "That new wife of mine, I'm telling you, she's going to wear me out . . . if you get my drift."

"You're no spring chicken Joe, maybe you oughta take it a little easy."

"Man, I can't keep my hands off of her and besides, I got to do all I can while I can," he winked.

"Sounds like quite the frisky relationship, but don't tell me she can't keep her hands off of you either."

"Of course she can't," he chuckled some. "The funny thing is she's twenty years younger than me."

"Well, keep a stock of Viagra on hand," I said as the driver pulled up outside.

"Don't need it Truman," he replied as I headed for the pickup truck thinking . . . I'm twenty years older than Laura, so, what if?

The night air had returned to balmy. The guard grunted some sort of greeting as I climbed into the cab. "Evening," I replied, just to let him know I'd heard his attempt at being human. We covered the half mile to the slaughterhouse in silence. He pulled up, came to a stop, and grunted "night," as I got out and none too gently closed the door.

He was one of the surly types.

The night had turned chilly from the change house to here, a time lapse of about two minutes.

I stood there after the guard spun away, thinking about Laura and ravens. As much as I'd tried to prevent it, she was involved, and if there was any danger, she was in its way.

Sonofabitch.

Instead of going straight inside, I took a stroll around the building looking for . . . what, I wasn't sure, clues, answers, a body lying in the grass or hanging from one of the roof beams. Who was behind all this spooky shit and why was the question I needed answered.

The waist high dead grass across the gravel road rustled, causing icy fingers to run up and down the length of my spine. It wasn't because of the chilly air. No breeze blew.

Twenty feet beyond the high grass was a split rail fence, gray and rickety, like the skeleton of a giant snake all of a sudden stopped dead. Between the fence and the gravel road, the grass rustled again, caused by what I at first thought was a drifting mist, an isolated stretch of wispy fog moving along the split rail fence.

Then, a low grunt-growl came out of the wavering grass, rumbling deep inside a cavernous chest, and it was sincere, very sincere. I heard one more rumble, then . . . silence. The grass stopped moving. The hair on the back of my neck stood up. My scalp tingled. My spine turned to ice and the rest of me froze, I couldn't have moved if my life depended on it.

With the earth-shaking roar of a lion, the boarwolf exploded out of the high grass, its front paws and rear hooves raising pillars of dust as it shot across the road, its great white tusks gleamed in the moonlight, its eyes red with blood lust.

It wasn't, it couldn't be real I thought, as the beast launched itself at me and hit me in the chest with its huge front paws, knocking me on my back as it hurtled like a freight train over the top of my body, drooling putrid smelling saliva onto my face as it passed over.

I was up on my feet in a split second. I turned to see the boarwolf skid to a stop in the short-cropped grass behind me. I squared up to the beast and took a step forward.

As he turned, he was broadside to me, his gruesome head to my right, his hindquarters to my left.

In two long quick steps I was next to it and let fly with a right front snap kick, hitting it square in the throat, then again and again over and over until the beast dropped on its side, it's legs moving, jaws snapping, and making gurgling sounds somewhere between rage and agony.

I looked around for something to club it with and spied a two by four leaned up against the building not far away. Gripping it firmly, I stood over the beast as he struggled to get up. I raised the piece of lumber high above my head and brought it down with all my strength smashing it against the boarwolf's skull, hoping to bash its brains out.

The board hit with a dull thud, the impact causing only a slight amount of give in the monster's skull. I raised the two by four up over my head and looked down at the . . . ground? What the hell?

I focused. There was nothing but the ground covered with short cropped grass. Lowering the board, I let it slide loosely through my left hand. The butt touched the ground. I felt something wet and sticky at its upper end. It wasn't mud, or dirt, or grass. It was blood and bits of bone and a few pieces of bristly hair.

The dream had manifested and run its course and now the nightmare had begun.

Sweat dripped from my forehead, my breath came in heavy gasps as I stood in the balmy air looking up at the full moon.

Balmy air? Full moon? The air had been chilly and the moon three-quarters a moment ago . . . hadn't they?

Certain I was losing at least part of my mind, I leaned the two by four against a corner of the building, double-checking to see if the blood and the bone and the bristles were still on the end of it. They were.

Then I checked the road, and on it were the prints of the boarwolf's charge, deep gouges in the moonlight.

So where had the monster disappeared to, and how?

My head spun and ached. Suddenly exhausted, all I wanted to do was lie down and sleep and forget about the whole damn mess for a while.

"Hee—hee—hee," the little demon girl's laughter taunted me, but from where? Was it in my head? Around the corner?

Looking around I saw nothing that, in ordinary reality, should not be there, no spooks, no goblins, and no boarwolfs, but where the hell had it gone?

I'd answered my own question. It went back to hell where it came from. That meant if there was a hell, there had to be a heaven. Definitions by contrast, you can't have one without the other.

Weren't those some song lyrics a long time ago?

"Hee—hee—hee," came the tinkling laughter as I approached the door to the slaughterhouse. I had to start thinking of it as the cannery and not the slaughterhouse. Cannery didn't seem so foreboding.

"Hee—hee—hee Ichabod Cain was so insane. Truman Struck is such a dumb cluck," the little girl with the blond curls sang from somewhere.

My emotions had run from romantic, to a life and death struggle, to a questioning of my own sanity in less than . . . what, two hours. Drained of energy it was hard for me to stand.

Exhaustion gripped me like a vise.

"Truman Struck is such a dumb cluck."

Bring it on, I was too tired to care, let alone fight back.

Unlocking the door I flipped on the light switch, flooding the break room with bombardier fluorescents.

Empty. Okay.

Crossing the room, heels clacking on the concrete floor, I entered the hallway leading to the main cannery on my left and down to the basement on my right. I couldn't hear anything in either direction, and all was dark, darkest down the stairwell.

From nowhere chills of fear joined my exhaustion.

I flipped the light switch over the stairwell; the single bulb chased away what shadows it could. The stairs descended through a dark canyon of concrete walls. The ceiling above was flat, the wall at the far end like a giant tombstone.

I began my descent with no small amount of trepidation. To my amazement I no longer felt drained, but I was scared, so scared I thought I might vomit. I grabbed the handrail for support as I descended in to the tomblike basement.

Run? I couldn't do that, it wasn't an option. It was stand my ground time. No backing out of facing whatever or whoever I was up against. Maybe it was my destiny or more likely my fate. Or it could be genetics. Was I born for this, or to this?

What was that prayer? "Our Father who art . . ." I flicked on the light switch in the main room, only more dim light, but enough to drive away most of the shadows, even the one that flitted over by the tunnel.

". . . in Heaven . . . now and at the hour of our death, amen?" Something like that, close enough for now anyway. Maybe I'll go to church next Sunday, if I see next Sunday, if . . . what a huge word that is.

Swallowing the lump in my throat, I crossed the distance to my room without incident. My room, I should give it a special name. How about room number 666 at the Hell Hotel. Finding the light switch in its now familiar place, I flipped it up to the on position. The fluorescents obediently hummed, then buzzed, and then flared on, causing me to shut my eyes against the glare. Regret tore at my insides when I opened them.

She hung in the center of the room, swaying and twisting. Her skin looked like alabaster porcelain under the light.

Gasping for breath, I recovered somewhat from the initial shocking sight and staggered to the middle of the room to stand before her. No reason to check for a pulse, she was cold to the touch.

Removing the noose I gently laid her on the bed. How was it possible for this to have happened, for God's or anybody else's sake? So senseless, so macabre was this deranged incident that I wouldn't have believed it had I not seen it with my own eyes.

My stomach quivered as I returned to examine the noose, made of angel hair twisted together to form a thin rope with a hangman's noose dangling from the end. The other end was attached to a screw that protruded from the overhead light fixture.

I glanced over to where the statuette of Our Lady of the Mountains was lying on my bed. I wouldn't have been surprised if she was gone or had even come to life, but she lay exactly as I had placed her.

I unhooked the angel hair from the screw in the light fixture and returned it and Our Lady to the top drawer of my nightstand. After turning on the reading lamp, I crossed the room, shut off the overhead, and sat in my chair to ponder the situation.

"It came upon a midnight dreary as I pondered weak and weary . . ." Poe didn't have a corner on the raven thing anymore, or rather, nevermore. Then again maybe he did, maybe stories and poems and songs are inherently prophetic, and become real sooner or later.

"Good morning America how are you? Don't you know me I'm your native son. I'm the train they call the city of New Orleans . . ." We know all about New Orleans now since hurricane Katrina.

"Sergeant Peppers Lonely Hearts Club Band" Check out the 'net and all the lonely hearts sites where you can look for love. 1984 and Big Brother. It's here. Takes awhile for some of them to come around, but come around they do. So maybe I was caught up in Edgar Allen Poe's prophecy.

God, I was going nuts.

Who the hell had hanged Our Lady, and why? It was one thing to see spirits and apparitions; it was another to have them do things in the physical world.

It was just a single simple nightmare and nothing more.

I could call the guards I suppose. "Hey, there's things up here way spookier than you guys are, and they're hanging little sacred statues by their neck with rope made of angel hair." Right. I'm sure they'd be up here carrying a heavy canvas jacket with arms that buckled in the back.

"*Hee-hee-hee,*" the little blond spook giggled, her voice chiming inside my head. "*Truman Struck, he's such a dumb cluck.*"

Yeah, maybe that was true, but right now I didn't give a rat's bladder, lights out.

Chapter Forty-Three

The thing in the tunnel knew Truman Struck wouldn't scare easily; he was either brave or stupid. Too bad, feeding on fear was always a treat, a precursor to the devastation he liked to bring to a soul before reducing it to a sponge filled with terror, anger, hate, bloodlust and murder, and plain old greed, even though it was acceptable and promoted, and had become so common it was almost unpalatable, but it was always there, like potatoes or rice at a meal.

Like the legends of the vampires, the thing in the tunnel was held a prisoner by his own need, the price for eternal life being confined to the dark and possessed of an insatiable need for blood. The thing in the tunnel had an endless need for souls, and now, like the Count, he could not leave the entrapment of his granite prison until he received an invitation to come forth by one of the creatures upon which he fed.

The fool Cain had come close to freeing him, but his bloodlust, the drawing that brought him, had also foiled his escape. If he hadn't slaughtered one human being after another, the twisted thing in the tunnel would have persuaded him to ask to see his face. But, oh, the terror he had created, a true feast! The ravens, and the souls they brought, sustained but never fully satisfied his lusted hunger. At least Cain had given him that.

This Truman Struck was a strong soul, perhaps stronger than any he'd run up against—and he'd run up against many a saint and sinner alike—and the strangest thing of all was, the man wasn't aware of the strength he had. He'd probed his mind to plant paralyzing fear, and at times was successful, but it was always transitory. He'd probed his soul for footholds that would enable him to plant unholy and obsessive desires, but all he'd managed were a few scratch marks, and those always from far away.

Yes, Truman Struck had a secret line of power behind him, as yet unknown, but the thing in the tunnel would soon find out. He was ready to call forth his army, spoken of in the lore of old as demons. The haints, the angel, the boarwolf, and the blond curly headed girl were merely probes. The demons would peel him layer by layer, revealing what was underneath.

They would be more difficult to summon from inside his granite prison. Nevertheless, once they felt the drawing of his will they had no choice but to obey. They were all his creatures.

He pushed against the wall of Truman's room, listening to his heartbeat, probing his soul, implanting nightmares in his subconscious allowed to run free in his sleeping mind.

He knew exactly how to begin his attack, nothing too hard, nothing too serious, just a little confusion to soften up the being of the man.

He would send out his will, and no material substance could stop it. No living thing could resist it. But doing so tried his patience to the limit. He was used to moving at the speed of light, and by comparison his current state was slow and sluggish, being confined to the Continental Divide. But, he could still wreak havoc along the spiny mountains north to south and back again, creating concentrated pockets of evil disguised as glorious and beautiful cities.

Babylon Rising, and he would be its God!

He needed the services of his most powerful demon, and that of many of his empty headed but amusing imps.

Withdrawing deep within himself he gathered the energies of his will into a single focused point then cast it outward with one summons—Dethel.

* * *

"I heed your summons High Lord," said Dethel as he solidified out of a vaporous mist.

"Have you been watching for me?"

"Of course High Lord."

"Report."

"There are three who are behind the man Truman Struck, High Lord."

"I know of two, and one of them remains vague, but who is the third?

"The two you know are the woman and the medicine man. The third is a white haired man whose body is harmless but whose spirit is made powerful by his beliefs."

"Which are . . . asked the High Lord?

"Those called for in the incomprehensible book they call the Bible."

"Does he pray then?"

"Yes, High Lord."

"To God?"

"Yes, High Lord."

Dethel felt himself seized by the throat with a grip more powerful than he could ever hope to break.

"You forget your place Dethel, for I am God, am I not?"

"M-m-most certainly High Lord," he gasped.

The High Lord savored the nectar of fear.

"Of the three you mentioned, who is the nearest?"

"The medicine man, High One."

"You may attend to him as you wish, but take him out of the way. Have some fun with him if you like. Use your imagination."

"Thank you, High Lord." The Dark One released his grip. "Now go, and do not forget your place again."

"Thank you High Lord," gasped Dethel as he disappeared like mist in the wind.

Medicine Horse was deep in thought as he walked to the infirmary, the evening air cool and refreshing. The lights along the walk cast white halos on the concrete path. The white man's ways never ceased to amuse the Lakota. Why were they so afraid of touching nature? Would they find the Everywhere Spirit there if they did? But he understood the white man's culture would collapse if they were to suddenly realize that their God, the Creator, was everywhere, was of one nature toward all people, and could not be contained in an artificial box of their own making.

The concrete path made his feet hurt, to walk on the earth would not. A small example of the truth he knew.

But in realty who was Ishtay Wakanka? Horse wasn't sure.

Wally had charged him with keeping a watchful eye on him, and he always offered prayers for him in the sweat lodge and in the Pipe Ceremony.

And what was a philosopher, someone who daydreamed all the time, pondering unanswerable questions?

WHOOSH, a shadow shot past the corner of his eye.

It was just his imagination and nothing more. But a philosopher had to be more than a daydreamer, or a thinker in circles, or a ponderer of possibilities and what ifs. A philosopher sought more than that. A true philosopher sought wisdom, and wisdom's twin, truth. The truth, thought Horse. What does indeed live beyond the veil of everyday? What lies underneath the visible? That is what an Ishtay Wakanka is, a seeker, and that is what makes him dangerous to what lives beyond the veil or lies underneath the visible.

A dark shadow, the size of a man, stood in front of the entrance door to the infirmary, blocking his way. Two darklings materialized from out of the night and grabbed each of his arms, holding them out sideways. The dark shadow flew into Horse's chest and out his back, and along with the darklings, was gone as suddenly as they appeared. Medicine Horse doubled over at the twinge of pain in his heart, weak and out of breath. Dizzy, he stumbled toward the infirmary door.

Clutching at his chest, he waved his arm at the nurse in the control cage, and then collapsed in a heap outside the locked door.

She happened to look up in time to see him and she charged out of the cage, pushing the emergency button before leaving.

She turned Medicine Horse on his back, her finger on his neck to feel for a pulse, her ear to his chest to listen for a heartbeat.

She's pretty, he thought, with her blond hair and sapphire blue eyes. He tried to speak but couldn't. He pointed at his chest. The nurse nodded.

A couple of paramedics and two guards showed up. As gently as they could, under the time compression of an emergency, they hoisted him onto a gurney and rushed him into the building and down a highly polished, bright-lit hallway.

Horse wasn't sure where they were taking him in such a frenzy. The only reason he'd been to the infirmary over the last five years was for six month check ups, and each one revealed nothing wrong with him.

He assumed it was the emergency room, and his assumption was correct.

Hooking up the EKG monitor, watching the screen, and rolling in the IV tray, they had him under complete surveillance in less than a minute's time.

Meanwhile, Horse had found his voice, but how could he explain what had happened after they found no reason for his apparent heart attack.

"I'm fine," he said to the blond nurse with the dazzling blue eyes.

"Your vital signs are good, and your pulse is strong, but we'd better let the doctor decide whether you're fine or not," she said and smiled.

Beyond her, up in the corner at the intersection of two walls and the ceiling, a couple of darkling's waited, like chattering spider monkeys, to be alone with him.

Horse didn't feel their intended fear, knowing they were nothing more than pests. But where was the man-sized dark shadow, that piercing spear of a demon?

"How are you feeling?" asked Doc Greene, a kind old man who had a genuine concern for the inmates. To him, they were more than just slabs of meat in which the wonders of biology operated.

"I'm just fine, Doc. How are you?" asked Horse in return.

"Feeling any pain?"

"No Doc, none at all."

The doctor scrutinized him and then put the stethoscope to his chest and said "Breathe" as he moved it around.

"Nurse Peters thought you may have had a heart attack, but nothing indicates that to be the case. You're sure you're not feeling any pain in your chest area?"

"Positive, Doc."

"Well, just the same, we'll keep you overnight for observation."

"That's not necessary Doc. I'm feeling fine," objected Horse, looking up at the darklings grinning like wolves ready to pounce.

"You're not at all scared, are you?" said Doc Greene. Horse knew where the man-sized dark shadow was now.

"Not of you, demon."

"You will be yet tonight," replied the demon then flew to hover in the corner of the room, as the darklings dropped from the ceiling onto its shoulders.

"You will be well tonight," said Doc Greene rather absently. After all, he'd, been laid dormant for a few seconds.

"Well, you're the doctor, but I will say again, I will be fine."

"Do you need something to help you sleep?" asked the doctor.

"No."

"I'll have the nurse check in on you now and then, just in case, and I'll see you in the morning. Good night."

"Night Doc."

Nurse Peters came in and showed him where the emergency button was, where the lamp switch was, and how to operate the television remote. He thanked her; she bade him good night and exited the room, leaving the door partially open.

The darklings sat patiently on the demon's shoulders, saliva drooling from their teeth filled mouths.

The demon morphed from a shadow into the form of an elderly man with long white hair and skin like saddle leather. Dressed in a breechcloth, the apparition, his eyes black as onyx, stared into the soul of Medicine Horse.

"You do not frighten me," said Horse. The darklings screeched and leapt from the demon's shoulders, one landed on his chest, the other one pulled the emergency button out of reach before joining the other. Like two heavy stones they began to squeeze. They nipped at his chest, each bite a sharp, piercing pain that stabbed his heart.

Horse tried to sweep the creatures away, but the demon had moved around to stand behind his head and pinned his arms, rendering him helpless.

The EKG monitor continued to register a strong steady beat.

"Let me loose," Horse bellowed and his arms sprang free at the power of his words.

He slammed his palms together over his chest but struck only air. The darklings had retreated at lightning speed to their corner of the ceiling.

A night nurse stuck her head in the door to check on the commotion, not the blond with the stunning blue eyes, but a plain looking, gray haired woman wearing round eyeglasses.

A real life Norman Rockwell painting of everybody's grandma.

"Very well, Mr. Horse, hoka-hey asshole," she said and then disappeared, cackling "hee-hee-hee," like the mischievous little blond haired girl.

Medicine Horse stood up, looked down and noticed there weren't any bite marks on his chest, no evidence of the darklings morbid work. He removed the heart monitoring electrodes, but the monitor continued to register a strong and steady beat. He looked up at the ceiling but the darklings were gone.

"Hoka-Hey," he looked out the open door, in the hallway stood the man-sized sooty demon with the darklings on his shoulders. They flew at him, one after the other and hit him in the chest. Medicine Horse groaned as his knees buckled. The demon flew at him, hit him in the chest and continued out his back, causing him to stagger. His knees buckled completely and he collapsed on the floor.

The EKG monitor continued to register a strong and steady beat.

CHAPTER FORTY-FOUR

THE NEWS OF Horse's death was shocking but not surprising. How the thing in the tunnel had caused it, I had no idea, but felt certain I would soon know. I knew it could manifest itself in different ways, like an angel or a boarwolf, but they were only illusions once you got them figured out.

Exactly who or what the thing in the tunnel was, I couldn't say, I could only say that it was there, and some strange shift in fate had brought me just a breath away from the creature on the other side of the wall. A creature that played a game of cat and mouse with me, and the stakes were . . . my soul. But what did the creature have to lose? Probably nothing, yet the idea intrigued me. I hadn't seen a game yet that the outcome, though predictable, was one hundred percent certain. Maybe I had a fighting chance after all, in spite of my sleep becoming sporadic and my waking hours filled with unanswered questions, like, where had the boarwolf's blood gone from off the two by four I'd used to bash it's skull in? It had disappeared.

Was Shakespeare too far wrong—if at all—when he wrote, "We are such stuff as dreams are made on." Could it all be just a dream? I couldn't say one way or another, not with certainty. But, in the end analysis, it didn't matter, because whether awake or asleep I was trapped within it.

Chapter Forty-Five

WE GOT A new cannery worker by the name of Darius Kenelty. I'd never laid eyes on him before and at first sight he was just another face in a blue shirt. He was around five and a half feet tall, stocky, and two hundred pounds of solid muscle. His complexion was naturally dark. He kept his head shaved, a no-neck brute with dead black lifeless eyes which seemed to see nothing at all and at the same time see everything at once. When I got close to him my stomach would crawl. There was just something utterly . . . wrong about the man.

Conversations, like the other parts of my life, had become meaningless, so I didn't talk to Darius, or anybody else for that matter. But I kept a close eye on him as I went quietly about my duties of sanitizing all parts of the building except the processing room. The people that worked there were responsible for cleaning it at the end of the day, which led to a lot of bickering. "He's lazy. He's bossy. He won't help. He tries to do too much and make the rest of us look bad. He's a leg rider." You know, complaining like little children.

In order to do my job I had to pass through the process area, a thirty by sixty utility room filled with steam from the retorts, large steel baskets used for cooking, and from vats filled with boiling water, several times a day.

The guys appear like shadows in the heavy steam filled air. Those near ones very dark, those farther away are almost invisible. From out of this background, Darius came walking toward me, his eyes, glowing with an unholy light, fixed on me. He appeared in full color, not as I expected to see him as he emerged from the mist, a shadow changing from the shade of light gray to the color of charcoal. But no, he was full color as he drew near me, except for one thing, a thick and very dark outline surrounded him, extending about half a foot out from his body.

"See my new tattoo?" he asked, lifting up the sleeve of his white smock, flexing his right bicep in front of my face. It read *"DEMON"*

Not knowing the man's intention, I replied, "Nice," as the world came to a complete and sudden stop, all the background shapes and colors and sounds fading into a singular undefined haze of gray mist.

"I thought your name was Darius," I said.

"Nope. Once was, but now, just for today, it's been changed to Demon." The black aura surrounding him bristled outward to a foot thick.

On the edge of panic I peered through the heavy steamy mist, looking for an escape route, or for potential help, but I found neither, only the shadows of the other workers, standing still as death, looking distant and indistinct and observing with little interest the drama unfolding before them.

The black aura of the demon bristled larger, spreading further from his body until it separated entirely, and stood, as a distinct entity, in front of me. Darius stood detached and expressionless, as if a switch somewhere inside of him failed to make a connection.

The dark shadow formed into the shape of a man of indistinct form and feature. The crew of gray shadows formed a semi-circle behind it and they all knelt down on one knee.

"No where to run?" it asked, as I glanced quickly from side to side, looking for a way out. None. I took in a deep calming breath—as much as calming could be at the moment—and remained standing, ready to confront what stood before me, knowing it was only an illusion, created by the thing in the tunnel.

"Going to make a stand, are you Truman?" it asked, reading my thoughts.

"You know my name. What is yours?" I asked.

"Death and Hell, but you can call me Dethel my friend."

"What makes you think I'm your friend?" I asked, a sudden strength surging inside of me, a strength I had never felt before and had no idea where it came from. My best guess was genetics.

"Now, now Truman," said the demon with a mocking tone underneath it, "everyone is my friend, because everyone comes to visit me sooner or later. Surely you can see this?"

"I see it as a fact, but they come to you against their will and in fear, not as your friends. Isn't that so?"

"In the end all are mine, all say yes to me."

"But they have no choice, do they?"

"Do you?"

CHAPTER FORTY-FIVE

"I suppose not," I answered.

"You will kneel to me, will you not Truman?"

"Never by my own will," I replied.

"Don't be such a martyr. No one ever is, even those who believe they take their own lives, and you are no different. In the end you will kneel," he said, and then pointed upwards as two dark shadows, resembling spider monkeys, dropped from the ceiling to land on each of my shoulders, driving me to my knees, pinning me to the concrete floor.

It would be useless to struggle. I was indeed at the mercy of Dethel standing straight above me, grinning with demonic amusement.

"You see Truman, I could keep you here forever if I wished. You can therefore choose and become my servant now, or kneel to me later against your will and let your fear feed the Dark One as all fear does."

"Who is this Dark One?" I gasped, my knees feeling as if they were imbedding into the concrete.

"Why . . . your neighbor downstairs, of course, you really should invite him out some time, meet him face to face. I know he'd love to meet you. In fact, he's been waiting a long time to meet you."

"He is your master then?"

"Oh yes, and I live only to do his bidding. I Live, get it, you dumb cluck?" He hissed a mirthless laugh as I watched him transform into the white haired angel looking down on me with otherworldly kindness and compassion of such a magnitude I could not stop myself from melting before her.

"You're . . . you're not real," I managed to say, more to convince myself than to try to dispel the apparition.

"Oh but I am, Truman," she said as the darklings jumped off my shoulders and into her arms. She shrank down to the form of a young girl wearing a light blue dress, her hair hanging in long golden curls.

"Hee . . . hee . . . hee," she cackled with mirthless delight. "Truman Struck, he's such a dumb cluck," she said, and then swirled and became the dark shadow that was Dethel.

"The shape shifter, I should have known," I groaned as I struggled to stand.

"Feel your heart, Truman. What does it say to you?" Dethel asked, the darklings resting in his arms.

"Pain . . . excruciating . . . in my chest," I gasped.

The thing in the tunnel twitched at the sweet taste of fear.

"Don't underestimate me, Truman. That would not be sporting of you, would it old chap? And so when I want you, I will come for you, and because you would not kneel to me, I will torment you first, maybe for a short time or maybe for what will seem like an eternity, however long it takes until your fear is ripe enough for my master."

"You and your master can go to hell," I said as the pain inside my chest increased.

The demon broke forth in mocking laughter.

"Dear Truman, don't you understand yet? I am hell . . . and death . . . and the next time we meet, I won't be quite as pleasant. I'll squeeze just a little harder in order to make a true believer out of you, as the saying goes."

I couldn't catch my breath as the heaviness and pain in my chest increased by the ton.

"Jesus Christ!" someone hollered, immediately followed by the sound of a slamming door.

The pain in my chest lifted. I blinked. Dethel had disappeared with a shriek with the darklings clinging to him.

The process room was filled with a lighter mist. Six men were standing in a semi-circle behind Darius, mouths agape, staring down at me.

"Sorry dude . . . I didn't mean to . . . I didn't mean to," Darius was saying to me. Dumbfounded, I looked closely at his right bicep, no tattoo.

"I'm . . . I'm alright," I muttered as I struggled to get to my feet, the room swirling around me as I stood.

"What the hell happened here?" said Larry the supervisor.

Hell had paid me a visit is what had happened.

My focus sharpened as my vision cleared, bringing Larry into view. He was hustling toward me, the tails of his blue smock and his white hair flying out behind him. Stooping and kneeling down, he looked intently at my forehead. I reached up and touched it, bringing my hand away slick with blood.

"I . . . I'm not sure," I responded, suddenly aware of an acute pain in my skull.

"My fault, boss," said Darius from beside Larry as he cast me an apologetic look. "I swung a full retort around as he was walking through, it was real steamy in here, and I clocked him on the head with it."

After giving Darius a long inquiring look, Larry said, "Come with me Struck so I can get a band-aid on that cut and stop the bleeding."

I stood with his help, followed him into his office, went into the bathroom, and washed the blood off my forehead. It wasn't much more than a scratch, but it had raised a good-sized lump.

Larry handed me a band-aid through the door. After applying it I sat down on the well-worn office chair across from his metal desk.

"What happened out there Struck?" he asked.

"I honestly don't remember. I must've been knocked out for awhile."

"You look a little pale. Take the rest of the day off . . . with pay. Can't be too cautious with these kinds of things you know. Otherwise, it could develop into something serious."

"I'm fine."

"Oh no, I insist. Grab some aspirin on your way out."

I did have a throbbing headache.

"Alright, thanks." I stood up, poured a few aspirins into my hand and was at the doorway when Larry's voice halted me.

I turned slowly. Through the window, behind him, I could see Darius standing with one hand resting on the retort, an iron basket filled with one hundred forty evenly spaced cans of carrots, the holes in the basket allowing the steam to cook them evenly. He grinned at me.

I looked at Larry. The dark aura had shifted and now surrounded him. "Why don't you invite the Dark One for a visit? He'd be more than pleased to meet you."

The window behind him hinged at the top with the bottom pushed out toward the process room. Through it I saw the darklings dancing and twisting on the broad shoulders of Darius. He kept his silly grin and then said, "Truman Struck, he's such a dumb cluck." At that, Larry stuck his head out the window and hollered at Darius, "Who you calling a dumb fuck, Kenelty? Better watch your mouth or I'll fire you in a heartbeat." The darklings on Darius' shoulders twirled faster. Larry pulled his head back in the room, looked at me and said,

"A heartbeat. By the way, how is your heart, Truman?" he asked with a malicious grin plastered across his face.

I turned and walked out the door. I had never felt so alone and trapped in my life, and there was no way out. I had no choice but to stand and fight.

But who and how was what I didn't know.

And how was my heart? The pain was gone, but it trembled within from fear as I descended the stairs, holding on to the handrail as I went, steadying my rubbery legs.

Fear, yes of course. It was what the Dark One wanted, and he was getting it from me.

I slumped down in my easy chair after switching on the lamp and then switching off the overhead.

Fear. The Dark One. Dethel. What the hell.

Light, of course, is the opposite of dark, so what would be the opposite of fear in this world of definition by contrasts? Courage? Yes. But what is it, and how is it discovered or defined? How does a person know if they have it, or some of it, or any at all? Is it even real? Fear certainly is, bad and heavy. I sunk further into my easy chair, with a fool's hope that I might sink all the way into it and disappear from this nightmare altogether.

Death could come at any moment at the hand of Dethel.

I need a drink, no, more than that, a fifth of whiskey. But that just makes problems hazy for awhile and gives false courage. I knew at least that much by now.

Who could I trust? Anyone? I didn't think so, knowing what I did now, knowing Dethel could enter and control who . . . anyone? Maybe. Probably. Oh shit.

"Satisfied you son of a bitch?" I blurted toward the concrete wall, but there was no response, no growling, no flames of fire or dancing demons or pinching of my heart. Is that where one finds courage as in "Richard the Lionhearted?"

I knew in my mind fear was what the Dark One wanted, what he craved. But knowing something in my mind doesn't make it real in my heart. Like love, though undefined, you know when you're in it because the heart doesn't lie.

Laura, maybe I could trust her. I hoped to God I could. God? Where did he fit in all of this, if anywhere at all, if he even existed? And if he does exist does he give a rat's ass about humanity? I don't know. Sure doesn't seem like it, and frankly, right now I didn't give a rat's ass myself.

While I was unconscious and Darius became demon, I'd felt that strange surge of power, a strength that enabled me to stand up to him in my mind. But where had it come from? I felt no great fear even when my heart of flesh had been squeezed.

Owen Barfield, a British philosopher, wrote, "The relation between the mind and the heart of man is indeed a close and delicate one and any substantial cleft between the two is unhealthy and cannot long endure."

All right, I'll buy that as true, for that is how it rings, loud and clear. Maybe it's a truism on a larger scale. I know Montana has lost its heart, America too.

But how to bridge the cleft between my heart and my head was the problem I faced, because, in my heart there was still some fear, and in my head I knew there shouldn't be. And so, did that make me a coward? I didn't know, and it didn't matter because I knew I wasn't a hero nor would I ever be. If I had my druthers I'd be far away from this place. But I'm not and likely won't be any too soon. I need to face up to it, and maybe that's all there is to courage, facing up to your fears and grinding situations, come hell or high water.

Hell had already visited me. High water was probably right around the corner in the form of torture and then death.

I glanced over at Gideon's Bible lying undisturbed on the table. I reached over to pick it up.

"Not yet, Truman."

"What?" I exclaimed, jolted out of my morbid reverie. Looking around I saw no one.

"I'm not satisfied yet," the voice replied.

The Dark One, but unlike in the movies his voice was smooth, elegant, soothing and hypnotic, not coarse or raspy or reverberating. Oh no, the Dark One's voice was the kind that invited a fireside chat, yet was authoritative and full of subtle power.

The Dark One would remain trapped inside these mountains against his will, unless someone asked to see his face.

"You're no match for me, Truman Struck," he said.

And, he could discern my thoughts, at least at close range. My heart once again constricted as the small spark of hope that he couldn't read my mind died out.

"You could be my ally, maybe even my friend," the Dark One continued. "Your rewards would be very great," he said, and before I could ask, "What's in it for me?" he said, "Untold wealth, fame, women, power, and prestige. All the things money can buy and more. I *could* make you a king if that was your desire. I can give you all of your heart's desires."

"Laura?" I felt, more than heard, the Dark One draw in his breath with a pronounced hiss.

"Is she the one?" he asked.

"Just a question," I countered. I knew I'd made a mistake speaking her name, drawing her deeper into this, and that was probably what the Dark One had been fishing for.

"What about Dethel? How would he fit into that scheme?" I asked through the concrete wall, trying to divert his focus, if that were possible.

"You sent him to kill me, didn't you?"

"Dethel is my servant and does my bidding. I sent him to bring terror to your soul in order to make you believe in me. But as for you, I offer you a partnership with me, subject to me and me alone. Just imagine having all of your hearts desires."

"Immortality?"

"Extended life."

"The woman I want?"

"All the women you could ever want."

"Power?"

"Over nations and people."

"Authority?"

"Next to mine."

"Wealth?"

"More than you could ever dream of."

"And what must I do to gain all of this?"

"Simply invite me into your room that we may talk face to face."

"That's all?"

"You will know the rest when we speak face to face."

"How do I know you can do all of this?"

"Dethel, remember?"

"I wouldn't have to deal with him?"

"Not until the end of your very long enjoyable life. Don't forget, I hold his leash," he said, his voice smooth and containing a feigned kindness. "All your troubles would be over, all your desires would be fulfilled."

"How long a life?"

"A thousand years."

"As a crippled old man?"

"Oh no, you can choose your age and remain there for the entire time, as a youth in perfect health if you'd like. Wouldn't you like that Truman? Think of it. All the time in the world to indulge in and enjoy whatever you desire."

"And if I refuse?"

"Then, regrettably, Dethel will come for you."

"How do I know you will keep your promises?"

"I could have had you killed by now Truman, and any relationship needs trust to work. You will simply have to trust me, just a little."

"I'll need some time to consider."

"Take all the time you need, but consider it well. When you're ready to speak with me just come to the wall, call for me and I will hear you."

So gentle, so soothing, so enticing was his voice.

"Just exactly who are you? The Devil? Satan? Lucifer? What is your name?" I asked.

"Those are all creatures of myth Truman. I am much more than that. I am the fountain of time and the foundation of the world. I am all myths, all legends and the answer to all the unanswerable questions of . . . why? To know my true name, you must speak with me face to face. But, as Dethel said, you can call me the Dark One if you like, for in the end isn't it always darkness that prevails?"

"Your kingdom is the Kingdom of Darkness?"

"Yes."

"Are you God then?"

"I am ... the God of this world."

"But you are trapped in these mountains, are you not?"

I could feel a sharp wave of rage as the Dark One recoiled from the question.

"Did I hit a sore spot Dark One?" I asked, unable to stop myself from exulting in this one brief instant of triumph.

"Do not presume to trifle with me Truman. My patience is not infinite, neither is my good favor."

An acute pain pinched my chest, making it hard to breathe, and after a few seconds it eased up.

"Point taken," I said, attempting to mask my fear.

"Ah-h-h ... fear ... so sweet, but yours is not what I desire."

"Why me then?" I asked.

"Because you are here and convenient."

"If I don't help release you?" I said

"Short life, agonizing death for both you and ... what was her name ... Laura? The choice is very clear and all yours to make. And Truman I hope you make the right, no, the only choice."

The Dark One had a very strong presence and I felt it withdraw as he moved away from the wall.

I hadn't noticed until now that I was drenched in sweat. I lifted my hands and looked at them, they trembled. I felt drained, exhausted, as if a part of my life had been sucked out of me, right down to the marrow of my bones.

But no wonder, it's not everyday that a man bargains for his life and his soul at the same time.

Chapter Forty-Six

Faced with two choices, I could set the Dark One free by taking his offer, or suffer an agonizing end at the hand of Dethel. And there was Laura to consider. She was more involved now than she could ever have imagined and her life was in jeopardy. The Dark One no doubt could make good on his threats.

Me and my big mouth, well, I've never been accused of being overly bright, but I wasn't stupid enough to believe the Dark One's words without question.

"Dark One," I hollered in the direction of the wall.

"Well, that's much better than son of a bitch. What can I do for you my friend?"

Oh . . . so . . . smooth.

"You had Medicine Horse killed didn't you?"

"I cannot tell a lie, Dethel did it."

"At your bidding?"

"Of course."

"Why?"

"An attention getter, was it not?"

"It was that," I replied.

"Therefore, the reason," said the Dark One.

"Leave Laura alone," I said.

"Invite me in to your room."

"No, not yet."

Not yet, a very good sign, thought the Dark One.

"Then I'm afraid you jeopardize the young woman. You don't want that on your conscience, do you? Besides, if you choose my offer, I promised you a kingdom, with you as its king, and Laura as its queen. You'd like that, wouldn't you Truman?"

He was so smooth, so soothing, so convincing. I felt like I was becoming spellbound, despite knowing that was, in part, how he operated. I snapped myself out of it by shaking my head side to side.

"I'll let you know what I decide," I answered.

"You only have one choice Truman. I think you know that by now, don't you?"

It was hard to disagree with him.

I felt his presence withdraw. Our conversation was over, for now.

Reaching across the table, I picked up Gideon's Bible, the lamplight reflecting a comforting glow off its golden letters.

Feeling disoriented from my encounter, I needed to search my memory for the reason I had the Book out in the first place.

So much had happened in such rapid sequence my senses were all askew, but none as great as my sense of time.

Some say time isn't exactly linear anyhow, perhaps it is part of some grand illusion I don't understand. Maybe the Dark One does. He claims existence from forever and to forever, and, knowing he was for sure real, perhaps I could speak with him about it. My God, that's like thinking of him as a friend! Had my soul already been gripped and stolen? I didn't think so. No, I wouldn't talk to the Dark One, it upset my stomach anyway. Besides, according to Einstein, at the speed of light, time expands and distance contracts. That's good enough for me.

Now, why was I holding this heavy book in my hand? I did remember finding it in my nightstand.

I opened it up to the book of REVELATION, the thirteenth chapter, there I read,

MYSTERY
BABYLON THE GREAT
THE MOTHER OF HARLOTS
AND OF THE ABOMINATIONS OF THE EARTH

"Dark One!"

"Yes, my friend."

"What do you know about the Bible, and about Babylon?"

"The Bible . . . it is a myth. Babylon was a real city, I know, I was there."

I began to read aloud, ". . . I saw the woman, drunk with the blood of the Saints. And the woman whom you saw is that great city which reigns over the kings of the earth . . . and the merchants of the earth mourn over her, for no one buys their merchandise anymore . . . gold and silver, precious stones and pearls . . . and the bodies and souls of men."

"Dark One! What is this Babylon the Great? What does it mean?" I asked. No answer. The Dark One had retreated to some foul place.

If I accepted his offer, I would be a king, answerable only to him. "... great city which reigns over the kings of the earth ..." and he would reign over me, as it said.

Was he Babylon in reality? Anything seemed possible at this point. It said it dealt in the "... bodies and souls of men." Souls got captured in many ways and it didn't happen only at death.

Religion operates by implanting the hook of guilt and then the seeking of forgiveness as a never-ending cycle, or promoting sacrifice for some self-proclaimed righteous cause as a means of redemption.

"... the bodies and souls of men ..." perhaps the bible is not a myth I mused. Perhaps the Dark One is a liar. That seemed the most plausible of all possible answers. But, philosophies and possibilities aside, how was I to face and defeat him, my enemy from beyond the land of lore?

CHAPTER FORTY-SEVEN

EXHAUSTED AFTER TWO days of searching through genealogy records, Laura sat staring at the computer screen but not seeing what was on it.

She took a long drink of the dark coffee, eagerly swallowing the stimulating liquid, letting out a sigh of satisfaction, and set the cup down on its coaster.

The computer continued to grind away, searching for answers to her inquiries about the names Struck and Whitherby. She'd been able to trace her ancestry back through her family's arrival in the New World easy enough. Truman's had been a little more difficult.

She laid her eyes on the oak buffet, bequeathed down the family line by her great-great-grandmother, but that was as far as she could get in tracing the antiques' history, except that it had come across the Atlantic from Ireland.

And what about Truman? If there was or wasn't some connection with him from the past, there apparently would be in the future, and it was self evident one existed in the present.

But what was it and why was it? She couldn't use the shotgun approach to find the answer. Danger was too close and coming in too fast.

She asked herself, "What was happening in Ireland just before the first major immigration to the New World?"

Genealogies, concocted mainly by enthusiastic hobbyists, wouldn't answer that question. History, supposed to be written by unbiased experts, should. She decided to explore that avenue. She typed in 'Irish History' and then clicked on 'search'.

An entire universe of information assaulted her eyes and her mind, already on the verge of exhaustion.

Instinctively she clicked on Dublin as a starting point. Maybe she'd get lucky and find some piece to the puzzle, even though she didn't know exactly what the puzzle was, let alone how to go about solving it.

The number of choices on the screen pared down by half, still leaving a lot of information about the capital city. But she wasn't looking for the usual facts and figures and dates associated with history. She was searching for . . . beginnings, ancient lore, myths, and legends.

Listless, she clicked on "Early History of . . ." and as the machine chunked through its list, picking what choices to display, she stood up, grabbed her coffee mug, and headed to the kitchen for a refill, refusing to give in to her weariness.

A tired body and a swirling mind were not a good combination for research, but she'd pulled all nighters before, studying for finals in college and she could do it again. In this case she had to. To pass the test meant to live, to fail the test meant to die.

That realization gave her the extra jolt she needed and her alertness level spiked upwards in proportion. This wasn't an academic exercise or a matter of satisfying curiosity. No prizes waited at the end of it. People's lives were on the line with hers and Truman's at the forefront.

What was the thing in the tunnel, she pondered, seating herself in front of the computer screen with a fresh cup of coffee. Who was Truman Struck for that matter? He'd worked with her for a few months. They'd shared a dream, well . . . her dream, to him it had been a nightmare. Maybe the guy was simply insane.

What had Medicine Horse called him, oh yeah, Ishtay Wakanka, a true philosopher. But what did that matter to her? What did it mean? And most important of all, how did she get drawn into all this in the first place? And why should she care about an old drunk whom she really knew nothing about. Besides, it was quite possible he had destroyed enough of his brain cells with alcohol to make him delusional.

But her heart told her it was right. It was as simple and as true as that and all the reason she needed for involvement.

The phone rang, jarring her out of her reverie. As she turned to answer it the screen stopped gyrating and settled on a list of possible answers to her inquiry, stopping her.

"In the early days, around the years 900 to 1100 AD, legend has it that the name Dublin became a contraction of its original name of Double Lane."

The phone rang again.

I'd better get that, she thought, but her interest piqued by the information on the screen caused her to hesitate. Rising off the chair, she took the four steps to the phone on the stand next to the buffet. She valued quiet private moments too much to have a cell phone ringing, whistling, or playing tunes in her ear wherever she found herself, day or night. No thanks.

"Hello," she said into the receiver.

"Laura, this is Truman."

"Oh hi, how are you? I was just thinking about you . . . us . . . uh, are you alright?"

"I'm just fine my dear, and how are you?"

My dear . . . it sounded very unusual but nice, kind of soothing and fatherly.

"Good . . . I'm good, uh . . . what's up?"

"Do you have that sacred object we looked at before?"

Truman? He sounded distant and far away, lost deep in thought, or . . . not himself.

"The rosary?" she asked.

"Yes, that's the one. Would you mind retrieving it and bringing it close to the phone for me? I think I may be on to something."

"Yeah, sure, I'll be just a second," she said.

Opening the top drawer of the buffet and taking great care she removed the sacred object.

"Uh, Truman, do you remember what legend surrounds the rosary?"

"Please, hold it against the phone, will you my dear?" his voice soothing and compelling. Her mind blanked, her suspicions abated, she did as he asked without hesitation.

The Dark One had expected to feel a dangerous power from the sacred object and had braced himself for the offense, but nothing came, no wave of purity, no force of rightness, no rebuke from the heavens.

"Truman, what legend surrounds this rosary, do you remember?" asked Laura, her mind clearing.

"It . . . belonged to . . . St. Patrick." Truman's voice sounded strained and distant and then very sudden said, "Good bye, Laura." Click. The dial tone hummed hauntingly in her ear.

She dialed Truman's number and after the fourth ring someone picked it up. She wasn't sure who it might be.

"Hello," answered a lively voice.

"Truman?"

"Yes, this is Truman. Is this you Laura?"

"Yes. Did you just call me?"

"No, I didn't, what's happened?"

Laura's pulse spiked upwards. She needed to take a deep breath before telling him about the recent phone call, made in his name.

"It had to have been the Dark One," said Truman over the phone. She was certain it was Truman speaking by the familiar spark of life in his voice.

"What makes you say that?" she asked.

"I've had a recent conversation with him myself."

"Are you sure? I mean, you could have been dreaming, or you could be overworked or overstressed. Truman, are you certain?"

"Well, didn't you just have a brief conversation with him . . . or her . . . I'm not certain which. We'll use the masculine gender as a matter of tradition, okay?"

"Uh, yeah, fine, him it is," she said.

"And if he can call you and speak over the phone to you, then he can probably listen in on our conversations also."

"Right. So I'll have a guard bring you to the education building tomorrow after dinner. Will that work out for you?"

"Sure, we can talk then about what we've found out. In the mean time . . . be careful."

"I will and you too. Truman, I'm beginning to get a little scared. This is not a game is it?"

"No, I'm afraid it isn't. What we need to do first is find out exactly how and why we got caught up in this. I'll see you tomorrow night then."

"Bye Truman," she said, her hand in slow motion as she hung up the phone.

She returned to the computer and sat down in front of the screen, but her nerves, rattled to the extreme, kept her attention unfocused.

*   *   *

The Dark One curled up in front of the tunnel's north door, smug with satisfaction. It had been a good night's work in spite of exposing a minute fraction of his ability. He now knew that whatever the sacred object was that Laura possessed held no threat to him.

THE AWAKENING

CHAPTER FORTY-EIGHT

AFTER SEVERAL LONG gulps of coffee, Laura was able to focus on the screen in front of her.

". . . the original name, Double Lane, was due to the fact that the main route into the coastal villages was a lane twice the width of a normal lane. The doublewide lane led to the further development of the twin villages, separated by a narrow strip of woods. The separateness was not only geographical, but cultural. The names of the original twin villages are lost in time. The only known fact about them is one was built and inhabited by the Celts and the other was built and inhabited by the Vikings. According to legend, a Norse king by the name of Bukwold was the first to rule over the twin settlements, his rule lasting for a decade."

Fascinated, Laura read on.

"The twin villages, because they were situated at the end of the double wide lane, were soon called Double Lane and then Dublin, which has become a prominent city and the capital of Ireland."

Laura, her heart racing, quickly typed "Bukwold" in the search engine box and then pressed enter.

"The Norse king Bukwold, known as the Slayer, ended his long career of conquest by settling on the east coast of present day Ireland. Legend persists that after beheading the Celtic queen Lucretia in battle he buried his axe into a nearby oak tree and swore with an oath, "Here and no further." The Norsemen then established and settled a village that became, "Where Bukwold Struck the Tree." In actuality it encompassed more of a region than the confines of the small village itself."

Something inside Laura's mind clicked and solidified. She wasn't sure what, but she felt prompted to printout the stories of Bukwold and the naming of Dublin for further reference. Maybe together they meant something that could help solve the puzzling nightmare from which they had awakened, and must now face.

Looking forward to her meeting with Truman on the following day, she turned the machine off, intending to go to bed.

Before getting up, she felt something brush against her forearm. It was the rosary. She had been holding it while searching the Internet.

Rising, she stood and walked over to the buffet, opened the top middle drawer, and placed the rosary in it.

Why had the Dark One wanted her to hold it near the phone in the first place? Perhaps he was afraid of it. Did it hold some power he couldn't overcome? Was the whole convoluted puzzle as simple as Good versus Evil, no not yet, because Evil was clearly seen and defined, but Good remained a puzzle. The war between the two had raged since time began, a war whose balance seemed to be falling rapidly on the side of Evil.

The reports of evil acts were constant everywhere in the newspapers and television, but the evil itself dwelt in the people who the reports were about, reports of rampant chaos and cruelty.

The earth itself seemed poised to strike out against the violence done to it and on it, most of it perpetrated in the name of profit, and there's no way out. The damage done is far too great and goes far too deep to correct.

No ... Good remains undefined, while Evil manifests itself as a juggernaut for all to see that takes away any hope to deal with it.

Laura gently closed the drawer with St. Patrick's rosary resting on its bed of purple velvet cloth. Underneath that drawer was another one the same width of St. Patrick's, but it had twice the depth. It was locked, it had always been locked, and as far as Laura knew, the key was lost forever, somewhere between her home and the emerald isle, sometime between now and five centuries past.

She ran her fingers over the top of the buffet, feeling the same smoothness she always had, the same warmth of the wood, as if it were still alive, or the essence of her ancestor's touches had remained with the ancient piece and now, in some way, offered her comfort.

She circled it, trance like, caressing the wood as she did so, hoping to find some clue, or some way of opening the large drawer to reveal it's hidden secret which she felt stronger now than ever before. She knew the buffet's history, who had crafted it, how and when it had come with the courageous souls who sailed on wooden ships to explore and settle the New World, its journey thus far culminating at the place where it now stood.

She used to think of it only as an heirloom, a link to the past, a vague promise of the future.

Now though, seeing it as more than a sentimental piece of furniture, she felt compelled to discover what secrets it may hold, what tales it could tell, and what power it may contain.

The Dark One had been concerned about a sacred object, was it the buffet itself?

The piece was elegant and flawless; a minor miracle considering the distance it had traveled over rough seas and even rougher lands, and the time it had taken to traverse that great distance to stand where it now stood.

Laura had examined every detail of the piece many times before, and all she had ever noticed and now could find, was that single thin cut mark on its left rear leg. It wasn't a gouge, but a definite cut, smooth and not too deep, that ran across the width of the supporting leg.

The buffet emanated increased warmth, perhaps reflecting her warm surmising's about family from the long ago.

There are auras, there are genetic memories, and the wood came from a living thing, so how could one say with certainty that it didn't . . . *know*, or that it didn't hold the touch of those who had touched it?

Laura stopped in front of the buffet, one-step back from contact with it. Holding her body and mind still, she hoped for something to open her understanding or her insight, or perhaps a revelation to strike her, revealing any secret mysteries that she now pondered.

So she stood, still and absolute, not thinking, but feeling for anything instinctual or insightful, breathing deeply to help maintain her calmness against her growing fear.

If the Dark One could manipulate the phone lines and speak over them, what else was he able to do? He knew who she was and that she could have in her possession a possible threat to him, but what could it be? The only thing she could think of was the rosary carved by the hands of the patron Saint of the Emerald Isle, but it seemed to have no affect on the Dark One, and that was puzzling. Whatever trouble was brewing, she was certain she'd have a part in it because of her connection to Truman. She shivered and then opened her eyes, surprised at the tautness her face reflected in the mirror mounted on the wall above the buffet. Dropping her eyes, she looked at the buffet's backboard, focusing on the mural carved in high relief and running across the length of it. She moved one-step forward, pressed her stomach and abdomen against the front of the buffet as she reached out and began to run her fingertips over the high relief carvings.

She began at the foot high center, at the largest of the carvings, a magnificent oak tree full of branches.

To its left was an exquisitely detailed rose, about half the size of the tree. To the right of the oak an axe stood out, about three fourths the size of the tree, the type used in ancient warfare. To the left of the rose and to the right of the axe were carvings of leaves on vines that extended to the ends of the backboard and edges of the buffet.

She stared at them and wondered why such a strange and unconnected set of symbols were there in the first place. Were they simply the choice of the artist, or did they have some hidden message?

Again she ran her fingers over the high relief carvings. The wood actually felt warmer to her touch, warmer than she had ever noticed before, and she felt it was imperative to understand all she could about the oak buffet. Imagination? Possibly. Reality? That was possible also. The universe is full of possibilities.

Truman had said the theories of relativity and of quantum physics had their basis in possibility.

He also told her that scientists are beginning to believe, through strong evidence, that the original theories are coming closer to reality, that the past and the future exist simultaneously with the present, and information can flow in to the present from either direction or it can flow out from the present in either direction, the directions being the past and the future.

The ideas of space, time, and matter confined to the finite, "out there", are proving to be false. Quantum physics has also discovered that the behavior of some subatomic particles can be, and in fact are, affected by the expectations of the observer. In other words, the mind touches the "stuff" of matter at that level.

Medicine at one time popularized the idea of "psychosomatic" illnesses, diseases brought on and physically manifested by the power of a person's mind. Those with multiple personality disorders—schizophrenics—often witness other realities or other beings in their presence. In fact, if a person does have multiple personalities, it could be that if there are parallel universes, and a parent, through sexual abuse, traumatizes Jane then Mary from a parallel world takes over, allowing Jane to retreat in order to cope with the devastation. Because only a small percentage of the population experiences this, it does not mean it is abnormal, just uncommon.

The universe is full of possibilities most of which have not been understood unless one has been around since beyond remembering, like the Dark One. He may very well know all things.

But I'm a teacher, not a philosopher, thought Laura and continued to run her fingers over the carved relief of the backboard. It warmed further to her touch and felt vibrant and alive.

To the right of the battle-axe were oak leaves. The oak leaves to the left of the rose were the mirror image of those on the right of the axe, exact in detail and number. She ran her fingers, like feathers, over both sides one more time. Just decoration, she thought, leaning as far as she could across the top of the ancient piece, inspecting the leaf carvings with exacting scrutiny. In very minute detail, underneath the bottom row of the leaf carvings on both sides, she noticed what appeared to be some form of primitive writing, consisting of a combination of odd looking and unfamiliar symbols and letters. They began just underneath the roots of the oak tree and extended from there along the lower edge of the backboard to the edge of each side.

The writing was small. She couldn't help but wonder how she had missed seeing it before, and concluded that she just hadn't been paying attention. Or was it a timely intention? She wasn't certain if they had been there all along or not. She only knew of her discovery now and of the utter importance of finding its meaning.

Was it a voice from the past speaking now and for a reason?

That was a possibility she could not ignore.

Retrieving a piece of blank paper from the telephone stand, she copied the lines of symbols and letters, which looked to be a hybrid of hieroglyphics and ancient Greek, onto the paper, assuming it was ancient Gaelic in its most primitive form.

Chapter Forty-Nine

Buzzing with excitement, Laura turned around so quick she banged her knee against the man down on one knee before her, his face bowed low and hidden.

She gasped while the sudden shock caused her to drop the piece of paper on which was copied the ancient writing from the buffet backboard.

"Who are you and how did you get in here?" she asked her voice high and panic stricken as she pressed her back against the oak buffet. A heartbeat ago, it was a source of comfort, but now a captive, blocking her way of escape.

A cloak of royal blue draped over the man's shoulders covered his entire body. Tailored from a heavy woven material, it had a high collar crafted from threads of gold. The high top of a shiny black boot covered his exposed left knee.

His hair, black, wavy, and slicked straight back from his forehead, stopped at the golden collar of his heavy cloak.

"Do not be afraid, my lady," came a deep and gentle voice from the man's bowed and hidden face.

Guided by instinct and fear spiked adrenaline, Laura stepped to her side and reached for the knob of the top drawer of the buffet. Her heart thundering, she pulled it open and fumbled for the rosary. Her fingertips touched the beads. She grasped it and lifted it out of the open drawer.

"You didn't answer me," she stated.

"There is no need for fear," said the faceless voice. Laura's internal alarms told her different. They were clanging away like the bells of an old-fashioned fire engine. She held the rosary tight and close to her chest.

"Again," she said, her voice firm, "who are you?"

The man lifted his head up, exposing his face. Laura gasped, her breath escaping her, taken away by the rugged beauty of the man's features. His was the face of every woman's Prince Charming, forthright, strong, self-assured, as if made of chiseled marble, and just as pale.

She grasped the rosary tighter.

"I bring you a message from my High Lord," he breathed, as soothing as a Chinook wind in deep winter. But her alarms kept clanging.

It might be safest to play along, she thought. "Please rise messenger," she said.

Again she gasped as he was on his feet quicker than her eye could follow, his cloak fluttering down to settle on his shoulders. He stood perfectly still before her, and seemed not to draw breath.

Taller than any man she had ever seen, the width of his shoulders matched his height, being a yard wide. He reminded her of a knight at leisure in medieval times . . . except for his eyes, they were large and somewhat protruding. Looking into them she could see only deep cold. Her breath caught in her throat. The knuckles of her hands whitened around the rosary. Her knees trembled as she leaned back on the buffet to steady herself. The room swam before her eyes, but the man remained in focus.

Nausea roiled in her stomach.

"Who . . . who are you?" She asked again with the little amount of breath she could muster.

"A simple messenger, my lady," he answered.

Her palms wetted the rosary with sweat.

"Why do you call me that? I don't know you and you don't know me."

"Oh, but I do," he replied so charming, so smooth, so deadly. "And I call you my lady because my High Lord has chosen to make you a Queen."

"The Dark One!"

"If you choose to call him that, then yes, that is his name."

"I will not be his Queen . . . ever."

"No, not his Queen, but the Queen of Truman Struck, would you not like that? Truman is not yet a King, but if he chooses to be one, it shall be his, this my High Lord has promised. Imagine, wealth and all that comes with it, and all you've ever wished for with Truman at your side, and a life that will last a thousand years."

"And in exchange?"

"You simply use your powers of persuasion to get him to say yes to my High Lord's offer. Simple enough, is it not?"

"It is not, and I will not," she said. "What is your name?" she demanded.

"My name is of no consequence. My High Lord calls me Dethel.

Laura's mind raced in time with her pulse. Who knew what the creature was really planning, or what evil it was capable of doing? Lying and deceiving certainly. Perhaps it was only toying with her, and its true intent was to cause her to suffer the pain and the terror that precedes death by torture.

She had no way of knowing and nothing to rely on but her instincts and her wits, which hung on a thread and were very difficult to keep about her.

Every molecule in her body vibrated with alertness, the product of adrenaline coupled with a large dose of fear.

The man closed his deadened eyes and inhaled deeply, breathing in her fear. Her fear increased, he breathed deeper, and when he opened his eyes, they were aflame with a desire unknown to mortal man.

Sweat dripped from her closed palms.

"Dethel, if I would truly be a Queen, then hand me that paper, will you?" she said, pointing at the piece she'd dropped at her first fright.

She'd kept her wits about her.

"As you wish, my lady," he said, with an elegant bow. Then he grasped the paper with the mysterious writing on it from off the floor. His hand was a blur as he gave it to her. His face a grimace of pain as a tiny wisp of smoke rose up from his fingertips.

"This paper causes you pain?" she asked with feigned innocence.

"Yes, my lady."

"Why?"

"I do not know, perhaps my High Lord will. May I have it back?"

"Wouldn't you risk burning it or your hand?"

"I'll place it safely here in my cloak," he said to her.

"They're gathering intelligence," a small voice whispered inside her mind, her intuition speaking.

"No Dethel, the answer is no, to your offer and to your request."

"My High Lord is patient, my lady, but also very powerful. The former will dissipate long before the latter. He will not be pleased."

"That is no concern of mine," Laura said, feeling very powerful herself, knowing that for the moment she had the upper hand. But why didn't Dethel just take it from her by force? He'd have no trouble overpowering her.

She held the crucifix upwards so that he was able to clearly see it—she was aware of the vampire stories—Dethel laughed, he'd heard the stories also. But he stayed where he was.

Permission, he needed her permission, that was her discovery.

"You may leave now Dethel," she told him, and in an instant, amid the swirl of his royal blue cloak, he disappeared.

Laura, holding both the paper and the rosary close to her chest, collapsed in a faint.

She awoke shivering from a cold that penetrated to the marrow of her bones. Shaking, and with painstaking effort, she stood up, clutching the rosary and the paper close to her breast.

The clock on the wall read five past midnight. She'd been out only a few minutes, but remembering the reason for her fainting, a choking gasp stuck in her throat.

Tightening her grip on the rosary, she glanced around the room, her eyes unfocused by disorientation and enlarged by terror.

CHAPTER FORTY-NINE

Nothing.

She felt violated, but not in her body. It was her soul that felt like it had suffered rape. Still shaking, she climbed, fully dressed, into the comfort of her bed where she drifted off into a night of tossing and turning, caught in that hazy world between sleep and wakefulness.

CHAPTER FIFTY

THE CONFINES OF his entrapment were closing in tight, fast, and suffocating, and the Dark One raged in fury. He twisted and then exploded, dematerializing and caroming off the tunnel walls as deadly as random strikes of lightning. Throwing his head back, he howled out his ferocity, fixing his blood red eyes on Dethel, as his gaping jaws drooled with acidic saliva.

Dethel cowered, plastered against the tunnel wall.

He alone could hear the howling of the Dark One's fury and see the grotesque and twisted features of his master's true nature; all the evil from beyond remembrance to an imagined future not yet exposed, and evil does not like to lift its cloak.

This caused another furious howl to erupt from the Dark One's cavernous throat.

True evil loves darkness and secrecy, subtlety and cunning. It loves creating lies wrapped in illusion, the setting up of false hopes, just to tear them down with gleeful and malicious vengeance. Why? That is its nature. Pride and arrogance are its wings, lies and murder are its heart, treachery is the engine that drives its mind and directs its motives, fear and hate its banquet, greed and lust it's playground. And its throne is called confusion.

The Dark One fixed his eyes on his cowering servant. Dethel's fear was helping to soothe his blood red rage. He became very still, staring at the black shadow that was Dethel. Further down the tunnel, a hoard of darklings, the spider monkey imps, waited, eager to feast on the demon at the wave of their master's hand. Chattering and dancing, twisting and twirling, their frenzied yellow eyes glaring at the shadow huddled against the wall.

"You have failed me!" shouted the Dark One, his voice like a roaring lion's, causing Dethel to shrink even more. The Dark One waited to hear his string of excuses, and they came at once.

"She is very strong willed, I could not charm her into co-operating, even though I treated her as if she were a queen," said the cowering shadow.

"You gave her a taste of possibility. That is good."

Dethel relaxed a bit.

"What form did you take?" asked the Dark One.

"The form of the handsome and charming prince."

"Good."

He relaxed a bit more and straightened his back, but kept it plastered against the cold concrete wall of the tunnel.

The spider monkey imps retreated further into the shadows, to Dethel's visible relief.

So amusing, thought the Dark One. "What else?" he asked Dethel with feigned interest.

"She asked me to retrieve the piece of paper she dropped when frightened by the suddenness of my appearing."

"A piece of paper, what is the significance of that, what was written on it?"

"Very odd scribbling that looked to be some sort of text. I was unable to read it High Lord. But it was written on today's paper and therefore was not ancient. And one other very strange thing ..."

"Yes ..."

"When I retrieved the paper, it burned my fingers, but not hers when she took it from me."

"A sacred object on new paper or some new incantation, perhaps that is what I felt from this Laura woman. But what did the text say? It's related to the Prophecy no doubt." He finished talking to himself, not expecting any answers from Dethel.

The Dark One fixed his eyes on his trembling servant. "Perhaps you have discovered much more than you thought," he said to him.

Dethel smiled a weak and sickly smile.

"Perhaps," repeated the Dark One, the relief showing on Dethel's face another source of amusement for him.

"High Lord, with your permission, I would learn of this Prophecy," requested Dethel.

"Presumptuous of you, is it not?" the Dark One replied, secretly amused. "Of course you cannot be trusted with such knowledge, can you Dethel?"

"No, High Lord."

"Good, then I will tell you of the Prophecy, but whether it is true or will come to pass, you will have to decide for yourself. Yes ... the Prophecy ..."

* * *

"Thank you High Lord," said the darkened spirit leaning against the wall. "May I enquire as to the origin of the Prophecy, High Lord?"

"It is very ancient, passed down from a Celtic or Druidic culture or a mixture of both. I took it serious from the first and nestled in the tree of which it spoke. I got pinned there by some unknown foreign object until a young man felled it. After my release I rode the winds around the earth, traveling in all conceivable directions, my fury driving me, my lust for souls insatiable."

Dethel marveled as the Dark One's twisted features settled into a look of pure rapture.

"I lost track of time after the Civil War which I caused in this New World. Oh to wade in the knee-deep blood such as I had at Gettysburg! I was glutted and satiated and drifting at my leisure until I became lean and hungry once again. So I caused two wars, what the fools call World Wars, the feast of all feasts! Again I drifted off across this New World satiated. I propelled slowly toward these mountains for some solitude, taking time to savor the triumphs of my latest work.

As I drifted, content and contemplative, I did not notice the dark thunderheads gathering in front of me, pregnant with rain and lightning, and their underbellies about to burst open. Are you listening, Dethel?"

"With utmost fascination High Lord," he lied, but no matter, the Dark One continued on.

"And so, I drifted closer to the clouds until I was underneath them, they then spewed lightning, cracking the mountain peak below me. Another lightning strike hit me, driving me into the crack opened in the mountain peak. It closed behind me, and I was trapped." He snarled at the thought. "So there I was, trapped again, and I had such magnificent plans! But I found I could travel within these mountains, moving through the veins of gold and silver and copper that run like rivers deep within them. So maybe the joke will be on he who calls the lightning, if such a being exists, for it is quite possible that Truman Struck and the Laura woman are spoken of in the damnable Prophecy."

"Why don't you just send me to kill them?" asked Dethel.

"You insufferable fool!" raged the Dark One, causing Dethel to shrink down and press even tighter against the tunnel wall. "I may need one of the descendants written of in the Prophecy to see my face to be freed from these mountains. Now, go and play, but do not kill."

"Yes High Lord, thank you High Lord," said Dethel, holding his hateful thoughts in check lest his master should discern them before he could leave.

CHAPTER FIFTY-ONE

ONLY THE DARK One was more fearsome and had more power on the face of the earth than Dethel. He could make any being on the surface and those below it cower before him, except of course his master and he hated him for it, but he also loved him in the twisted way of evil, for his master was also his maker. The Dark One had never told him that, but somehow, and it didn't matter how, he knew it to be true.

Even so the continual humiliation had become insufferable.

A mortal asking to see his face, maybe he could use that to his advantage and ensure the Dark One's demise, if the Prophecy was true.

"Fool indeed," muttered Dethel. "We will see," he said, as he flew off to pay Laura a surprise visit.

He stood before the buffet in her dining room, looking in the mirror above it, not liking what he saw—a sooty black shadow with sickly yellow eyes—he morphed into Prince

Charming and began searching for the paper that could burn his fingertips.

Still seething over his humiliation, he considered harming the woman sleeping in the next room, or, better yet, telling her the story of the Dark One's entrapment. If she and that Truman fellow knew, they would not consider confronting him or asking to see his face, and his master would remain trapped in the mountains to rage forever in that forlorn tunnel he had no choice but to call home.

If only the Dark One were removed Dethel would rule over all that was, kings and kingdoms, presidents and politics, economics and education, films and music, and communion and communication. What a field day he would have! If mortals thought the world was a twisting, downward spiraling juggernaut now, wait until he got his hands on it all, *ALL*, and he could taunt the Dark One daily.

As of now, the masses dwelling on this piece of cosmic dust bent the knee and bowed the head to the Dark One, the Prince of Undercover Darkness. Why he kept it that way, he couldn't understand. But it would be different with him. He would see to it that he received the worship of the inhabitants of the earth or they would suffer consequences far worse than death.

Dethel, the King of Darkness! If only.

His fantasizing of grandeur abated his raging hatred as he strolled around the room, checking the table, the shelves, and the floor in the dimness of the night. Walking back to the buffet, he stopped a few inches from it and reached out with his hand to touch the velvety smooth wood.

It was warm, and growing hotter, but his fingertips didn't burn as they dropped closer to the wood. He stopped his hand a fraction of an inch above the top of the flat surface and let it hover there as he studied the carvings on the backboard. A huge tree in the center, a rose to its left with oak leaves to the left of that running to the far edge of the backboard. To the right of the tree was an axe with oak leaves to the right of it running to the outer edge of the backboard. Ancient symbols of everyday life back when, he thought.

Noticing a different kind of carving under the bottom row of the oak leaves, he leaned forward for a closer look. His fingertips touched the wood surface and burst into flames. Letting out a stifled scream of pain and rage, he withdrew his hand, stepped back from the buffet, and covered his hand with his cloak, smothering the stinging flames.

Expecting his shriek to have awakened the woman in the next room, he focused his attention and listened, but heard only a soft murmur as she stirred under the covers.

Lust gripped the shape shifter.

Moving without a sound into the next room, he stood by her bedside watching her sleep in the soft light.

He could morph into an incubus and take her in her sleep. She would think it was only a dream, an extremely pleasant dream, one from which she would not want to awaken.

He burned hotter. His loins throbbed with desire.

How long had it been? No matter, what he wanted was here and now. But . . . a dream from which she would not want to awaken . . . and sometimes they didn't. Many had been unable to take the unendurable pleasure sustained over the length of the night, and passed from their bodies, their death in the throes of ecstasy a savory banquet of incomparable delight.

His loins ached with desire and swelled with passion.

"Go play, but don't kill," rang his master's words, halting him. He couldn't take the risk, not right now. His High Lord needed this one alive in order to increase his chances of escaping from his granite prison. If he killed her there would be more than hell to pay.

"Not now my sweet," he whispered as Laura stirred under the covers. Her sleep would be fitful. She had felt his desire and wanted to respond.

Dethel stood in front of the mirror above the oak buffet. His Prince Charming mask had changed into a twisted reddened mass of frustrated lust.

The strength of the pull to the bedside of the Laura woman was near overpowering, but only to draw him to an inexorable fate he did not want, could not tolerate, and would not survive.

He had witnessed many times the furious destruction wrought by his master's rage, the rending and tearing of thousands of bodies and thousands of souls until he would become gorged and satiated.

But that was nothing compared to what his master did to those who betrayed him. He would take them apart in little bites, piece by piece, over centuries of time as they hung suspended over a raging fire that never died, while they screamed for a merciful death, their screams falling on hard rock, their tears hissing into steam as they would strike the fire below. And worst of all, the Dark One taunting, saying how much it hurt him to have to treat one of his most beloved and trusted servants in this manner.

The color of Dethel's face turned to ashen gray as the heat of lust gave way to the iciness of terror.

He forgot about the woman, stepped up to the buffet and leaned forward, very careful not to touch the wood. Again, he scrutinized the high relief carvings on the backboard. His intense concentration revealed carvings underneath the oak leaves. They were an exact match of the word symbols he had seen on the woman's piece of paper, just before it set his fingers on fire.

A killing anger flared for an instant, but as cunning set in, it subsided. He looked around the room for a piece of paper and a writing instrument. He would copy the word symbols and present them to the Dark One, thereby pleasing his master and gaining back his favor.

But, as is its nature, more cunning crept in, and he caught himself, intercepting centuries of behavioral thinking instilled in him by the Dark One, what if the meaning of the word symbols proved to be instrumental in setting his master free?

Dethel decided to work against his master's release. After all, it was the Dark One that had taught him, "What they don't know won't hurt them." Maybe in this case it would. Maybe not knowing what the word symbols said, would indeed hurt his master.

Chapter Fifty-Two

Laura awoke shivering in spite of the warmth of her bed. She glanced around the room, her breath catching in her throat from the expectation of seeing somebody, maybe Prince Charming. She'd tossed and turned all night on the verge of a dream, his face going in and out of focus before her but impossible to grasp.

She let her breath out and shuddered, not from cold, but from the sense that someone had violated her soul exposing her very essence to an unnamable and unholy desire.

Disoriented, she shook her head from side to side, trying to clear the sense of her violation, the reason for her confusion. What had happened to her? What had Truman Struck gotten her into? Remembering Prince Charming kneeling before her in the night just passed, she felt a surge of anger toward Truman. It didn't take her long to realize it was a reaction to feeling vulnerable, she dropped it, got up, got out of her rumpled clothes, tossed on her robe, and was ready to get ready for the day. Another day, drive to the prison, try to teach men who didn't want to learn. But this day may prove to be different, she thought, depending on her meeting with Truman. The brief flare of anger gone and feeling less disoriented, she had a general direction to go in.

Bending to make her bed, she saw the piece of paper with its undeciphered writing lying next to the rosary. The scorch mark on the side of it, compliments of Prince Charming, made her let go with a little chuckle. It had served the bastard right. The bastard . . . yes, he was indeed real. But in spite of that, the humor and the laughter made her feel an unusual buoyancy.

The rosary hadn't affected the old Prince, but why, she wondered. The paper itself could be the description of ordinary so it must have been the words written on it.

The symbol words . . . what did they say . . . what could they mean . . . and most of all, what power did they contain? Just exactly what had Truman Struck gotten her into anyhow? Once again anger surged and she determined to find out and then give him a piece of her mind, or maybe all of it, depending on what she found out. She'd never invited any of this on herself, a waking nightmare that refused to stop its torment.

Glancing at the alarm clock on her bed stand, she saw she'd gotten up a couple of hours early. She'd heard it go off, hadn't she? She thought so.

Regardless, she didn't feel sleepy and resolved to ready herself for the day. She finished making her bed and headed for the shower.

Stepping out of the long hot shower, she felt cleansed from the remembrances of the night before.

She wrapped a bath towel around her and stood before the steamed up mirror above the lavatory. Removing the hand towel from off its chrome rack she wiped the steamy residue off the mirror, only to see the face of Prince Charming towering over her.

Gasping and shrieking she whirled around, causing the towel to come loose and fall to the floor, exposing the nakedness of her body and adding a searing insult to her soul.

Nobody was there.

Shuddering from the shock she dressed, applied what little make up she used, and made her way to the kitchen.

Was her imagination now betraying her, causing her to see hallucinations? Or had the demon actually been present? Or could it appear and disappear like a puff of smoke? The questions made her skin wriggle and her nerves prickle.

She poured herself a cup of coffee out of the time controlled brewer and moved over to the computer desk. Her hand trembling, she set the coffee on a coaster and sat down in front of the screen. Its initial glare hurt her eyes. She turned her head to the side, and they landed on the sheets of paper she'd printed out the night just passed, now so long ago.

Her brief and piercing encounter with hell had caused a shift in her lifelong belief system, now skewed in so many directions it held no resemblance to a system. Her self-confidence had lost its equilibrium and teetered on the edge, ready to topple her over at the slightest nudge.

The reality of unreality has a way of slapping life long boundaries to the side.

But ... the day ... focus, she told herself.

She picked up one of the printouts and tried reading it in the dim light emanating from the screen. It wasn't enough; she flicked on the desk lamp.

Chapter Fifty-Three

Laura had pursued the avenue of Genealogy to an ending that concluded in what ifs and maybes and guesswork when it came to pinpointing actual beginnings.

Reading one of the printouts from the previous night, she was given hope as she read the history of Bukwold the Slayer and of the two villages that first became Double Lane and were eventually condensed down to Dublin.

The Norse village was named, "Where Bukwold Struck the Tree," yes, she remembered that. But what was the name of the twin village that gave it the double in Double Lane?

She took the piece of paper with the scorched edge and word symbols and, trembling because of its attached memory, held it up next to the computer screen as she went to the home page of Encarta, typed in Languages, clicked on European, clicked on Ancient and then made her final stop at Gaelic. Bypassing "History and Development of", she went directly to the "Alphabet and Structure of" site.

Comparing some of the symbols on the screen with those written on the paper, she saw many that matched up. Her excitement brought her to full wakefulness.

She glanced down at her watch and it said go, start your day. She felt like a treasure hunter who had just stumbled on a major clue, exhilarating her. She couldn't wait to tell Truman and work with him on the research. It would be a painstaking endeavor, but her confidence had returned and she knew they would be equal to the task.

Slipping the demon's scorched paper into her purse, Laura truly began her day.

She drove nervous from her house to the prison, half expecting Prince Charming to materialize in the passenger scat, or show his face in the rear view mirror when she glanced in it. Her palms were sweaty by the time she stopped at the guard kiosk for clearance to enter the main prison gate.

She pushed her sunglasses up to rest on the top of her head. The weather, somewhere between Anaconda and the prison, had turned from a promising brightness to a sullen gray, contrasted only by darker shades of gray that were the towers, walls, fences, buildings, and trees prematurely stripped of their leaves by an early fall.

The calendar said today was the first day of autumn, but it felt more like the dead of winter.

She had no explanation for shivering as she rolled the car window down, ready to say good morning to George the guard.

"Mornin' Miss Whitherby," greeted old George, a veteran of three decades of commendable service and was now semi-retired snug within his kiosk. Laura looked up at him to return her usual "good morning."

"Good . . . God, George!" she rasped, her mouth dropped open, her eyes widening in disbelief at what they saw. The thing had George's voice, but that was all. In place of his usual round, jolly, grandfather's face, was a pale gaunt one, like a skull looking back at her through empty eye sockets, his standard prison guard's cap rode high on his head and was skewed to the side on his hairless head.

"G—good morning George," she replied, her voice shaky. As usual, he raised a finger to the tip of his hat, a skinless bony finger. "Have a nice day," he said, as usual, his razor thin lips pulled back in what substituted for a grin, exposing jagged yellow teeth.

Laura returned a weak smile, rolled up her window and started forward as the double gates swung open, her vision blurred by the drizzle that ran down her windshield.

She clicked on the wipers against the drizzle, glanced in her rear view mirror, and saw the old familiar George waving good bye to her as she drove through the open double gates.

Nothing was moving about in the prison and it felt deserted as if the slow drizzle of the rain had kept all living things behind closed doors, those with bars and those without.

Pulling to a stop in her designated parking space, she flipped the hood of her light parka up on her head before shutting off the engine and getting out of the car. Nothing in her vision stirred as she hurried across the pavement, the heels of her shoes click clacking loud enough to echo off the nearest of the prison's forbidding walls.

The wind picked up.

The rain fell heavier.

The echoes of her footsteps softened.

She approached the pedestrian gate, the last one to go through before she was in the main compound. The chilly air penetrated further, working its way through her light blue parka. Again she shivered, but it wasn't from the increasing cold, it was from the *aloneness*, the utter dead stillness that pervaded the gray prison yard.

No visible living thing moved.

No flag on the flagpole flapped in the wind.

No ravens rode the air currents.

No sounds, just the lonely wind and the soft patter of the rain.

She looked behind her, nothing but the same stillness.

Once through the last gate she increased her pace to almost a run and by the time she reached the bottom of the four steps that led into the education building her breath gave out to heavy breathing, not from the scurry, but the sudden shrieking of the wind.

Taking the steps two at a time, she grabbed the handle of the heavy metal door and yanked it open, surprised at her own strength. In front of her was nothing except more emptiness, more stillness, and more aloneness.

Turning to her right she walked as if in a trance up the flight of stairs that led to her department and the library.

Pitter-patter, the rain splattered against the lone window situated half way up the stairwell, a sound she had never noticed before and was surprised she could hear above the boom of her heart as she climbed to the top of the stairs.

Reaching the landing between her department and the library, its barred doors closed and locked, she found only more emptiness.

Nobody stirred down the hallway to the left as she turned in that direction. Like a child lost in a dark cave, she held her hands palms out and in front of her as she groped her way down the hall towards her classroom.

The hallway was silent, eerie, and dark. She looked down at the prison yard through the rain-streaked window on her left. Nothing moved that she could see.

Framing herself in the open doorway of her classroom, her eyes fell on even more emptiness. Slow gray snakes of rain crawled down the windows at the back of the unlit room. Taking two steps into the empty room, she turned and looked up at the clock on the wall. One hand was moving, the smaller of the three keeping a perfect sixty beat minute. The other two were stuck on the six, giving her the feeling that time had stopped, replaced by a sentient emptiness, stark and cold, no matter where she might find herself in the day.

She shivered once more. Taking three steps she was out of the room and into the hallway.

With her rationality shutting down and putting her on the edge of panic, she reached inside her purse and felt around for an anchor of sorts, the piece of scorched paper. Finding it gave her a small sense of direction, but she knew not where to focus it. What did the mysterious word symbols have to say and to whom did they speak?

Call Truman, cut across her swirling mind.

She knocked on the wood veneer door to her left. No answering voice, of course not, and she hadn't expected one. She tried the doorknob, it was unlocked. The Director of Education had always believed in an open door policy.

Laura chuckled and reminded herself to lobby him for a phone in her classroom someday . . . if someday ever arrived. She could not be sure of anything right now.

"Don't be morbid," she told herself with unsuccessful conviction. They hadn't taught her anything about things like this in college. She'd had no preparation for . . . what, the reality of the unreal, the manifestation of myth, the visibility of the invisible, all of the above or none of the above? Her mind reeled, only the chill within keeping it from spiraling totally out of control.

"FOCUS!" she screamed silently, jarring herself back.

She plopped down in the Director's chair, picked up the phone and dialed the cannery, four rings and then silence. God she felt so alone, as if the world had stopped and every living thing had spun off into space and all color had bled off into the ether leaving only a gray-misted world of emptiness devoid of anything except the certainty of impending death. And maybe that was it, she was dead, killed by Prince Charming and she was now condemned to haunt the prison, living as a shadow without substance.

Ring . . . ring, no answer.

She *was* dead and alone, she knew it now. Ready to break into sobs, she moved the receiver in slow motion toward its cradle.

"Hello," a faint voice came from out of the almost cradled receiver, then louder, "Hello!" Laura caught it an instant before the phone was snuggled dead in its own resting place. It was probably the Dark One, but she put it against her ear just the same.

"Truman?" she asked.

CHAPTER FIFTY-THREE

"Yes, Laura where are you?"

"I'm in the education building, in the Director's office," she answered. So what if it was the Dark One, she was dead anyway.

"What's going on?" he asked. Maybe it was Truman, might as well go with that, she figured she didn't have anything to lose.

"The world feels so empty Truman, as if all the force of life has been sucked out of it."

"No one's come up to the cannery today either. I guess it's everywhere, this vast . . ."

"Emptiness," finished Laura. She wasn't dead. It *was* Truman. "What *is* happening? Have we entered a different world?" she queried.

"No," answered Truman. "This is the work of; I'm not exactly sure what to call him, or her."

"We agreed on him, remember?"

"Oh, yeah, and I Live is his name."

"Or the Dark One," said Laura. "At any rate, we don't know his true name, and I believe that would be a key to understanding all of this."

"So do I," replied Truman.

It really *is* Truman, exulted Laura to herself. "I'm coming out to get you. We need to talk face to face so the Dark Thing Living in the Tunnel won't be able to listen in."

"In a few then, and take extra care," replied Truman.

"Sure, in a few," she replied and hung up the phone. In a few what, she asked herself. Time had become meaningless.

Stopping briefly in the hallway to gaze down at the prison yard through the rain-streaked window, she saw that nothing had changed, it remained deserted and steeped in emptiness.

Across the yard and past the three separate cellblocks were the guard towers, also deserted as far she could tell.

So how had the gate opened to let her in on this side of the compound? The guard manning the tower usually opened and then closed it, but how this time? The towers were deserted. And if she was trapped inside the prison, then who else?

Hurrying down the stairs and thrusting open the main door she was again on the concrete sidewalk of the prison yard. In a fast walk she approached the pedestrian gate, the rain falling harder, dampening her light jacket.

She had four steps to take before reaching the gate; two steps. The electric motor hummed and the gate slid back just enough to allow her to pass. Once through, she turned and looked up at the guard tower. The skeletal features of old George, his grin sardonic, waved with one bony hand.

Spinning around, Laura ran to her car, found her keys, opened the door and fired the ignition in one seamless motion. Backing out of her spot, she threw the transmission into drive and screeched out of the parking lot, tires smoking on the wet pavement. She didn't bother waving good-bye to old George as she sped past the kiosk.

She heard laughter, looking in the rear view mirror, she gasped at the face of Prince Charming. She slammed her foot down on the break pedal. The car slid side ways and screeched to a complete stop. Flinging the door open she stumbled out, her purse in hand. She rammed her other hand into her purse and yanked out the rolled up piece of scorched paper. Thrusting it through the open door of her car, she hoped in desperation to stick it in the demon's face and burn the sonofabitch, but nobody was there, of course not.

"Get ahold of yourself," she murmured, and climbed back into the still running car. Much easier said than done, she thought, as the chill deepened and further jangled her nerves.

Checking the rear view mirror, she sped down the gravel road running outside the prison fence and toward the cannery.

She had to see Truman. They had to face what danger may lie ahead. The inevitability of it roared up from her depths and smacked into her consciousness. Unknown to her it was the Gift of See and had always been there, dormant, but was beginning to manifest in this, her moment of need.

CHAPTER FIFTY-FOUR

LAURA, ALWAYS THERE and always on time, it was uncanny, I thought as I hung up the phone.

See you in a few, a few what, seconds, minutes, hours, days, gobbledygook's? It was just another slang expression that catches on, and which everybody seems to know, when in fact it means nothing at all. A few heartbeats? I hoped so, because my heart was thumping hard, partly at the thought of seeing Laura, and partly because I felt like something big was about to go down. Pardon the slang expression.

"What's up?" Everything over the top of my head I suppose.

"Dark One!" I hollered through the concrete wall, after returning to my room, "What are you doing in there?"

"You must ask to see me," he replied, "so I can explain to you face to face."

"Explain what? Who you are? What are your motives? What is your game?" I shouted at him.

"Don't be so impatient, Truman. I suspended time to show you that I can, and therefore showing you that I can indeed make good on my offer to make you a king, with your own kingdom and all that goes with it. Your future queen has arrived. You should go greet her, don't you think?"

Without responding I tore out of the room, took the stairs two at a time, and reached the door at the same instant Laura knocked.

"Want some coffee?" I asked, stepping aside to allow her room to enter.

"Yes I would, please."

I wanted to hug her, I was so glad to see her and relieved that she was safe, for now anyway. I filled a cup for her from the stainless steel urn I'd made for the non-show crew earlier. I handed her the cup as she seated herself at the table.

Through the open window, the sound of bleating sheep came from the foot of the hills to the south. Cattle were lowing to the west, income for the prison, not food for the inmates.

Laura unfolded the story of the night before, her meeting with the demon, and of her recent journey into the present netherworld of the prison, taking sips of coffee in between sentences. That explained the uneasiness I had felt all morning, it was the netherworld into which our world had been plunged.

It was, of course, the work of The Dark One, and something beyond common knowledge had gripped our known world.

I had a good background in physics, and this surreal reality was beyond my comprehension, but at the same time it was ingrained in my nature to try to find an explanation.

Ishtay Wakanka, a true and good philosopher, according to the book Hanta Yo. I had always considered philosophy as circular, head-in-the-clouds, maybe this, maybe that speculative type of thinking, mainly about unanswerable questions. But since then I had learned that the word philosopher comes from the Greek language and means, "a lover of wisdom."

There are two types of philosophers, those who turn within to contemplate behavioral questions of ethics and morality, and those who turn without to contemplate the phenomena of nature and the universe, the natural philosophers. The Greek word for natural is physicos, from whence we get our word physics.

But it is without meaning now, I thought as I gazed across the table at Laura. We were captives and there was no turning back and no escaping it.

She looked so serene in the face of all this madness. Was she possessed? Was I? She was probably wondering, as I was, if the thing in the tunnel possessed the other. At this point, anything within the realm of imagination was in the realm of possibility. So, where would that leave us . . . without trust. Directed earlier into the book of Revelation I had read, "Who is like the Beast and who is able to make war on him?" The Dark One could very well be the Beast, and who is able to make war on him? Until now, no one, but we were in a definite war, a psychological one of nerves. And trust was paramount to having the slightest chance of success. I perceived Laura to be in a mild state of shock, and so approached her gently. "How has your morning been?" I asked.

"Don't patronize me Truman," she shot back and then smiled as if she knew all I had been pondering, and maybe she did know . . . back to possibilities. Then, reaching across the table, she placed her hand on my forearm, and with gentle force said, "You have to trust me Truman. I'm stronger than you think." Did she *really* read my mind? Anyway, she managed to dispel any doubt that had been plowing through it, attempting to plant its seeds deep in the furrowed soil.

Finishing her coffee, she placed the empty cup on the table and said, "Let's go downstairs." Her voice didn't match the insistence in her eyes.

"It could be dangerous," I replied.

She simply nodded as she pulled the scorched piece of paper from her purse. Together, we descended the dimly lit stairwell.

"Dark One!" I called as we entered the main basement room, its single dangling bulb feebly attempting to light it.

"Ah, the King and Queen approach," he replied, his voice smooth and enticing. Laura boldly held up the piece of paper. "Dark One . . . if that is your name . . . what do you make of this?"

He didn't respond, but instead we felt him recoil from the words written on the paper. The truth and its inherent sacredness was far more powerful than he had imagined from Dethel's description, and it caused his throat to tighten, rendering him unable to speak.

"Cat got your tongue?" she tantalized.

The Dark One burned red in fury, like molten metal with the gray slag floating on top, red streaks sizzling in between the scaly material.

Laura handed me the paper. The word symbols meant nothing to me yet. "We need to decipher this," I said.

Laura had already turned, headed back toward the stairwell. I stepped into my room where Gideon's Bible was lying open on the table. I read aloud, "Who is like unto the Beast and who is able to make war against him?" The Dark One hissed from the other side of the wall. The odor of rot and roses permeated the basement. He had seen the word symbols and probably knew what they said but didn't know the relevancy of their meaning. Alone they were nothing but nonsense.

His fury could only increase and he only wanted to kill, as was his nature, and so summoned Dethel.

Chapter Fifty-Five

The library, like the rest of the prison, was deserted and empty. Fortunately, the power was on, so we settled down in front of the computers and returned to Encarta.

We found some sketchy history of the Gaelic language, but didn't find a way to decipher any written words.

"Explain to me again about the word symbols," I asked Laura. She reiterated what she had told me before. "I copied them from off the backboard of the buffet. They were intermingled among the carvings of the oak leaves."

"They were on both sides of the backboard?"

"Yes."

"We need to know what they say, and more importantly, what they mean. The Dark One could not answer to them for some reason. I'm guessing they pose a threat to him. How or why, I have no idea. Maybe some ancient curse . . ."

"Or some ancient prophecy," added Laura. "We need to go to my place," she said with finality as she turned off the computer and stood up, "and get on the 'Net," she finished.

"Your place, uh, Laura, I don't need an escape charge, I'm an inmate, remember? Besides, you could lose your job; maybe even get charges brought against you for aiding and abetting."

She rolled her eyes. "Truman, look around you and see what the Dark One has done. Time is warped, but more likely brought to a complete halt. He sends demons to be his hands and feet while he's trapped. He infiltrates telephones and who knows what else, people's minds perhaps? For a brief time I wasn't willing to trust you, thinking he could possess you if he willed, or at the very least, influence your mind to do his bidding. Truman, we need to know what we are up against, who we are up against. Don't you see, the stakes here are much greater than just you and me."

I rose up without a word and went to the technical bookshelves. There I found what we might need, two texts on ancient Celtic and Gaelic languages. I grabbed both of them. They might help us find out what the word symbols had to say.

Laura had turned off the computer I'd been on and was joining me to leave. I noticed a charcoal gray overcoat hanging on a tree rack on the other side of the counter.

"Wait a second," I said, pointing at the coat. She instantly knew my intent and stopped—Laura, always there—so I could retrieve it. Might as well add theft to my upcoming escape, but it would disguise my much too obvious prison blues . . . just in case. I slipped it on. The fit was slightly large but acceptable under the circumstances.

I could be mistaken for an official and the thought made me chuckle.

We walked with deliberate casualty making our way to the main gate. As we approached I had to restrain myself from looking up at the guard in the number one tower. Laura had told me about him and about old George in the outer kiosk.

The gate slid back and we exited the compound without incident. I could no longer resist. I turned and looked up at the guard in the tower. He was as Laura had described him, a living husk of a human being, skeletal, with empty black holes where his eyes should have been. His uniform hung like dirty dish rags from his fragile frame, and, through the open sliding window, he held a high-powered rifle pointed directly at the middle of my chest.

"Laura," I said with my voice down low, "don't turn around. Keep walking toward your car."

"Why?" she asked as she kept moving forward. I took slow diagonal steps backward away from her, increasing the distance between us.

The rifle held by the skeletal guard didn't waver, following me as I moved.

"The guard has a rifle pointed at the middle of my chest," I answered her. She gasped, but kept walking steadily forward.

I began to sweat in the cold drizzle. Glancing down at my chest, I didn't see any exposed blue. The overcoat had done what I had intended, so . . . why?

"It's okay, he's with me."

Responding to her voice, I looked to my right. Laura had turned around and had shouted up at the skeleton of a guard, brave girl.

The guard lowered the rifle, and then, grinning absurdly and waving as if we were old friends, hollered down at us, "Whatsa matter sonny boy, can't take a joke? I wish you luck, Truman Struck, in spite of being such a dumb cluck!" he cackled with high-pitched glee. Then the sonofabitch turned around, let his baggy pants fall to the floor, and mooned us with his bony ass.

I couldn't stop myself, my laughter burst like water from a dam that cracked. A second later Laura joined me and teary eyed we reached her car and drove off, not stopping at the guard kiosk as the other zombie inside of it waved, with a herky jerky motion, good bye.

The release of tension by the laughter did us both a world of good, and God only knows how badly we needed the remedy for what lay ahead.

CHAPTER FIFTY-SIX

I LEANED OVER THE top of the oak buffet and compared the word symbols with those few I could find in the commandeered library books.

Laura was in the kitchen, preparing chamomile tea. Maybe it would help to calm our jangling nerves.

I compared the symbols on the scorched paper with the carvings on the backboard. Satisfied they were alike in every detail, I moved to the computer desk with the piece of paper in one hand and the book of Gaelic in the other.

Laura unhurriedly entered the room, set the tea down, sat herself down, said, "Help yourself," then focused her attention on the task at hand.

"Thanks," I replied in the guise of nonchalance as I gazed at her profile, strong, decisive, and beautiful. Her beauty emanated from deep within and contained a pureness I never believed possible to exist in a human being.

Laura, always there and always at the right moment, I hoped she trusted me as much as I trusted her.

"Nothing," she said.

"Huh?"

"I've found nothing so far on the 'Net. Where have you been?"

"Uh . . . I think I might have found something," I replied, but didn't tell her that the *something* was the beauty I saw in her.

Get a grip, you have a job to do, and nothing more, I told myself.

But of course that was the story of my life. Just when I'd find something I wanted or had nearly reached a goal I'd set; it would be yanked away from me by some malicious perversion of fate, always, but then, what is life but a whisper of time, a vapor of breath, a two step dance into death. *Holy shit! Get a grip, Charlie Brown.*

"We've got work to do," Laura said from somewhere far away, *had she been reading my mind or feeling my feelings again?* Well, anything was possible, I supposed, in this dark world into which we had been thrust, like it or not, believe it or not.

"Where do we start?"

"What?"

"Truman, snap out of it, we have work to do here," she said, giving me a quizzical look.

"Yeah right, uh, well, exactly what do we know about the Dark One?" I mused aloud.

"He can manipulate time."

"He can send out freaky little emissaries," I added.

"He can talk and he's afraid of these words," said Laura, holding up the scorched paper.

"And we need to find out what they say."

"Bingo!" she exclaimed.

"So, for starters, we need to find out what the words say and then why he needs to speak with us face to face," I said.

"He needs us in order to be freed from these mountains," she replied.

"But why . . . why us, why not just any-old-body?"

"I don't know, can't say, maybe we're his last chance, somehow," she said.

"Or else he could be trapped inside these mountains forever?"

"Possibly," she said.

She scoured the Internet while I scoured the book and after being at it a long time, like hounds on a cold trail, we switched from chamomile tea to strong coffee. And bit by bit we found symbols that matched those on the paper. Each one was like discovering a hidden treasure.

So one by one, piece-by-piece, the puzzle came together, we came up with t's and r's the most. Many blank spaces were in between them until we stumbled on an h.

Can I have an e please, how about an s?

The letters arranged themselves into fourteen undeciphered words, just a smattering of t's and r's and h's, all common letters in any language.

We continued to a point where, after we'd exhausted our supply of symbols, patience, and energy, the words seemed to jump off the page becoming clear to us.

"whither by the sea, where buccwold strucc the tree, there lies the hidden ccey."

"Well, that's it, I'm sure of it," I said.

"So what does it mean?"

"Who knows, who cares, I'm too exhausted to talk about it. It hurts my head to think," I replied.

She looked at me with some degree of sympathy, which I thought was much better than disdain.

"I'm tired too," she remarked, suggesting we needed to go on.

"Look Laura, I'm no flippin' comic book hero. We're talking our *lives* here. I don't give a rat's hat about Montana. So let the damn thing live here in these mountains, and it would serve the place right, right?"

Laura just smiled, waiting for me to continue my rant.

"Look," I continued, "it wants us to free it . . . him. Why not just leave him locked up. *He needs us,* otherwise he'd have had us killed a long time ago, don't you see? We could simply just split."

"Split?"

"Leave." The generation gap was in place, dammit.

"You mean . . . run?" she asked.

That hurt, but it was true in a way.

"Not me," she continued, "you can if you want, and then you'll for sure be a fugitive, and I'll be charged with aiding and abetting. Have you forgotten so soon that we just talked about him stopping time? Then he can certainly start it again, or send out demons, and who knows what else? He reads minds; you know that. He could be listening right now and have the cops here before we could snap our fingers. We're caught in his game and have no choice but to play by his rules."

"Okay," I said.

"Okay what?"

"You're absolutely right, and on my tombstone they can put these words, "Truman Struck really was a dumb cluck.""

"Not funny," she said, as she stared at the array of word symbols showing on the lit up screen.

CHAPTER FIFTY-SIX

"Anything else?" I asked.

"We still can't be sure of the translation of the message."

"I know. The c's, are they hard or soft sounding, and so what if they're either or," I said.

"Cynical aren't we?"

"You're still young."

She turned and looked me straight in the eyes. "Age doesn't mean a lot. In fact, it doesn't mean a thing when it comes to how we feel, does it?"

Right again.

"Anything else you can think of that could shed some light?" I asked, veering the subject back on course, I was afraid to hope. But, what if?

Laura looked around her desk, drumming the fingers of her right hand on the surface as she sifted through a small stack of papers with her left. Stopping, she pulled a single piece of paper from the now disarrayed pile. "Here's a printout I made last night," she said, her hand trembling slightly as she held it out for me to look out. "Last night," she continued, "it seems like a lifetime ago. What have you gotten me into, Truman Struck? How are we to fight this . . . this beast?" Her lips trembled as a single tear trickled down her cheek. I brushed it away with my finger, my heart almost breaking as I saw and felt her anguish.

"I'm not sure how we got into it," I said. "Fate? Destiny? But I know we're in it together and there's no running, remember?" She nodded. "And the only chance in hell we'll have against it is to face it together and trust each other, agreed?" She nodded her head yes.

Brave lady.

"This printout, as I recall . . . God Truman, it seems so long ago that I printed this . . . ," she said once again. I had no words to say to her, I reached over and touched her arm. She smiled a slight smile at me, the appreciation glowing in her eyes, eyes that just for an instant took on a violet hue. I was sure I'd never seen that before, or maybe I'd just failed to notice it until now, but I knew one thing for sure, they were beautiful beyond description.

"I'll be all right," she said. "Anyway, this one is a brief history of the east coast of Ireland, and more specifically of Dublin and the surrounding area."

She read the printout to herself, beginning where she'd left off the night before ". . . from the general name of the twin villages at the end of the double lane came Dublin, which has since become a prominent city and the capital of Ireland.

Legend further goes on to say that the Norse king Bukwold ruled the twin settlements for a decade in their early years."

She realized she'd done this last night. But why hadn't she seen it before? Well, no matter, she saw it now and her heart beat increased its tempo. She understood it could be that buccwold was the original spelling of Bukwold, and so, the double c's were pronounced hard. She read what came up on the screen.

"The Norse king Bukwold, known as the Slayer, ended his long career of conquest by settling on the east coast of Ireland. Legend persists that, after beheading the Celtic queen Lucretia in battle, he buried his axe into an oak tree and swore with an oath, "Here and no further." The Norsemen then settled there in a village known as "Where Bukwold Struck the Tree . . ." Of course, she thought, as the words carved on the backboard became clear.

Her excitement spiked by adrenaline caused her to grip my shoulder with near otherworldly strength.

"Look at this!" she shouted in my ear, shoving the printout in front of my face. After scanning it, I looked at her with a question mark, not getting her drift, let alone her point.

"Now look at this!" she exclaimed, shoving the piece of paper with the translated word symbols in front of my face.

"whither by the sea, where buccwold strucc the tree, there lies the hidden ccey."

"It's a hard c sound, pronounced like our k!" I exclaimed.

"Let's look further," she said, her excitement infectious. Quickly she typed in "Where Bukwold Struck the Tree." Up it came, "a region established by the Vikings, sometime around 900-1100 AD, near present day Dublin.

The town eventually became known as Struck Tree, which was finally reduced to the one word Struck."

Laura looked at me with focused intensity, the odd violet hue in her eyes making them all the more beautiful. "That's your name," she stated, her excitement undiminished.

"That's odd," I remarked. "Could it be possible I'm descended from there? I mean, I know I'm of Norse ancestry, but . . . from there?"

"Why not, it makes sense at least, doesn't it?"

It did, but so what, I thought. "So our best guess is that the words on the backboard read: "Wither by the sea, where Bukwold struck the tree, there lies the hidden key!"

"Yes, I'm absolutely sure of it!" she exclaimed in jubilation.

I wrote the translation down on a piece of scrap paper and stuffed it in my shirt pocket.

The clock had revolved through twelve hours and outside could still be called daylight, the light a dull gray pall.

"I should be going," I said to Laura, "they could be looking for me by now, for all we know."

She nodded; we flung on our overcoats, hopped in her car and headed back toward the prison.

"I'll take the back road, that way we can bypass the prison and its gates," she said.

"And the zombies," I remarked. She chuckled as we drove off, the windshield wipers ka-chunking in time with the water splashing up from the car wheels.

The gravel road we were on went by the cannery, providing a direct link to Anaconda, which could prove useful in the future, as bleak as it appeared to be.

Laura wasn't the least bit cautious as she drove up to the south facing entrance door, out of the view of the prison.

Time hadn't started up again, at least not in this tiny, but at the moment, very important, corner of the world.

Laura pulled to a sloshy stop, letting the engine idle. "Want me to come in with you?" she asked. It wasn't a possibility I had thought of along the way, but my decision was instant.

"No . . . I think we may be getting to a critical point, and a dangerous one, in this game. But thanks for your concern."

She smiled and nodded. "Do me a favor then, go on in, check things out, and if you feel okay and don't sense any danger, come back to the door and wave at me . . . okay?"

I nodded in agreement. "Five minutes," I said, leaving the car to enter the former slaughterhouse.

Chapter Fifty-Seven

I NOTICED NOTHING UNUSUAL as I entered the cannery break room, except for a black shadow flitting across the window, catching the corner of my eye. I wasn't surprised. What once had been unimaginable was now imaginable and close to being reality and normal.

I walked nonchalantly to the top of the stairs and, after glancing backward down the short hallway toward the process room, peered into the dim stairwell below. I no longer felt fear, it had been scattered, not by courage, but by simple acceptance. I was ready to face what I knew to be inevitable, and the realization brought on a weariness like the weight of a large stone embedded in the middle of my chest.

I turned away from the top landing, moving like I was wading in wet cement. I recrossed the break room, opened the outer doorway, and smiling, gave Laura the thumbs up, assuring her everything was all right.

She returned a wan smile. I waited in the doorway as she backed onto the gravel road.

After closing the door, the morbid thought that I may never see her again surrounded me.

I knew if the Dark One could suspend time, he could set me up with a kingdom, an idea that was becoming more and more appealing as I pondered his offer.

Maybe I can negotiate with the bastard, I thought, as I slogged through the imaginary pond of wet cement down the stairs and across the empty warehousing space, my footsteps echoing off the hardened concrete walls.

Entering my room, I plopped onto the single comfortable chair and flipped on the lamp beside it. The heaviness inside my chest lifted, replaced by a feeling that my soul had been convoluted and twisted into a tightly wound knot, one which I had no idea how to untie, like the legendary Gordian knot faced by Alexander the Great. He got right to the heart of the matter, drew his sword and whacked the thing in half. But I was only Truman the Mediocre, the reluctant hero, and without a sword

The bed stand clock read straight up twelve. Whether it was AM or PM I didn't know, but then again, it didn't matter. I only knew I was weary to the bone, and last I looked, it was still daylight with the world suspended in the dull, gray, chill of it. So I sat in utter weariness, suspended out of time, lost in the undefined mist of it all, a three pronged spear piercing my soul but leaving the knot tightly wound.

"Dark One!" I called, sending my voice toward the opposite concrete wall. No reply, I tried again, same result.

I set my alarm clock for seven AM and went to bed "to sleep, perchance to dream," as the old coot with the puffed out collar once said.

It would be better than facing my destiny at least, or was it my fate? Wait a minute; destiny good, fate bad, but who or what determined either was the question and right now, who cared? Not me, I thought, as my bones collapsed into powder, my soul turned into water and I fell into a deep and dreamless and welcome sleep.

Outside, the ravens gathered atop the guard towers, the building parapets, and the razor wire that topped off the chain link fences. The drizzle beaded up and rolled like silver liquid mercury down their black bodies the size of eagles.

Not at all comfortable with the idea of her and Truman being separated, Laura backed her car away from the cannery. Getting it turned around with the cannery in the rear view mirror, she circled downward and to the right on the gravel road, bringing the prison into her view.

Her discomfort turned to acute apprehension.

The prison scene below her flashed from color, then to black and white, and then back to color, a mild surreal scene at the least, a trick of the Dark One at the other end of the spectrum of possibilities. It was due to fatigue she told herself. But regardless of the reason, she didn't see the shadow like creature coming straight at her until the instant it crashed into the windshield, leaving a spattering of blood and a spider web crack on the passenger side of the window. Laura's fragile nerves felt as though a bolt of electricity had shredded them raw. She screamed and screamed again and slammed on the brakes, spitting up a wave of gravel as she slid to a stop. She focused on the dismal prison scene in the shallow valley below, and on the cloud of ravens rising up from it.

Throwing her car in reverse, she arced backwards into a narrow side road, and then shot forward up the hill toward the cannery, mud and gravel spewing like small fountains from underneath the tires.

* * *

The sound of footsteps pounding down the stairwell jolted me awake.

"Truman! Truman!" the urgency behind the voice pierced the fog in my mind and I was fully awake and up in an instant.

"Laura, down here!" I hollered as I pulled on my blues and was lacing up my boots when she burst through the door, her face pale and panic-stricken.

"We need to get out of here . . . NOW!" she said. She had already turned and was running up the stairs with me not far behind.

"The ravens are back!" she cried as we reached the outside door. My understanding was immediate as she placed her hand on the door knob, ready to give it a turn.

"Wait!" I hollered and placed my hand against the door, preventing her from yanking it open. "We need to be careful," I told her as calmly as I could. I felt helpless, not knowing if I could protect her or alleviate her fears. What was it I'd read a while back? "God is the strength of my heart." If ever that could be true, I needed it to be true now.

Gideon, do your stuff.

A couple black streaks shot past outside the break room window. They were here all right, either to kill us or to feed the Dark One.

I opened the door a crack and peered out. Laura stood close behind me. No black cloud of birds, her car within a couple of steps, the engine idling along as if nothing in the world was going on, except all hell was about to break loose.

"Let's go!" I shouted. We jumped off the concrete porch and were in the car before our hearts could beat twice. Laura took the wheel; I stared out at the world through the spider web embedded in the windshield.

As we rounded the first curve on the descending road, we saw the ravens rise from their prison perches to form an ominous black cloud of living beings against the gray pall of the lifeless sky.

Laura shoved the accelerator to the floor. I didn't know how fast ravens could fly, but surely not more than fifty-five miles per hour, which the speedometer read, the tires continuing to spit gravel.

I turned and looked out the rear window. The ravens were shooting toward us, formed, as before, in the shape of a gigantic arrow.

The speedometer hit sixty. I held my breath.

The arrow dipped and entered the cannery, like before.

"They're going into the cannery," I said as I turned and looked through the spider web. She didn't take her eyes off the road or ease up on the accelerator. We sped along in silence until we reached her house, the town of Anaconda down below, oblivious to anything but its normal sleepy functioning.

"They're feeding that thing in the tunnel," she said without looking at me.

"I know, strengthening it," I added.

She shut off the car and looked me square in the eyes. "Truman, right now we must find out all we can about our . . . the how and why we are linked . . . which at times seems mythical or mystical . . . to that thing in the tunnel, the Dark One." She drew in a deep breath, and then let it out very slowly.

"I know. Nothing else really matters at this point, does it?" I said.

She shook her head with an agonizing no.

We got out of the car. Sometime between the cannery and her house, the sky had turned stygian black, thick and palpable. We ignored it, hooked arms and went inside.

CHAPTER FIFTY-EIGHT

"The double c's, like in strucc and ccey have to be pronounced hard, like a k. Don't you think so?" I asked Laura. "Yes, it's the only way it will ever make any kind of sense," she said.

"Whither by the sea, where buccwold strucc the tree, there lies the hidden ccey," I read again the words copied off the buffet backboard and onto that scorched piece of paper. Laura was in the kitchen, busy making tea.

"Where Bukwold struck the tree," I mused, wondering how my name derived from that phrase.

"Where Bukwold struck the tree," I spoke the words slowly, letting them roll off my tongue. "Then the village name condensed to Struck Tree, and then to Struck," I continued.

"Laura," I called as I heard the clinking of teacups on platters coming my way.

"Just a minute," she answered as she entered the living room. Setting two cups filled with tea on the low coffee table she turned to me and asked, "What's the urgency?" She had relaxed a little and that was good to see. I was strung as tight as a catgut string on a violin.

"I need to know how you spell your last name, and yes, it is urgent."

"You don't know?" she asked.

"I don't. I've only heard it pronounced as Weatherbee."

"That's close, but slightly off. It's spelled W-I-T-H-E-R-B-Y, and technically pronounced Whitherby."

"Read out loud the phrase on the left," I said, indicating the scorched paper lying on the table between our cups.

"Whither by the sea . . ." she read slowly, and then, in a whisper, "Whither by . . . Oh my God!" she exclaimed.

"I believe we have found our link," I understated.

"Wither by . . . Witherby," she whispered, as the magnitude of the realization dawned on both of us at the same instant.

Our eyes, wide with wonder, locked into each other's in a moment of time that pulled us out of time and we just *knew*.

She threw her arms around my neck, mine naturally encircled her waist, and we hugged in the joy of our mutual relief.

While wondering at the wonder of it all, we finished our tea and returned to the computer, intent on verifying, if possible, the newfound knowledge that our last names had come from the twin villages now known as Dublin. It seemed self evident, but there was no room for guesswork.

Exploring the areas of history and genealogy once again, we discovered that the husband of Lucille, the seventh descendent from Lucretia, had indeed crafted the mysterious oak buffet in Ireland.

"And you," I said to Laura, "are the sixth descendent from Lucille which makes you the thirteenth from Lucretia, the Queen of the Celts. So then, according to the myths and legends, the Gift of See should reside in you."

She gave me a doubtful look, and then the idea sank in to acceptance.

"I guess it does," she said. "At least I'm here with you, as if it were predestined." She smiled and touched my hand. "Now it's time to find out about your ancestry."

After much agony researching genealogy, we discovered that I was in fact descended from Bukwold, the thirteenth generation from him.

So there we were, the thirteenth generation from Lucretia and Bukwold, Laura and Truman, live and in color.

"You don't hold a grudge against me do you?" I asked her.

"No, why would I?" she returned.

"Well, my ancestor killed your ancestor, but I think it was a fair fight," I added.

"Of course not, silly," she grinned at me.

"So, what does it all mean, other than we've met, or rather, been brought together," I asked.

Of course the question was rhetorical in nature. So without attempting to answer it, she stood up from the computer table and then stood in front of the mysterious buffet. I joined her. We stood silent before it, like it was some kind of shrine, and perhaps it was, without us knowing it or acknowledging it.

What we did know is that there was still a piece or two of the puzzle missing and we needed to find them to solve it.

"Whither by the sea, where Bukwold struck the tree, there lays the hidden key," she murmured, again reciting the message carved on the backboard. "Okay," she said, "we know our intertwined heritage, but now what, I'm not even sure what we're looking for . . . there lies the hidden key . . ." she mused, "But where?"

I shook my head and gave her a look that could not be mistaken for anything but dumbfounded.

"The tree . . ." Laura said as she stood stone still beside me. "The tree carved in the center, that has to be it. "Look," she said and pointed, "an axe on the right, symbolizing what . . . the Norsemen? A rose on the left symbolizing what . . ."

"Has to be the Celts," I replied

"Perhaps, but it could be something more specific than that. A rose can only grow out of rosewood, right?" She backed up a step, taking me along with her, and then, opening the top drawer of the buffet, pulled out the rosary and held it up in front of my face.

"The rosary . . ." she said.

"Carved from rosewood," I finished. "Makes sense," I added, not exactly sure what kind of sense it made.

"Wait a minute," I said, and pulled the buffet out away from the wall. "I was thinking . . ."

"Oh, oh," she said, lightening up the moment. We both knew by now the proverbial showdown was imminent and loomed on the near horizon.

Outside, the dull gray continued unchanged while the clock had spun through another twelve hours. Laura had left the TV on. Grabbing the remote, she clicked over to the news channel.

So far, I hadn't heard any reports of a prison escape, in fact, I hadn't heard anything at all. The local station was frozen in some idiotic commercial pose; babes in bikinis selling national brand name snow tires. It never ceases to amaze me what people will do for money.

"I was thinking," I said, smiling back at her, "that the person who made this piece of furniture would have used the very strongest part of the wood for the legs."

Chapter Fifty-Eight

"Probably," she agreed, not certain where I was going.

I walked around to the back of the buffet and closely inspected the cut line on the left rear leg. She had earlier pointed out it was the only flaw on the piece. I determined it didn't happen after the piece was built or while it was in transit from Ireland to here. It wasn't an accident, but a clean cut, made by a very sharp, very heavy instrument.

"The very strongest part of a tree is the heartwood, and this," I motioned for her to come around and feel the smoothness of the cut, "I believe was made by the axe of Bukwold."

"Where Bukwold struck the tree . . . ," she whispered feeling the cut.

We looked in wonder at each other, knowing we had somehow received this truth by a mystic revelation not to be questioned.

"Then this buffet is quite possibly . . . no, is . . . made from the very tree Bukwold buried his axe into, symbolized by the oak tree carved in the center of the backboard," declared Laura.

"And the axe to the right of it is a symbol of Bukwold's," I said.

"And the rose on the left . . . it's still a little hazy how the rose works as a part of the puzzle."

"I think it references the rosewood of the rosary, or the rosary itself," I offered.

Breathlessly we moved to the front of the ancient piece. We stood and gazed awestruck at the relief carvings on the backboard.

"Laura," I said, laying my hand on her shoulder and turning her toward me, "what is in the large drawer beneath the one that holds the rosary?"

"I . . . don't know, and as far as I do know, it's never been opened. No one has found the key, if one exists."

"Time to use the Gift," I told her.

"The Gift? Oh, my supposed ability to See, I don't know . . ." Inexperience gave her reason to doubt.

"Come on, try it, we've nothing to lose. Look at the backboard. The rose on the left symbolizes the rosary, St.

Patrick's rosary, in the buffet, the axe on the right symbolizes Bukwold's, and so, is there a connection between the two that we need to find and understand? Close your eyes and give it a try," I urged.

She closed her eyes and placed her fingertips as light as a feather's touch on the top of the buffet. Drawing in several deep breaths, she began swaying back and forth.

"Whither by the sea, where Bukwold struck the tree, there lays the hidden key," she repeated two more times, almost making it into a chant, and then ended with repeating, ". . . there lays the hidden key." She stopped moving and stood motionless, as if in a trance. She opened her eyes and then placed her right index finger under the loop of the rosary lying on the top of the buffet and dangled it in front of my face. "The hidden key," she declared with a Mona Lisa smile.

"What?" I asked. Without giving an answer she took the crucifix, inserted the crossed piece into the horizontal slot of the large drawer, twisted a quarter turn to the right, and something inside the drawer went click. Keeping a grasp on the longer piece of the crucifix, Laura pulled on it, opening the drawer about an inch as I stood breathless, watching the scene unfold. Hooking two fingers into the narrow gap, she pulled the drawer open to its full length. "And here it is," she said, as if expecting whatever was there to be there. Still breathless, I leaned over and peered into the drawer's interior. Lying there, silent and still, was an ancient battle-axe.

"Yes! It's Bukwold's! I have no doubt!" she exclaimed, "It must be ten centuries old."

"At least," I added, having a hard time believing my own eyes.

CHAPTER FIFTY-NINE

THE AIR BEHIND us sizzled and snapped. We whirled around in unison. There, in the middle of the room, stood Dethel.

"My master awaits your answer," he said without any fanfare or theatrics. He appeared as a harmless choirboy, dressed like the "Blue Boy" in the famous painting by Thomas Gainsborough, circa 1770.

We kept our guard up despite his harmless appearance.

Reaching behind me into the bottom middle drawer, I grabbed the axe by its handle, lifted it out, and then held it up in front of me. Dethel took a step back.

"The answer to what, I'm afraid I've forgotten the question," I said.

"When are you going to invite the master to speak face to face with you? He has infinite patience, and you will ask eventually. So what will it be, sooner rather than later I hope."

"Never," Laura bluntly replied.

Dethel glowed with a red aura. "What is that in your hand?" he asked me.

"An axe," I answered, figuring the less information the demon had, the better off we would be.

"Not just an axe," he replied, "but the axe of Bukwold the Slayer." We twitched in surprise at the quick confirmation of what we had believed to be true.

"I'll let you in on a secret," spoke the demon. "Take a close look at the edge of the axe head, both of you."

We examined the still sharp edge, and along the full length of it there appeared to be a line of rust, about a half an inch wide.

"It is not rust," said Dethel, "it is the blood of Lucretia of Whither by the Sea, the first queen of the Celts. It must remain on the blade. When Bukwold buried it in the oak tree, he pinned my master in its branches. The wood of that same tree is in this very room. Oh yes, the history of him and the both of you go way back, as I'm sure you are aware of by now."

We nodded our assent, remaining on our guard.

"This is the axe you will need to battle the Dark One," he said.

"We don't believe you," I replied.

"Indeed . . . and why should you? I am the master's little go-fer, am I not? But I have reached my limit of taking his malicious and humiliating treatment. I'm grossly under appreciated, you might say."

"Don't tell me you have feelings that can be hurt," I quipped with unmasked sarcasm. "Or have you suddenly gotten soft hearted?" I added.

"Do not underestimate me, Truman. If you do battle the Dark One, and, by some miracle vanquish him, I also will cease to exist, for I am nothing more than an extension of his persona. That being said, my only emotions are those of the dark, hate being the foremost, which of course leads to revenge and that is what I seek, that is what is driving me on. I would advise you not to turn me against you.

From here on out I will remain neutral. If my master calls me I will not hear, and as an obvious consequence, will not do his bidding."

"Thanks for small favors," I said, again letting my sarcasm run free. Then, I leapt forward and swung the axe at him. He vanished, but not before dropping the "Blue Boy" disguise. He flashed as the Angel with the snow-white hair, then the little girl with the golden curls, and then we saw his true self. I recoiled at the revelation that he was indeed Death and Hell, and whatever anyone had ever imagined them to be was there to be seen.

"It's all backwards!" he screeched, just before disappearing.

I turned to Laura, her jaw dropped open, her face gone pale.

"Why did you do that? Are you insane? Are you *trying* to get us killed?"

"I . . . I'm not sure what I was thinking, maybe it was impulse, but I'm not certain of that. It was like the axe had a mind of its own and wanted to slice into the demon. I just went along with it. Sounds incredible, doesn't it."

"Truman," she said laying her hand on my arm, "I'm sorry I panicked and yelled at you."

"It's alright, but you do believe me, don't you, about the axe having a mind of its own?"

"Of course I do. We have to believe anything and everything now. And we especially have to believe in ourselves and in each other."

"So, you don't think I'm crazy?"

CHAPTER FIFTY-NINE

"No, and even if you were, it wouldn't matter to me."

I held the battle-axe in my hand, wondering over its independent action as I turned, ready to return it to the drawer. With my left hand I felt along the bottom of the drawer, exploring the axe's original placement. I felt a substance that wasn't wood. I laid the axe on the computer table in order to investigate further. Reaching into the drawer again, I pulled out a sheet of leather. It wasn't chamois cloth soft, but far from saddle leather.

I took it over to the coffee table and set it down in front of Laura.

"What's this, something new?" she asked, her face a picture of inquisitiveness.

"Something old," I replied.

"Something borrowed?" she quipped.

"It could be, but certainly not something blue."

We laughed at our word play, relieving some of the tension.

Laura reached out and turned the sheet of leather over. On the upside, carved into the leather, were words in ancient Gaelic. All we had to do was decipher it.

"At least we know what the language is," she said.

"Looks like back to work we go," I said, standing up from the sofa with the leather sheet in my hand.

With a heavy sigh, Laura joined me, and being the superior typist, sat down at the computer keyboard. I placed the leather sheet face up on the table to her left for easy scanning. "Thank you," she said, as she hit "enter".

The screen didn't clear, but instead remained dark. She checked the machine. It had power and the on button glowed positive. She turned it off, waited a minute, and then turned it on again. This time the screen glowed but was fuzzy, snowy, like an old black and white television set that wasn't getting reception.

"It's never done this before. Maybe the Internet is down, or, maybe the Dark One . . ."

The possibilities were myriad. I looked down at the leather sheet, and could not believe my eyes! "Laura, look!" I said, pointing down at the piece of leather. The letters were swimming, forming themselves into words we could understand.

"Are you seeing what I'm seeing?" I asked.

"It's forming words," she said.

"Yes!" I exclaimed. Laura quickly scooped up two sheets of writing paper along with two pens.

Handing one of each to me she said, "Write down what you read and I'll do the same. We need to be sure we get the exact same message."

I started writing as the words clarified into the English language.

> *The Queen's blood with the heartwood mingled,*
> *stays the Slayer's hand.*
> *The branches from the root removed to a foreign*
> *land.*
> *From east to west seed is scattered in places far*
> *between.*
> *Until twice seven, less the one the Son shall meet*
> *the Daughter of the Queen.*
> *They twain shall gaze in fear upon what 'til then*
> *remains unseen.*
> *The ancient blade will be their need to slay the*
> *beast that cannot bleed.*
> *If to twice seven the beast survives*
> *Rell~Ik Ra~Il shall remain alive.*

I placed my paper next to Laura's. They were a perfect word for word match. We could only stare at the leather sheet and watch in awe as the words returned to their original form of ancient Gaelic.

"What do you think it means?" I asked.

"I think you know," she answered. "I think *we* know."

For the most part I guess we did.

No turning back.

CHAPTER SIXTY

LAURA WAS FIRST to break out of the semi-trance the prophetic poem had put us in. "Let's go over this line by line and see if we can decipher it," she said. I was more than ready to try, parts of it were like thick evening fog.

I read aloud the first line.

"*The Queen's blood with the heartwood mingled stays the Slayers hand.*"

"Seems self evident since the demon pointed out that Lucretia's blood remains on the axe blade," I said.

"Yes," she replied, "and legend verifies it, as does the cut on the buffet leg, which we thought must be carved from the heartwood of the oak tree, and that was also verified by Dethel. So, we're clear on the first line?"

"Right, your turn," I replied.

"*The branches from the root removed to a foreign land.*" she read.

"I think it speaks of two things; the wood itself being removed from the tree to the New World, and the moving of the generations from both villages to America, which was then a foreign land," she offered.

"Sounds right," I said, and then continued,

"From east to west seed is scattered in places far between."

I looked quizzically at her, not sure how to interpret that line. She jumped right on it. "From east, Ireland, to west, Montana, seed, meaning generations, has been scattered from there to here. And the buffet itself first landed in Boston, then Chicago, then Minneapolis, then Billings, and finally, here."

"Makes perfect sense, in fact, the only sense," I said, causing her to smile, the kind that lights up a room.

"Until twice seven less the one the Son shall meet the Daughter of the Queen," she read.

"My God, Laura, that has to be us, you and me! We've already established that I'm the thirteenth from Bukwold.

"Until twice seven, less the one equals fourteen minus one

". . . which equals thirteen, and I'm the thirteenth from Lucretia," Laura finished. "And we are, in ancient terminology and thinking, the sons and daughters of our ancestors."

"I don't see how it could possibly mean anything else," I said.

"So this is the Prophecy and we're caught right in the middle of it," I concluded. I looked at Laura, she didn't say so, but I could tell she understood that to be true.

"This is where it begins getting murky," I said, reading the next line.

"They twain shall gaze in fear upon what 'til then remains unseen."

"I think it means that we will look upon the face of the Dark One and it will be fearsome," I said.

"So we will ask to see its face, as it has requested all along," said Laura.

"That seems to be the game plan," I said, adding a heavy sigh. Laura covered my hand with her own velvety touch.

"I'm so sorry I brought you into this," I said, turning to look in her understanding and beautiful violet eyes.

"You didn't," she flatly stated.

"I did."

"What are we reading here?" she asked, then answering her own question said, "A prophecy, a century's old prophecy and we're together because it's . . . destined to be. How or by whom I have no idea. But I do know, beyond any doubt, that we are here and together we are to call out and confront the Dark One."

I had no argument with that.

"Let's go on. My turn to read," she said and began,

"The ancient blade will be their need to slay the beast that cannot bleed."

"This one is a puzzler," she said after reading the line.

"It is and it isn't," I replied, "because it can only mean Bukwold's axe." I paused while she nodded her agreement. "But, to slay the beast that cannot bleed, that's the puzzler. We both know the beast is the Dark One, but how can we defeat it with an axe if it cannot bleed?"

"Which means it has no flesh or blood," Laura concluded.

"Yes, it all fits into the context of the Prophecy to this point, except for the last part. But why the blade, if the thing cannot bleed?" I mused.

"Good question, Truman. We'll just have to trust it for what it says, she paused. Wait a minute, what was it the demon said about the axe?" she asked.

"That it had pinned the tail of the Dark One to the oak tree. How? Don't know, but it gives a clue that the axe affects him, don't you think?"

"Yes, of course that's it," she answered.

"An act of faith, then," I said. "I hate this hero crap. Why don't we just forget the whole thing and leave the sonofabitch trapped where he is?"

Laura gave me an "Oh please," look. "The next line explains why we can't. Go ahead, read it," she said.

"If to twice seven the beast survives

Rell~Ik Ra~Il shall remain alive," I have no idea what that means," I said and shrugged.

"Nor do I," she said and shrugged.

"Up above, to twice seven less the one, we figured out to be thirteen," I muttered.

"And so, to twice seven must translate to fourteen," added Laura.

"You and I are the thirteenth from the King and Queen, if he survives to twice seven-fourteen, the fourteenth generation, then he lives", I paused, "forever. My God, if it means what I think it means, you and I are the last hope of saving this world. A world, by the way, I don't think is worth saving," I added.

"Maybe we're just buying it a little more time, a period of grace, or something. Either way, we really have no choice," she said.

Click . . . buzz . . . whir . . . the fact embedded itself in my brain and locked there, and no one, not even I, would be able to remove it.

I'm exhausted," I remarked to Laura. She glanced up at the clock. "No wonder," she said, "we've been up almost twenty-four hours. I'm weary myself," she said and then continued,

"Apparently the Dark One isn't going to let us go. He's going to suspend time until we return. And—I'm just guessing—if he wanted us out of the way he'd let it be known that you are not at the cannery."

"Then he must not know the words, or maybe the entire meaning, of the Prophecy. Otherwise, he could simply out wait us, and when we were dead, all threat to his existence would be over," I said.

"But then he'd be trapped forever in the mountains."

"And he's hungry because he feeds on souls," I said.

"With fear for the appetizer, so perhaps he's starving, but can exist, just barely, on what the ravens bring him, but his hunger is growing and driving him, and he's getting desperate, I'm guessing."

"Who is like the beast, and who is able to make war against him?" I muttered to myself.

"What was that?" she asked.

"Just something I remember reading in Gideon's book." *Who is like the beast and who is able to make war against him,"* it says. I guess we are able to, as strange and unbelievable as that may sound," I said to her. Her eyes, taking on an even deeper violet hue, widened. "Truman, I'm scared," she confessed.

"I am too, and bone weary on top of that. We should probably get some rest before we go back to the ... slaughterhouse."

"That sounds so ominous."

I sighed and dropped my head. No way out, I knew it and she knew it. I gulped, nearly swallowing my Adam's apple in the process. "Got an extra pillow and blanket? I'll crash here on the couch."

Laura placed her hand on my arm, looked in my eyes with a sincerity born of Eden, and said, "I don't want to be alone."

We rose up from the couch. She took my hand and led me into a part of her home I thought I'd never see, and a part of her heart I thought I'd never know.

We were in no hurry. All we wanted for the moment was to hang on to what we knew, to remember anything that once was normal, to hold each other through the night, and let our souls become knitted together. I had found my heart's desire. I wasn't sure how she felt. I think her main need was for comfort and closeness. But at least for a brief moment my heart was full with what was right and real.

She stirred next to me. I watched her, in the dim light, as her eyes opened, filled with the look of love.

"Thank you," she whispered.

"You're welcome."

"No, not just for sleeping with me and holding me, but for being you and *feeling* me, my soul, you know what I mean." I nodded. "And guess what else?" she continued, "This could be, and probably will be, the greatest adventure of our lives, and we're going through it together, and so, thank you."

"I never thought of it that way." I kissed her softly and we drifted off to the sweetness of deep sleep once again.

When we awoke, the grayness of the never-ending day had darkened, and the drizzle ran in slow silver streams down the window glass. I felt miraculously refreshed, and was in a place, spiritual maybe, but certainly one of extreme comfort and contentment, one that I never wanted to leave.

"We have no choice," Laura whispered, as if she could read my mind. Well, she did possess the Gift of See.

Neither of us was hungry, we had coffee and then, taking Bukwold's axe and St. Patrick's rosary, headed for the door, the axe in my hand, the rosary in Laura's.

She stopped in the drizzle to turn and take a long look, possibly the last one, at her home. What was it about courage? Face what you don't want to, what you fear, and do the best you can. She was a very courageous person, but at the moment, it didn't diminish the sadness that had settled on her. I slipped my arm around her waist. She smiled up at me with no fear in her eyes.

"Wait a minute," she said. "I think the computer came back on, and the screen cleared. I want to check on something."

"Want me to come with you?" I asked. She nodded yes.

Moving to the table, she typed into the search box the name Rell~Ik Ra~Il.

Nothing returned.

Sighing, she logged out and then turned the machine off. Without another word, we went outside, got in her car, and headed down the muddied gravel road to the slaughterhouse, to our destiny or to our fate, depending on the outcome.

THE OMEGA SLAYER

CHAPTER SIXTY-ONE

THE SILENCE WAS deafening as we rode through the drizzle, the slow beat of the wipers moving rivulets of water from off the glass. I kept my gaze out the side window rather than look through the spider web fracture on the windshield.

On the back seat lay the axe and the rosary. Strange weapons to go up against who knew what, except what the Prophecy had revealed, we hoped that was enough.

"The beast that cannot bleed," that phrase scared me . . . a lot. My mind twisted around itself as we drove along, and I was unable to concentrate. Concentrate? On what? Only the utter absurdity coupled with the stark reality of our situation, along with the myriad of possibilities it presented, all frightening.

"What are you thinking?" asked Laura, right on cue.

"I'm not. My mind won't quit swirling around in this vortex of madness we've been drawn into. I don't have the foggiest notion of a plan, or of who or what we are facing, or how to fight him, or it, or them. I just don't know, and to tell you the truth, it scares the hell out of me."

"Oh no, my knight has rust on his shiny armor, whatever shall I do," she quipped, causing me to chuckle. "I'm scared too," she said, taking her eyes off the road long enough to flash me a smile.

We pulled up to the slaughterhouse door. She shut off the engine, removed the keys, and stuffed them into her jeans pocket. I reached in the back seat, grabbed the rosary, handed it to her, and then grasped the axe by its handle, keeping it for myself.

Laura was waiting for me at the door. Grim faced, we entered the building.

It was dead still inside, the kind that precedes a predator before it deals the deathblow on its prey. While crossing the lunch room, I moved ahead of her and peered down the shadowy stairwell, seeing nothing, we began our slow descent.

"Can you hear my heart thumping against my rib cage?" I turned and asked her halfway down the stairs.

"There's no way I could hear it above the pounding of my own," she replied.

I turned to continue our descent, but before I could take a step, Laura grabbed hold of my arm, stopping me. "Look at me," she said. She was standing two stairs up. A soft white light pulsated all around her. Her eyes were brilliantly violet and aglow from an intense inner light.

Now what, I thought, and braced myself, thinking the Dark One had gotten to her.

"I am L'Aura," she said. Her words sounded like silver chimes ringing over running water, "The thirteenth from Lucretia, Queen of the Celts. You are Truman, the thirteenth from Bukwold the Alpha Slayer, and you are the Omega Slayer and your knowledge is your weapon, the ancient blade the instrument of your mind."

She changed back to her more familiar appearance, and shined a smile at me. "You forgot, I have the Gift," she said. Not being able to find my voice, I just nodded my head up and down.

She hooked the loop of the rosary around her right wrist, tightened it, and then, holding the excess length in her right hand, let the crucifix dangle free in plain sight.

I knew how to handle an axe, having been a logger in Oregon in my youth, but as an instrument of my mind? It made sense in a sort of Zen martial arts way, but I didn't think that was what Laura had meant.

My mind raced. The beast couldn't bleed. My mind was the weapon, the axe the instrument to employ it? Too damn late to develop any kind of plan, I thought, as we descended the final seven stairs. We paused on the bottom landing, just outside the open doorway to the basement.

In the tunnel, the Dark One moved about restlessly. His moment had come, the time of his freeing, the time of beginning the feast. Without a sound, he summoned his darklings.

We stepped through the open doorway only to be met by a hoard of the malicious imps coming at us through the far concrete wall, fangs bared and blood lust blazing in their eyes.

I raised the axe over my head, ready to swing, for all the good it might do. Beside me, from out of the corner of my eye, I saw Laura become L'Aura, the bright glow emanating out from her. I lowered the axe and stared in awe at the celestial sight.

She raised St. Patrick's rosary up and held it out at arm's length, her hand as steady as the bedrock in the mountains.

"Here and no further," she said with a voice neither loud nor shrill, but quiet and commanding.

The imps halted in mid-air and congealed into the dapper and dashing Prince Charming version of Dethel. Smiling like he was my best friend, he picked up a large bolt from off a dusty workbench in the corner, and hurled it at me, its velocity equal to a major league fastball.

I put the axe up for defense, one side of it facing Dethel, the other side about a foot from my face. The bolt hit the broad side of the axe head with a loud clang . . . and stuck.

Lowering the axe to waist level, I looked around, trying to locate the demon, but he had disappeared.

L'Aura still glowed, but not as bright as she had earlier when first confronted by the chattering, sharp toothed imps.

Turning to me she asked, "Are they holograms, projections of the Dark One's mind?"

"They are my children, and I give them the power to lie and to confuse and to kill," the Dark One spoke through the wall.

"Who are you . . . really? Are you afraid for us to know?" I asked.

"If you look upon my face, you will know. But you must ask to see, and you will ask. You know as well as I that it is destined to be."

"Yours is the very face of evil. Why would we want to look upon it?" asked Laura, as I pried the half-inch diameter bolt from the side of the axe head.

"What is evil, except that which already lies dormant in the heart of humanity, waiting to be awakened?" said the Dark One. "Arise from thy sleep, I call, and it answers to me. I only direct the slumbering evil into hate, greed, lust, the so-called seven deadly sins, which are taken lightly, but are oh so real.

I establish false gods that do not fail to let the worshipers down, hard, and the joy I get watching them crash is unimaginable. And then, personally and nationally, comes the fear, my sustenance. And all I do is awaken what exists, am I therefore evil? Come now, my king and queen, surely you can see that is not the case.

Good? A simple case of wishful thinking. God? A fabricated ideal, fashioned more to control than to comfort. Look around you! You can see, you know all I say is true. There is no stopping me, for there is no stopping the inevitable. Don't be foolish. Join with me!

World leaders? Mere puppets of mine. Wealth and power? Illusions of mine. Oh, what a sweet tangle of confusion! And oh, the tasty treats I receive when the frustrations I create break out into bloodshed! Bloodshed on any scale, from the Holy Wars—an oxymoron of which I am particularly proud—two World Wars, and on down to the self pitying serial killers."

"Like Ichabod Cane?" I asked.

"Yes, Ichabod, a minor player in the scheme of things, a fool in the end, but he did create many a delicious morsel of fear for me."

"What did finally happen to him?" I asked.

"Why, I simply absorbed him, that is all," replied the Dark One. "Do you not understand yet Truman? All things either do or will serve me, and you and Laura can be a part of the inevitable, a king and queen at my side. Consider it well, for it is an offer I have made to no one before."

"Why us and why now?" asked Laura, her glow beginning to increase.

"I have waited very long for people who have, shall I say, your special qualities, a power you share and that increases when you are together. A power you are not even aware of, and to have flesh and blood allies of such magnitude as yourselves on my side will help to expedite and smooth out my plans."

"You would have us become agents of evil then, like Judas?" I remarked.

He hissed an audible sigh.

"Ah, Judas, so many think he was the ultimate manifestation of evil, the very son of Lucifer. But he was only a heartless, petty thief who, like billions of others since, will commit any act for a few pieces of silver. Imagine what it is I am offering you!"

"Aren't you Lucifer?" asked Laura.

Again the Dark One hissed.

"Didn't you have Jesus, the Christ, crucified?" she continued.

The Dark One hissed louder.

"The Lucifer of your bible? Not hardly. And Jesus, who claimed to be the Christ, who really crucified him? Was it not the religious establishment of his time because he threatened their structure of power, their control? It was that fear that crucified him. But you do not fear me, do you, my little King and Queen?"

"No," we replied in unison, and it wasn't false bravado. He would have known that in an instant. In my gut I knew I held no fear, I was confident Laura didn't either.

"It is good you do not fear me, but you should. My business has and always will be, not so much involved in sweeping world events, no, they are a natural consequence of my real work, which is to wound tender souls as soon as I can, and to wound them so deeply, so completely, that not only do they not understand the cruelty of it, but they never heal, never heal, do you hear me? But they plod on, even though they would prefer death to life. Oh no, it isn't noble suffering, but cowardice, that keeps them going. And as they plod on, I create in each one the Empty, that place in every one where once was something cherished, but now there are only bitter thorns and the feeble hope that what they once knew, they may know again, and what once had filled the Empty, would one day fill it again, a false hope of course."

My stomach lurched. I knew the Dark One wasn't joking. And I saw how stopping him would give humanity a chance at redemption.

"I don't think you yet realize what it is I'm offering you, a chance to rise above and be beyond all of the normal hum drum suffering of man-unkind." He laughed maniacally, like the organ pipes played by the Phantom of the Opera.

It pealed like thunder, reverberating off the concrete walls, and then subsided, but ethereal music continued playing. "The piper pipes, and the children follow. Haven't you noticed generation after generation dancing to whatever tune is being played, until they dance into a life of helplessness and hopelessness?"

The power of the Dark One was becoming clearer as he revealed more of his sinister nature to us. Again his laughter pealed. His music began to mesmerize us.

"I am offering you two what men and women for century after century have longed for, have slain millions for in an attempt to obtain a very long life, wealth unimaginable, and power unquestionable.

ASK—TO—SEE—MY—FACE!"

CHAPTER SIXTY-TWO

LAURA BROKE AWAY from the mesmerizing affects of the Dark One. "And what is it to look upon your face?" she asked him. "Will it bring paralyzing horror at your ugliness, terror at your viciousness, or fear of such magnitude it will stop our hearts and deliver our souls up to you?"

"I cannot say. My face is all of the above and none of the above. In my face you will see the culmination of all fear, all hate, all rage, all confusion, all false beliefs, all false hopes, and all the tormenting nightmares and shattered dreams of humanity since the beginning of time."

Laura squeezed my hand hard, looked in my eyes and without speaking a word, said it was time and she was ready.

I laid the axe on the landing. *"They twain shall gaze in fear upon what 'til then remains unseen."*

"Are you sure?" I asked her. Her glow increased, she nodded.

Releasing her hand, but keeping her gaze, I backed through the open doorway to the stairway bottom stair. She gave me a puzzled look, I gave her a wink that said, "I know what I'm doing, trust me." Returning to her, I grasped her hand and both of us exhaled a deep breath, taking a long time to do so.

"Ready?" I asked her.

"Yes, this is it, the moment of truth. Wait!" she said, and standing on her tiptoes, kissed me lightly on the mouth. "I love you," she whispered.

Her words stunned me. I blinked three or four times before they hit home. "I love you," I whispered in return, and then we kissed, real lovers, right there in the face of the Dark One, in the face of our own demise, and in the face of the end of the world.

"Wanna do it?" I asked her.

"Yes," she replied in that husky voice women get at special moments, and then she grinned at me, she was so lovely. I let loose of her hand. We turned toward the front wall of my room and the concrete wall behind it. "Dark One! Let us see your face!" I hollered in as loud and as brave a voice as I could muster.

We should have expected the unexpected.

The concrete wall didn't explode outward to rain crushing chunks of it down on us. We heard no roaring like a ravenous beast hungry to rend and tear hot flesh. The only indication that the Dark One had heard our invitation was the seepage of light from under the door of my room. It came to a stop about fifteen feet in front of us, shaping itself into a lightning bolt stilled by a photograph. Then it shattered into a million tiny sparks twinkling and drifting like stardust, it was beautiful, there was no denying it. The scattered particles began to mold themselves into an oblong shape with the long axis vertical. As the features became more and more clear, the deeper the horror of what we faced penetrated my soul. I gasped for breath at what I beheld. For what I saw was . . . the mirror image of me!

"No! It can't be!" I whispered. I felt Laura grab my arm through the swirling mist of confusion that held me in its grip.

"It is so, Truman Struck," replied the Dark One. "Why are you surprised to find yourself in me? What makes you different from any other? Nothing. You are Truman, I am Everyman. The fear in you is part of me, as was the fullness of the hate in Hitler," he said and then sizzled into the image of Der Fuhrer with Sieg Heil being shouted by thousands of voices in the background. Then he was me again.

"I am the face of hope," he said, and morphed into George Washington "and the depth of hope lost," and became John F. Kennedy.

From there the Dark One became a pure white angelic being having long black hair, hollow eyes, and a gaping, fanged mouth. Covered in a tattered shroud, and with the shriek of a thousand demons, she launched herself at Laura. By instinct, Laura raised the crucifix, the sight of it stopping the beast woman in mid air. She hissed while blood dripped from her elongated canines.

"I am the stuff nightmares are made of, my dear," said the Vam~Pyre as she settled into the perfect image of Laura, the image smiling beautifully at her. "And I am also Everywoman."

Laura was trembling beside me.

"You see, it is as I said, I am merely a reflection of what is in the heart of all people, the image of the beast!"

He threw back his head and howled with laughter that reverberated off the walls under the slaughterhouse. We covered our ears with our hands.

"Stop! Stop it!" I bellowed above the cacophony as Laura shut her eyes tight.

Like a shock, there was sudden silence.

I uncovered my ears and Laura opened her eyes.

Standing in front of us was a young man with long hair, a beard, and a beautiful serene countenance. A crown of thorns had been crushed into his head. Droplets of blood trickled down his face from where the thorns pierced his skin.

"Blasphemy!" I cried.

The Dark One in his disguise smiled at me.

"Blasphemy because I take on an image you have created to atone for your evil, blasphemy because you have created an image of God, which your own bible forbids you to do? Do I blaspheme because I have caused much suffering and bloodshed in the name of your God, His followers more than willing servants of mine? Well then, how about this?" and in a sizzle of fire and vapor of smoke he disappeared and then reappeared as a serpentine creature with horns on its head, a forked tongue, a spiked tail, and the vertical reptilian eyes of the dragon.

"How about now?" he asked. "Do I blaspheme now, or do you? For now you think me evil, do you not, because of my appearance, and, oh yes Truman, you could easily justify killing me, could you not?"

I silently admitted to myself that I could.

"Images of your own heart and mind Truman and of all the hearts of man-unkind, who conveniently put God in a box and at the same time allow evil to run rampant, without any boundaries or chains upon it.

Blasphemy? Surely you see the foolishness of it all. So, come, join me. You and Laura will be a King and a Queen ruling over your own Kingdom."

"You are not Satan or Lucifer then?" asked Laura. The Dark One sighed, weary of the question.

"No my dear, I am simply the total of all fears and all hate and all murders, of all things done by reason of greed. Am I to be blamed then? Don't you think I deserve some sympathy? Join me."

"Where then *IS* God?" she asked.

"I cannot tell you. Perhaps I am, perhaps you are, perhaps *WE* together are, or perhaps God is all people."

"Pretty slick answer, Rell~Ik Ra~Il," I interjected.

He hissed and froze. He lost his composure. His countenance turned ghostly and he morphed into the shape of a man with jet-black hair flying back from his head, blown by an unfelt wind. His eyes became hollow black sockets, his clothing and cape turned to glistening shiny black silk, like the skin of a serpent. His eye sockets blazed blood red as the air surrounding him snapped and crackled. Blue sparks, like small stars, shot out from around his skull, spinning themselves into a mock halo.

"You have read the Prophecy!" he bellowed, as sparks flew from his bony fingertips. "Where is it?" he hissed, the face of his rage instilling cold fear in us, the force of it driving us backwards one step at a time, the wind of it driving Laura's hair straight back from her head.

She held St. Patrick's rosary up against the onslaught. It burst into flames. We moved into the open doorway.

"Where is it?" repeated the Dark One, as he, from a small distance away, moved along with us.

"Yes, where is it, Truman?" asked the sweet faced, white haired angel.

"Where, oh please tell me where," begged the little girl, her innocent eyes pleading with me, her blond curly hair hanging to her shoulders.

"I cannot tell," I replied as Laura placed Bukwold's axe into my hand. I held it diagonally across my chest.

The innocent little girl hissed and changed into a huge serpent coiled against the far wall with its hood, like that of a king cobra, spread out. Its face was like someone's who had once been dead and whose waxen features were now chiseled into concrete hardness. Its eyes, as cold as ice and as hard as steel, were first hollow and black, and then raging and filled with fire. A contrast of cold, unfeeling, directed evil, and rampant, murderous, blood lusting fury.

I shuddered, Laura trembled as we gazed in fear upon what til now had remained unseen.

"Rell~Ik Ra~Il," I said again, causing the creature to emit a thunderous roar.

"Your mind is your weapon," Laura reminded me. Then she flung the remains of the rosary at the coiled beast, and when it struck its essence, the sacred remains burned it, again the monster roared, not in pain, for it could neither feel nor bleed, but in fury at the insult of being touched by something sacred.

"The ancient blade will be their need to slay the beast that cannot bleed."

I raised the axe higher but the beast did not move. Instead, it coiled itself tighter against the wall, poised to strike. He showed no fear of the ancient blade, so what was I to do now? My mind raced at miles in milliseconds as I took another step closer.

"You fools," he spoke, "you could have had everything. Now you will simply add to my power, for I shall eat your pitiable souls. But before I do, shall I call a thousand ravens to come and tear your flesh? Shall I summon a thousand Dethels to make you dance as they torture you until you beg for the mercy of death? Do you like rats?"

I felt Laura cringe.

"How about angels?" he asked and a dozen of the beautiful beings appeared floating in the air around the coiled beast, and they looked as we picture them in our minds, except they had fingernails like silver knife blades, ready to slice our throats open as they gazed lovingly into our eyes.

"But none of these!" he roared as the apparitions departed into the nothingness from which they had come.

CHAPTER SIXTY-THREE

THIS ... THING HAD controlled the minds of millions, had set up kingdoms and nations for his ravaging, and my mind was my weapon? Come on, an ancient blade against Rell~Ik Ra~Il, what the hell.

"Would you and Laura like to look into the heart of evil, as you call it, before I rip your flesh in ribbons from off your bones and then shred your miserable souls? I am free now, and I want to show my appreciation by showing you your future." He raised a taloned hand, and using what looked like a thumb with a long blade for a nail, slit open his chest with a single vertical stroke exposing a panoramic view of the earth as it spun in its orbit. After several of its daily revolutions a darkening mist obscured it. Dark clouds of cosmic magnitude swirled around it, becoming first a vortex and then a completed black hole.

The world disappeared altogether.

Suddenly, from out of the mist, a child's face appeared where the world once was. Whether it was that of a girl or a boy I could not tell. But it was the face of all children, innocent, with beautiful blue and brown eyes and every color in between, aglow, like those of children who awaken on Christmas morning to wishes fulfilled and the dreams of magic realized. Then the child faded, sucked into the black hole that had quickly become its reality, and that reality was . . . aloneness. And at once, hundreds of thousands of agonized faces that had held innocence swirled in the mist, caught in a vortex from which there was no escape.

I lowered the axe as I stared into that void, feeling myself drawn closer to oblivion, Laura moving, as in a fog, with me toward the Dark One and the heart of evil contained within him.

What caused it to beat?

I would have expected gruesome pictures of bloody and dismembered bodies because of countless wars. Or I wouldn't have been surprised to see hundreds of thousands of slaves made from conquered peoples, people who were merely the pawns of some political system, whether a kingdom, or a dictatorship, or a democracy. All were only smoke screens made to cover up the only political system in the world, the plutocracy.

The whips are the same, the severity of their sting is the only difference.

So what did cause the Dark One's heart of evil to beat?

"Join me," he said. "To be consumed in me is inevitable.

I still offer you the choice to rule and reign with me for a millennium."

We continued toward him drawn to the void that was his being. And I realized that was it. The Empty is what kept his heart beating. His work there was his reason for existence.

"Who . . . who are you, really?" I asked in feeble resistance as Laura continued in silence beside me.

"I have told you who I am, and you have guessed my name. And what you behold in me is nothing more than the slaughter of innocence by the sword of abandonment. Is it not so? You know it as well as I, abandonment by parents, or brothers, or sisters; by priests and mentors and teachers, and by lovers. The abandonment by humanity of itself, and humanity's most hopeful illusion, God, until there is nothing but aloneness striking out against the abandonment in the form of hate, or purposelessness, or depression, or the disease of rampant raging greed, as if the acquisition of wealth could protect them from harm or insulate their hearts from pain. But in the end, all belong to me!"

"I know your name," said Laura, who I thought by now had been mesmerized. "It is, I Live, Rell~Ik Ra~Il."

The Dark One mocked us with laughter. "Close enough my little King and Queen," he remarked, his look or position unchanged.

"Then how about Evil I, Liar Killer?" she asked. "That is your true name and true nature . . . is it not?" she said.

The Dark One hissed violently, and then his chest closed up.

I took a step closer, raising high the ancient axe.

"You!" he exclaimed, raising a taloned finger and pointing its gnarled ugliness at me, his serpentine eyes having gone sickly yellow.

I felt strong and more powerful than at any other time in my life. My heart swelled, filled with the courage of a lion. The muscles in my forearms looked like the knotted ropes of a sailing ship. My hair had become blond and long and it swirled as I whipped my head around looking for Laura and she was there. Her hair wasn't copper colored, but flaming red and long down to her waist. Her eyes were deep violet and blazed with furious intent.

Turning back to the Dark One, my intention was to destroy him, and it was focused with razor sharpness.

"You!" exclaimed the Dark One again. "Bukwold!"

The axe possessed a mind of its own and moved in for the kill. "Liar-Killer!" I hollered, ready to swing the blade at the Ancient Enemy, but before I could, he exploded into a cloud of sparks hovering in front of me.

And then I understood how the Dark One had been pinned inside the grand old oak. The axe head held just enough of him to keep him there, but the wood acted as an insulator, preventing the total absorption of the Liar-Killer.

Instead of holding the axe as if to strike with its sharp edge, I held it broadside to the swirling mass of sparks. The axe drew me closer to the beast.

"Here and no further!" I bellowed, echoing Bukwold's words when he buried his axe into the tree. He must have known the Liar-Killer was there, and although he could not stop him, he at least slowed him down for a long while.

My intention was to stop him with absolute finality.

"Here and no further!" I hollered again holding the axe by the end of its handle high and with the head broadside to the King of Emptiness.

The Dark One shrieked from a mouth and throat that I could not see while his essence, the cloud of shimmering sparks, got sucked into the ancient blade, the Liar-Killer shrieking in rage reverberating in the concrete tomb of the basement walls. He understood his fate.

The silence was sudden. The storm was over. The air smelled of burnt ozone and electricity. I looked across the room, Laura had become L'Aura and she was beaming at me.

"You figured it out, didn't you," she stated rather than asked.

"Yes, but how did you know?"

"I didn't *know* a thing. I simply followed the Gift and had faith in who you are," she answered.

Chapter Sixty-Four

WE THOUGHT IT best to leave the cannery.

I laid the axe on the back seat of her car and we were halfway to Anaconda before she spoke. "Now what?" she asked, her voice so low I could barely hear it above the ka-chunk of the windshield wipers.

"I don't know," I answered. "Right now I don't know what day it is, or if time has stayed still or started again or reversed itself or spun on ahead," I said, confessing my total loss of the sense of time and place.

"Of course, first things first, we need to get to my house and sort out what we can," she said. I nodded, weariness catching up to me. Laura probably felt the same. But so far her intuitions had been right on, and we didn't know what the Liar-Killer could do. Though trapped, it didn't mean his influence was inoperable.

Ka-chunk, ka-chunk. Tick-tock, tick-tock.

I brought the axe with me into her house and laid it on the coffee table in the living room while she returned the charred rosary to its place in the buffet drawer. I followed her lead, rose off the couch with axe in hand, and headed for the buffet to return it to the bottom drawer. It seemed the Dark One was aware of his surroundings, the axe head taking on a rusty, not quite red, glow. But it didn't generate heat. Apparently, he didn't like the idea of being, once again, within the wood of the old oak tree. I put him there anyway.

"Home sweet home," I said as I placed the axe in the drawer. It vibrated at that one. I closed the drawer but didn't lock it.

Laura brought in some chamomile tea and, after setting it down on the coffee table, invited me to join her on the sofa.

The tea was soothing, but not as much as her company was. I felt like I'd been run through a meat grinder and needed all the comfort I could get.

I reached over and touched her arm. "You okay?" I asked. "Yeah … well … no, but I'll be fine after I get some rest and am able to relax. I feel like I've been run through a meat grinder and somehow survived."

"Me too," I said. Now we were starting to think alike, and I wasn't sure what the cause or what the result of that could be, but it had to be good. I did know we needed to sort some things out before we could make any further plans.

"How *did* you know?" I asked for starters.

"The Dark One's real name?"

"Yes."

"It was Dethel," she said.

"How? When?" I asked.

"Remember when he was last here?" I nodded. "Just before he disappeared, the last words he spoke were, "It's all backwards!" I thought he meant … I don't know what … the world maybe, or the Dark One, I wasn't sure. But then I remembered the name in the Prophecy."

"Rell~Ik Ra~Il," I said.

"Well, Rell~Ik Ra~Il, spelled and spoken backwards is Liar-Killer. He had also referred to himself as, I Live. So I took the chance on that being backward too and said, Evil I Liar Killer and it helped break him down, you see?"

I nodded. Brilliant she was, or perhaps gifted, probably both.

"Your turn," she said, looking at me with through beautiful, though exhausted, blue eyes.

"Again Dethel provided a clue. When he threw that half inch bolt at my head, I put up the axe for defense and the bolt stuck to the axe head."

"I remember," she said, taking a sip of her tea.

"That could only mean that the axe head had some how become a powerful magnet, and it took all my strength to pry the bolt loose. So anyway, I figured that was how Bukwold had pinned the Liar-Killer in the tree. The only question was, why hadn't he been sucked into the axe head then? There was too much insulation around him," I said, answering my own question.

"Insulation?" she asked.

"Yes, the wood itself, which means the Liar-Killer is made up of electrons, negative I'm sure."

"Of course," Laura smiled.

"The other clue was that he moved rather easily through these mountains. And what is Montana called . . . the Treasure State . . . and on its flag is the slogan, "Oro y Plata" which means . . ."

"Gold and silver," she finished.

"That tied in perfectly because the three major conductors of electricity, in order of efficiency, are gold, then silver, and finally copper, perfect vehicles for him. Veins of these metals must run like rivers deep in these mountains.

The final piece was when you broke him down by speaking his true name, "Evil I Liar Killer . . ."

". . . and he became those brilliant sparks in the air," she said.

"Yes . . . but I noticed one other thing, a slight mist intermingled with the electrons . . . which meant his true essence is plasma."

"Plasma, you mean blood?" she asked.

"No, this kind of plasma is a gaseous substance that also conducts electricity and the electricity intermingles with it. It's the stuff inside of fluorescent light bulbs.

This substance, the charged particles and the rest of it, can be contained in magnetic fields that are known as magnetic bottles."

"The axe head," she said.

"Uh-huh. I can explain how it works, in detail, if you'd like."

"None needed, I already know they work and that's all I need to know."

"Yes . . . and so, as you pointed out, my mind turned out to be my weapon as all these clues cascaded and came together in a single instant."

She turned to me and smiled. There was a hint of the mysterious violet color in her eyes. "I can't believe it's over," she sighed, leaning back against the softness of the sofa. I joined her by leaning back against the softness of the sofa at my back and the softness of her at my side.

I didn't have the heart, right then, to tell her what else needed doing.

Chapter Sixty-Five

Startled by something unknown, perhaps a dream, I awoke. Disoriented, I scanned my surroundings. Laura was asleep against my side. The house was quiet, too quiet it seemed. Not wanting to wake her, I sat still in the silence.

A short while later she awoke.

"We're at your place and safe," I reassured her. She nuzzled up against me.

"What day do you think it is?" I asked.

"I have no idea. Maybe the TV is working and we can find out." With that said, she grabbed the remote off the table and clicked it on. It was working. She surfed over to the weather channel. It was Saturday. She turned it off. "Now what?" she asked.

"I'm not sure."

"We can't assume you can stay here, you're likely to be discovered missing soon, and if you're found here, I'll be charged with aiding and abetting and harboring. I really don't want to deal with that. In fact, a little normal, hum-drum life right now would be welcome." I couldn't begrudge her for wanting that.

She gave me a very slight smile. It was hard, facing the "now what," never thinking we'd get to it in the first place.

The only thing I knew for sure was that I couldn't leave the axe of Bukwold anywhere but in my own safekeeping.

Outside the window, the gray broke apart to reveal that the sky was still blue.

"I understand," I answered, "and I've thought about my next step."

The surprised look on her face told me she didn't miss the fact that she had been omitted from my statement, but I think she felt a sense of relief.

"I have to leave and take the axe with me. I would never feel at ease if it was left anywhere but in my own hands."

"Are you going to take it with you back to the cannery?"

"No, I can't. It would just be a matter of time before it was discovered, or the Dark One figured out a way to escape, or the axe head could somehow become demagnetized."

"Then what *are* you going to do?"

"I'm going into the Bob Marshall wilderness, from there I'll work my way north into Canada."

"To escape the authorities?" Laura felt the first twinge of ache in her heart as she realized what was about to happen . . . her final separation from Truman.

"No, not at all, I'll go into Canada, out of the wilderness, and then work my way east toward Hudson's Bay."

"Why there?"

"That's where the true magnetic north pole is located. There, all the lines of magnetic force culminate and run through the center of the globe and then back again in a never-ending cycle. And so, that's where a magnetic field would never fail as long as the earth survives. And that would guarantee that the Liar-Killer would remain trapped within the axe head."

"The perpetual magnetic bottle," she said. "Truman, you might not make it. It could end up costing you your life."

"It could, but then so could have facing the Dark One, and your life too, by the way. I really have no choice. It's part of the deal, and I have to trust in it. That's all I can do."

Laura nodded as the ache in her heart increased. "Yes," she whispered, "I can see that now." With that she stood up and went to the back of the house. In a few minutes she returned, holding out a metal object dangling from a short chain. "Here's the key to the gun cabinet in the basement. Take what you think you'll need. I'll rummage some warm clothes for you."

Taking the key, I went down into the basement, Laura disappeared somewhere in the back of the house. Opening the gun cabinet, I removed a high-powered rifle with a scope, a forty-four magnum long barrel Smith & Wesson pistol, and, from out of the bottom drawer, a full size Bowie knife with a twelve-inch blade and a brass-crossing bar between the blade and the handle. I grabbed six boxes of ammunition, three for the rifle and three for the pistol.

I stuffed the Smith & Wesson, the Bowie, and the ammunition in a pack that was lying on the floor by the cabinet and hustled back upstairs. Laura returned with an armload of what must have been her father's, or perhaps an ex-husband's clothes, I didn't know and didn't ask.

"Hurry! I'll put these in the car. You can change while I drive." No argument from me. Grabbing Bukwold's axe from the drawer, we were about to leave when Laura said, "I'll be right back." She took off at a trot to the door of the attached garage. She wasn't in there more than a minute when she returned carrying a regular single bitted axe. "I thought you might need this," she said. Out the door we went.

The sky cracked a little more, showing off its blue. Off in the distance I heard the faint wailing of a siren, probably announcing my absence, telling us we had no time to lose.

Within an hour, we were at the southern tip of the wilderness. This was hard, harder than facing the Dark One, for I had found in Laura what I had searched for most of my life.

"Will I see you again?" she asked.

"It's hard to say, but I think the odds are against it."

"Well . . . thank you for giving me the greatest adventure of my life," she said, the tears welling up in her eyes.

"And thank you. And you can always remember and take solace in the fact that you helped to save this world."

"Or at least buy it some more time," she said.

Teary eyed, we threw our arms around each other, kissed long and deep, and said good-bye. What else could we do?

I stood and watched her drive away down the deserted and seldom used gravel road. I should have felt like a Hollywood movie hero. Hell, we'd just prolonged the existence of the human race, and maybe helped ease some of its suffering. But all I felt was the ache of losing Laura as that reality settled deep in my heart.

I turned into the woods after watching her car disappear and began my journey northward, hoping to ensure the continued captivation of the Liar-Killer.

EPILOGUE

Chapter Sixty-Six

"And so here we are, Joseph James, you and I, sitting across this table from each other," he said.

"Quite the fantastic tale old timer," replied the young photojournalist, "but I think you've been in these woods too long and you let your imagination run away with you. To be honest, I think you made it all up."

"Could have, but I didn't," he said and with that bent over and reached into the pack laying at his feet. The photographer grew attentive, expecting the crazy old coot to come up with a handgun. Instead, he produced a rolled up sheet of leather and laid it out flat on the table.

"Means nothing to me," said Joseph James.

"Take a closer look."

He focused on the word symbols inscribed in the leather. They began to swim before his eyes, forming themselves into the words of The Prophecy.

Truman looked amused as he watched Joseph read it twice. He pushed the leather sheet across the table toward Truman, his eyes wide, his mouth agape with wonder at his new found belief in the unbelievable.

"I can't deny that. But what says you're not some crazy kind of sorcerer steeped in the old ways?"

Truman snickered and shook his head. Reaching over to his left, he opened the leather flap of the case he had carried on his back, and pulled out Bukwold's axe.

"You could have made that, or bought it somewhere."

"Could have, but I didn't," he replied and grabbed the axe by the end of its handle. He held it straight up and turned it round and round while Joseph James watched with focused intent.

"How are we doing today you Dark Son-of-a-Bitch?" Truman asked, speaking to the axe head, holding it steady. It began to vibrate and glow red.

"Furious aren't you, now that you're cloak has been removed," he said, mocking the Liar-Killer. The mountain man grinned at the photojournalist. "Touch it," he said, "it's not hot. What you see is the color of fury." He put his hand on the axe head and left it there. "Your turn," he said. Hesitating, Joseph James placed his fingertips on the opposite side of the axe head. It was cool to the touch. He placed his palm against it and left it there. "It pulsates," he said.

Laying the axe down, Truman said, "Yes, and what you feel is the heart of evil. I aim to find a deep, deep place to bury it somewhere between here and the polar ice cap."

"I don't know what to say," replied the younger man, his voice a whisper.

"There's really nothing to say except that you believe my story and that you will write it down."

"I believe it, man, and I will write it down . . . get it out there . . . though I doubt many people will believe it."

"You know it's true."

"Yes, deep down in my gut I do."

"It's because we're connected by . . . what, I'm not sure . . . perhaps the Prophecy. I don't even know where it came from, or who wrote it."

"Does it matter?" asked Joseph James.

"Not one damn bit," replied Truman. "Here," he said, pushing the Prophecy across the table, "take this with you; it'll add credibility, along with the bear hide. Maybe you can sell it to a museum or something," he laughed, and held Bukwolds' axe in the air. "Take a picture of this, but not of me, for obvious reasons," he said.

The young man retrieved his camera, clicked several rapid-fire shots of all sides of Bukwold's axe, and, satisfied, returned the instrument to its case.

"You could notify the authorities," quipped Truman as he replaced the axe in its leather sheath.

"Could, but I won't. What purpose would it serve? Doesn't seem there's much of a chance you'll be doing any drinking and driving anyway," he chuckled. "What will you do once you're satisfied the axe is secure?"

"The axe will never be secure. The best I can hope for is that the Dark One will be forced into dormancy. Evil never dies, you know."

"I know, but what will you do afterwards?"

"Stay out of sight, of course. Maybe work my way to Mexico. I'm a bona fide fugitive now."

"Yes, but maybe they'll grant you a pardon or something for saving the world, or at least buying it some time."

"Not in this state. They demand their pound of flesh and then some. I'll be on the run and in hiding the rest of my life I reckon," said Truman.

With that the photojournalist stood up, gathered his notes, put them in his bag, and extended his right hand to me. We shook, bonding our word and our trust to each other.

"Anything else I can do for you?" he asked, as day was breaking outside the window.

"Yes, there is. If you happen to go check out the geography of the prison and Anaconda, will you please look up Laura, show her the Prophecy, tell her you've seen me, and that I'm okay and working my way north?"

"Yes, certainly . . . it would be a pleasure and an honor to do so."

Chapter Sixty-Seven

Laura ran her fingers along the beads of her rosary. Stopping at the crucifix, she picked up a small piece of cloth and gently rubbed the charred surface, removing more of the burnt material. She returned it to the top drawer of the oak buffet, pondering the events of not long ago.

An undemanding knock came upon her door. Closing the drawer, Laura moved gracefully across the room, and without any apprehension, opened it. Before her stood a young man, the outdoors type, with a full beard, longish hair, and clearness of eye that belongs to those who look on the wonders of nature with a sense of reverence.

"Hello," said Laura.

"Hello, my name is . . ."

"Joseph James," she finished for him, extending her hand. He took her proffered hand and shook it, noticing her grip was gentle but contained great strength underneath the surface, as she herself did.

"I still possess the Gift," she said, smiling as she released his hand and warmly invited him in.

In his lingering disbelief, his belief in the story strengthened as he entered her house. The first thing his eyes landed on was the oak buffet.

"Please, have a seat," Laura invited, waving her hand toward the living room sofa. "Would you like something to drink?" she asked as he moved toward the sofa.

"Got any beer?"

"I happen to have just one, and it's ice cold. Do you need a glass?"

"No thanks."

An outdoorsman for sure, she thought, as she brought the opened bottle of beer. Handing it to him, she seated herself in the easy chair opposite the sofa.

Soft music played from a local radio station.

Outside, the sky was cloudless, the air crisp and invigorating, the leaves on the birch trees shimmering in golden glory.

"I had the rosary out and was looking at it a moment ago. Would you like to see it?" she asked.

"Yes, very much so," he answered.

Rising without effort from her chair, Laura crossed the room with an undeniable sense of serenity and ease. She was L'Aura once again, and if asked, Joseph James would have said she glowed.

Returning with the rosary she held it out to him. "Here, touch it, hold it," she said. Placing the bottle of beer on the table in front of him, he took the object, his reverence apparent. After touching the charred crucifix, he looked up at her in wonder. "It is true, all of it," he exclaimed as L'Aura returned to her chair.

"Yes, Joseph James, and now I believe you have no doubt that you are a part of this."

"I haven't the slightest whisper of a doubt. Truman gave me the Prophecy, would you like to see it?" he asked opening the shoulder bag he'd placed on the floor bedside him.

"Yes."

Retrieving it, he handed it to her. As before, the words swam until assembling themselves into readable English. The last line was gone. The one that read, *"If to twice seven the beast survives, Rell~Ik Ra~Il shall remain alive."* She held the sacred leather against her breast, glowing brighter as she whispered a prayer of thanks.

"I want you to keep it," she said, handing the sheet of leather back to Joseph James.

"Truman told me the same thing."

"Do you have a picture of Bukwolds' axe?"

"Yes, he told me to take some for further evidence."

"Evidence?"

"To add credibility to the story, I also have the bear hide and the Prophecy. I'm thinking all that should be convincing."

"A bear hide?"

"Yes, he shot it while I was snapping pictures and it was sneaking up behind me."

"Do you have a picture of him?" she asked, pinning him with the light of truth shining in her eyes, a light he could neither resist nor lie to.

"A . . . distant one, a full figure of him, just as he shot that grizzly behind me, but his face is obscured by the flame out of the gun barrel."

"That's how you met?"

"Uh . . . yeah, fate I guess."

"Not fate, destiny," she said.

He felt the warmth of St. Patrick's rosary increase as it lay across his left thigh.

"Anything else?" asked Laura.

"He told me he'd work his way north until he found a deep crevasse to drop the axe in. He couldn't say for sure where, he did say it could be here in Montana or as far north as the polar ice cap. He charged me to warn others to stay clear of this country though, because, although he can't be certain, he has a good basis to believe the Dark One is still able to reach out with his will to influence people and affairs."

"Or possibly command them," she said. "Your resolve to write the book is firm then?"

"Yes, even more so after meeting you."

"What will you call it?"

"I hadn't thought about it until right now," he said and then after a brief pause said, "How about . . . *Under the Slaughterhouse?*"

"Sounds perfect," she replied.

With that Joseph James drove off in his Jeep, leaving the unfinished bottle of beer on the living room coffee table.

Laura watched him go, raising a cloud of dust behind him as he drove. *Ashes to ashes, dust to dust,* she thought as she watched him until he was out of sight. Well, maybe not quite yet, she told herself as she slowly closed the door. Maybe the sacrifice will be worth it, she thought, as she turned back to the living room, the ache in her heart eased by knowing that Hope remained alive and that that forces of Good and Evil were brought back into balance, maybe even tipping the scales slightly in the favor of Good.

THE END